The Perfect Couple

THE PERFECT COUPLE

JANE McLOUGHLIN

LUME BOOKS
A JOFFE BOOKS COMPANY

LUME BOOKS
A JOFFE BOOKS COMPANY

Lume Books, London
A Joffe Books Company
www.lumebooks.co.uk

First published in Great Britain in 2024 by Lume Books

Copyright © Jane McLoughlin 2024

The right of Jane McLoughlin to be identified as author of this work has been asserted in accordance with the Copyright, Designs and Patents Act 1988.

This book is a work of fiction. Names, characters, businesses, organisations, places and events are either the product of the author's imagination or are used fictitiously. Any resemblance to actual persons, living or dead, events or locales is entirely coincidental. The spelling used is British English except where fidelity to the author's rendering of accent or dialect supersedes this.

We love to hear from our readers!
Please email any feedback you have to: feedback@joffebooks.com

Cover design by Imogen Buchanan

Printed and bound in Great Britain by Clays Ltd, Elcograf S.p.A.

ISBN: 978-1-83901-572-4

To my brother Mark and my sister Anne

Chapter 1

"So what's it going to be, honey?"

The question hung in the air as the waitress put their drinks on the table, picked up the empty glasses, and glided away.

"A new start overseas, or staying where we are?"

Jacey couldn't tell if her husband was joking. The look on his face was serious, those clear blue eyes still and calm, but he was good at making fun of her without her even knowing, until it was too late to defend herself.

"I mean it, Jace. Minnesota, or England. It's your call."

Rob's voice faded for a few seconds, as the air around him seemed to thicken, and the music from the DJ inside the bar slowed down, almost stopping, getting lower and lower, dropping below a frequency that was audible to humans.

It was only when she looked around the shady beer garden and saw the college students drinking among the twinkling lights, chatting happily, oblivious to the changes in the sound and air, that Jacey realised what was going on.

The hollowing. It had been so long since she'd felt it – years ago, before she got married, not since she was a teenager – but what else could it be?

A year away from home, Rob was saying, his voice back to normal; that's all it would be. Twelve months. Nine months really, if they wanted to cut it short at the end of the academic year, or make a quick trip back for Christmas vacation or during the long Easter break.

He made it sound simple. And it was sweet the way he asked so nicely, and held her hand, and talked about doing this *before* the babies came, like doing an academic exchange to England was all part of the wonderful package that was their lives together.

It meant moving to another country, of course, Rob explained, but the country in question would be England, so it would be a familiar place, with the same language. And the English – sorry, the British, he said, you had to be careful in case you were talking to somebody from Scotland or Wales – wouldn't think of them as foreigners, not at all.

Jacey nodded, hoping that would slow down his rapid-fire words if not stop them altogether.

They'd be like cousins, you know? Family?

And the hollowing came again – no doubt about it – stronger this time, muffling what he was saying, so she could hardly hear his words.

They'd fit right in. Right, babe?

"*Right.*" Her throat was so tight, she had to squeeze out the word. She'd remember that later, the not being able to speak, the start of it all.

It would be easy, yeah? Simple?

And so it was. Easy, to get there at least. New passports applied for and issued, immigration forms filled in, Covid booster shots jabbed in their arms, and then two months later, a few days in Chicago so they could get the paperwork completed at the British consulate before the flight.

After the visa meeting, they celebrated by the Chicago River, at a bar on a wide terrace that overlooked the city's iconic skyscrapers. They watched the tourist boats float by, their engines sputtering and spewing out puffs of dark fumes, while Rob pointed out the most famous buildings and told Jacey about this scene from that movie and that scene from this movie and did she see the one where …

He never stopped talking, Jacey's husband. He knew so much about so many things, of course he'd want to share his vast understanding with the entire world. Who wouldn't if they had a brain like his, capable of retaining knowledge, finding solutions to problems, always ahead of the intellectual curve?

Jacey sat still, sucking in the sour cocktail – lime juice, Brazilian sugar cane rum – until the liquid was gone, and then more and more slurping through her straw until the ice melted and there was nothing left in the bottom of the glass.

She listened, too, at least she pretended to, while Rob explained. And she looked at his phone when he showed the pictures of the town in Sussex close to the university where he'd be teaching, and the amazing house they'd be living in once they got there. "Look at it, Jacey," he said. "That mansion will be our home."

She'd seen the pictures before, of course, but he was so excited …

And the historic town, nestled in rolling green hills, not far from the ocean. "Sea," Rob said apologetically. "I meant the sea – that's what they call it over there."

Old buildings. Dark stone walls, covered with ivy; narrow cobbled streets. The pictures gave her a chill even here, in the bright American sunlight that was reflecting up from the glimmering river and shining off the glass and chrome skyscrapers that loomed over them. She gazed up, awed, as ever, in her small-town Minnesota way. But she wasn't scared of them, despite their gargantuan size, because they were modern buildings. Safe. Knowable.

"And one of your grandmothers was from England, right?" Rob said. It was like he was still trying to convince her that they were doing the right thing, although she'd agreed to do it, and she'd packed up all her things, and said goodbye to her family and friends. It was as if his mind was searching out new positive angles, so he could win her over 100%. After seven years of marriage Jacey knew that merely agreeing with Rob was never enough; there couldn't be a scintilla of doubt that whatever he was saying was bang on the money. He needed her approval, because in his own way, he needed her.

"Something about World War Two?" he asked.

"Yes," she said. "She met Grandpa during the war. Cambridgeshire. A little town near an American air force base."

"You could go there," Rob said. "Find that town. Trace your roots."

"Maybe," she said, her heart beating faster, her chest tightening at the thought of following Nana Ivy's footsteps, visiting her grandmother's childhood home. The pictures her mother had shown her of 'the old cottage in England' as she called it, terrified Jacey as a child. Maybe it was because the sky – huge and flat – was always cloudy in the pictures, and Nana Ivy, even as a young woman, had worn a fierce, terrifying scowl; or maybe it was the darkness from inside the house that seemed to seep out of the windows and settle like a thin covering of soot on the grey stone walls. The memory of looking at those photographs, of feeling the hollowing when she saw them, and not understanding what it was, frightened her still.

* * *

They could have stayed in America, of course, instead of going for the year's exchange. Rob could have landed another job in a better university if he'd held out. After his book was published, he'd been hot stuff—in academic circles anyway. Number 20 in the New York Times non-fiction charts was nothing to sneeze at, even he admitted that, though his advance had been modest and the sales weren't all that, despite the 'New York Times Bestseller' sticker his publishers slapped on the front cover.

Bestseller my ass, Rob said, but not bitterly. He was philosophical about it: at least he tried to be, at the beginning. He had an agent; he got invited to events and conferences. But the book hadn't brought the riches or the guest slots on the late-night talk shows he'd been hoping for. He was still just Rob Gibson, PhD. Associate Professor at a small Minnesota state university, agent or no agent, book deal or no book deal, with or without the New York Times sticker.

And when the second book didn't get published because the imprint was making cutbacks and sales of the first were not what had been expected, and he hadn't earned out his (very) modest advance, he was pretty pissed off. OK, very pissed off. How *could* the book have sold, he said, when there was no publicity budget? Hadn't he busted a gut for them? Hadn't he gone on book tours, and written up pointless posts for academic blogs that nobody subscribed to, and that he'd never been paid for?

And so, with everything else going on in the country, this was the perfect time to take a break from it all, he said. The Brits were pretty messed up, too – all of Europe was, if you looked closely enough – but nothing compared to what was going on in the US of A.

No. America could kiss his ass. That's how he put it, like America was one of the lazy and know-nothing college freshmen he was forced to teach in Literature for Boneheads 101.

The waiter handed them the bill for Jacey's cocktail and Rob's large draft beer. "Thirty-five bucks?" Rob asked incredulously. "You fucking shitting me?"

The waiter pursed his lips and looked away as Rob reached for his credit card.

"That's a lot of money for two lousy drinks."

Jacey knew that tone of voice, recognised the look on her husband's face. Rob wasn't going to let the anger go. He could be like this sometimes, when he was stressed or felt taken advantage of.

There was more pursing from the waiter, with a touch of eye rolling for added effect, then a quick tap of the card, an awkward wait for the payment to be approved, and a curt "thank you" when the receipt was handed back.

Rob opened his wallet. "I'm going to put in a claim for this," he muttered, folding the receipt, ready to stuff next to his cash.

To whom? Jacey wanted to say. *Now that you quit your job.*

But the wind came up off the river, and the tiny slip of paper flew from Rob's hand and wafted over the safety railing and landed upright in the water several metres below. For some reason Jacey was tempted to go after it – instinct told her to dive in and save this bright white square that bobbed on the water's surface like a tiny boat before disappearing in the wake of an oncoming sight-seeing cruiser. It was like a magnetic pull, trying to hoist her out of her seat and into the water. She grabbed the arms of the flimsy metal chair, even though she knew it was silly to be frightened, that nothing was actually going to drag her in.

And then somebody screamed.

And there was a splash.

When Jacey peered over the railing, she saw a small body floating in the water, exactly where the paper had fallen.

Good God, what was it? A baby? Somebody's child?

People rushed to the side of the safety railing, yelling, pointing and shouting as the pathetic figure bobbed along, like a ragdoll, drifting helplessly closer to the river's main channel and the path of the boats.

Jacey heard a distraught wail – "Maisy! Maisy!" – but as she looked closer the numb terror subsided.

Slightly.

A small white dog, some kind of terrier, was fighting the current, paddling for dear life, ears perked up as if listening in vain for a recognisable sound, a familiar voice amid the din of shouts and warning bells and what must have been the deafening grinding of engines and churning of the water.

"Jesus," Rob grunted, pushing his chair back. "I'm not watching this." He sounded angry, like he had with the waiter, as if this poor little dog and its distraught owners were part of the conspiracy to ruin his day with their desperate cries of panic and misery, adding to the indignity of being overcharged for the drinks.

"Come on," he snapped. "What are you waiting for?"

Rob tugged at Jacey's arms, and she managed to prise herself away from the table she was now clutching for safety and let herself be whisked away from the scene. She couldn't see the outcome of what was taking place in the river, but the shouts and cries and the tooting horn of a boat made it clear that the dog was doomed, about to be sucked under a rusty hull, or mangled by a whirring propeller.

And in all that time, with so much upset, she never noticed the way everything had slowed down. How the air thickened, and the sound of the screams got quieter and quieter until, finally, they were nothing but whispers, harsh and shrill.

Chapter 2

Before heading down to their new home in Sussex, Jacey and Rob spent a week in London, negotiating the crowds at the usual tourist haunts, discovering little 'gems' as Rob called them – out-of-the-way pubs and small greasy-spoon type cafés that managed to survive the gentrification and commercialisation of central London, as well as the waves of terror and disease and other forms of bad fortune the arms of history could throw at a city.

London took everything in its stride: wars, terrorism, pandemics. That's what Rob said, and it appeared he was right. In fact, a few days before they left London for the quiet of Sussex, there'd been an attack on a police station in a part of town called Shepherd's Bush and several officers had been injured. To Jacey everything in the city seemed to be going on as usual: red double-decker buses lurched and halted on the traffic-clogged roads, shoppers jostled each other on wide pavements that were teeming with people.

They ambled across St. James' Park on their way to a pub where they were meeting an old college friend of Rob's and his wife. Nobody in the park seemed tense either: families were having picnics, children fed chunks of bread to the ducks, and young couples made out on blankets on the grass, lying on top of each other, acting like they were the only people on earth.

Jacey took Rob's hand. *We used to do that, didn't we?* she wanted to say to him. *Only a few years ago, remember?* One of those couples had a baby, too, asleep on the blanket beside them. She hoped Rob had noticed them, and that later, when they were alone, they'd talk about their future and he'd mention the little family, and how it made him less scared of the whole baby thing – that's what he called it whenever she brought the subject up – and they'd maybe even make love without a condom, just to be reckless, just for fun.

As they walked, they didn't talk about the couple, or the baby; they talked about the terrorist incident and Jacey made a comment – all right, a bad joke – about the name where the attack took place, Shepherd's Bush. Rob pulled his hand away from hers and shook it, as if he were trying to get rid of some plague-carrying germs. It wasn't the disrespect to the injured police officers – he called them constables – that bothered him, it was the laughing at the name of the place: 'Shepherd's Bush'.

"You'd better get used to those kinds of names," he said, "and not cackle like a moron whenever you hear a place with the word 'cock' in it, because there are plenty of those in this country."

Jacey spat out a laugh and Rob glared at her, appalled by her immaturity.

"But cock's a funny word," she laughed. "And so is bush. Anybody would think so, even you would have, before you put that corncob up your ass."

She was being brave here, mocking him. Gently making fun of his stuffy pretentiousness was bound to backfire.

"Cock," he said seriously, his face sober, corncob held firmly in place, sphincter tight as a drum, "means rooster here."

"I bet it means cock, too," Jacey muttered. "As in penis."

"Well, don't go around asking people, OK?"

Jacey didn't answer, but when she dared look at his face – they were walking more quickly now – he was still scowling. OK, so he didn't like that she had a joke at his expense, she got that, but was it something else, too? Was he embarrassed by her? Did he think she was an unsophisticated, undereducated hick? Were the silage and manure of her family's farm permanently encrusted into whatever shoes she was wearing?

On the grass verge beside the path, another couple was kissing on a blanket, while yet another baby gurgled happily in a pushchair next to them. *They had a kid*, Jacey thought, but they could still manage to act like a couple – showing affection, being nice to each other. Why were she and Rob behaving like crabby long-term marrieds? They'd only been together for nine years. She felt stupid for believing that England would be a good move. What had Rob called it? A brand new start.

"Come on," Rob said, making a big show about having to stop to wait for her to catch up. "We're going to be late."

She'd slowed down deliberately, looking over the park's vast lawn, groups of people dotted in clumps across the grass, and on the blue lake in the distance, bobbing on pedal boats and tiny canoes.

"Jesus, Jacey, I mean it." Rob was ruffling his hair, shaking out his arms, shifting his weight from one leg to another, like a runner waiting for the starting pistol.

"Well, maybe you could go ahead, if you're in such a hurry," Jacey said. "Find a table for us?"

She liked being out among all the people; she wasn't even sure she wanted to go to the pub to meet another American couple, who were on an academic exchange like themselves. Until today, it had been nice having Rob to herself in London; he was more relaxed when it was just the two of them, as if impressing her was a given. Yes, he had to constantly show off his vast knowledge of history and art and culture, but there was nothing more to strive for with her, no need for her further approval. She'd already married him, hadn't she?

These new people would just ruffle his feathers, bring out his need to compete, and she knew what that meant: subtle digs at her, the lowest rung on the ladder he always needed to climb.

"Are you serious?" he said. "What am I going to tell them? That you didn't care enough about me to want to meet my friends."

"They're not really your friends – Bex is just somebody you used to work with, and you haven't seen Jared since college, right?"

She was standing beside him, and for a few seconds, she felt taller, stronger, for having held her ground.

Rob's face changed; his jaw tightened, and Jacey knew that if they weren't meeting 'friends' she'd be in for the silent treatment. No shouting or anger expressed, just the Rob Gibson stone-faced blanking that could go on for hours, if not days.

Suddenly, she felt exposed. The world seemed to grow quieter – had everyone in the park stopped what they were doing in order to listen to them argue? And as the sun slipped under a heavy cloud and the air instantly got colder, she imagined the wide lawns clearing, the boat pond emptying, the sky darkening; until she was standing entirely alone and lost, waiting helplessly for someone to lead her through the gates that were creaking shut, locking her in.

"Jacey?"

She took a deep breath, waited for her head to clear. "It's nice here, you know?"

Without looking back at her, Rob strode away, and headed for a gap in the fence where they could get out to the main road. Why was he acting like this? Like impatient parents did sometimes when their toddlers lagged behind and wouldn't keep up. "That's it now," they'd say. "We're leaving without you."

So cruel of them, she thought, *to make such a terrible threat*. Once she and Rob had kids she'd never do anything like that.

But Rob wasn't a father yet, so he didn't actually stop.

They were meeting Jared and Bex at a pub called the Grenadier that was nestled in a side street off a busy main road, just a few hundred feet outside the park gates. Before they stepped inside, Jacey was warned about gawking at the décor or calling it quaint or historic.

"I've been to Boston," she muttered. "And Québec City, remember? Lots of old stuff in both those places, and I didn't drool over everything, or make a fool of myself."

She tried to sound angry – because she was – but her words came out as defensive and weak, the hurt toddler again.

"Well, this place is different," Rob said, holding the door open for her, but managing somehow to get into the darkened room first. "Nothing's as special as this," he sighed.

"Rob – Jacey! Over here!"

Rob waved and smiled at the Harrises, so nobody but Jacey would have noticed the way he winced when Jared called out their names. What was it that embarrassed him – the Harrises' loud American voices or how they'd just advertised to the entire pub his wife's tacky, trashy name.

"Jacey?" he'd laughed, the first time she met him, ten years ago, at a bar close to the college campus. "What kind of aspirations did your parents have for you, anyway, with a name like that? Head cheerleader? First runner up on *The Bachelorette*?"

"My mom thought it was cool," she answered. Hurt. Angry. Hating herself for even bothering to explain it. "She didn't like her own name and wanted something more individual for me. Not that it's any of your business." She turned away from him sharply and went back to her girlfriends, muttering the word "asshole" under her breath, but not loud enough for him to have heard.

A few minutes later a server came to their booth with a note saying how sorry Rob was, how he'd just meant it as a joke, and totally got how condescending he must have sounded, and offering to buy their next round. Her friends had already clocked him; they thought he was cute and said Jacey should call him – he'd written his number down – but that was only because he was tall and good-looking and looked like he shaved more than once every few days. But she ignored them and ripped up the number. The guy was a jerk. Obviously. No matter what he looked like. Jesus, how desperate for a man did they think she was?

Her roommate, Cara, was sure she recognised him from somewhere, and on the first day of the next semester she and Jacey found out where that was, when Rob strode into the front of their lecture hall wearing a tweed jacket over a light blue shirt and black jeans and introduced himself as Dr Gibson.

He wasn't a professor then; he was just an instructor, while he worked on his PhD. He didn't notice Jacey until he called out the register, and she saw his face get red and his hand shake while he waited for her to answer.

He looked up when nobody answered. "Is Jacey here?"

"Present," she said.

Jacey couldn't remember what he talked about. Something to do with symbolism or allusion in a boring novel by George Eliot that they were going to be reading with their real professor. When he droned on about feminist readings of the book, Cara leaned over and whispered, "Him, a feminist. Yeah, right."

Jacey was a liberal arts student, undeclared major, and in the first term of her sophomore year. Her humanities class was the Victorian novel and that meant long books that made her feel like she was wearing a tight corset and suffocating through the lack of air, and even longer lectures by sweaty bearded guys. One of them was Rob Gibson, who she ended up marrying, a year after dropping out because her family's farm went bankrupt, and they couldn't afford the tuition fees. When his lecture was over, Rob chased after her, sputtered another apology, and asked her out for coffee. Almost ten years later, walking into the pub and seeing the way he cringed at the sound of her name, she wondered if he regretted ever being so nice.

Whatever Rob thought, Jacey liked Bex and Jared straight away. Bex had a dumb-sounding name, too, although it was just short for Rebecca, so they had that in common. And even though she was as educated as Rob, and had the same job at a different British university, she wasn't arrogant like he was. She had grown up in a small farming town, too, so she seemed normal and down to earth. Jacey was happy to be meeting a potential friend in England, and she imagined visiting Bex in London, getting out and seeing the sights with her, exploring the city with somebody who wouldn't act like an expert on everything she saw.

Jared was wearing normal clothes for a warm, late summer afternoon – denim shorts and a Lone Star Beer T-shirt and deck shoes. He wasn't wearing a short-sleeved Oxford shirt tucked into his belted chinos, like Rob was, trying to fit in with the Brits, who were also mostly dressed like Jared and Bex, wearing shorts and T-shirts and ratty-looking Converses.

Jared and Rob went to the bar to obsess over the hops level of the different types of ale and cider. Bex and Jacey headed out to the beer garden, crammed with drinkers, full of toddlers on scooters and babies in pushchairs, and settled themselves at a little table hidden in a far corner, under a scraggly lilac tree.

"You'll like it here," Bex said. "Once you get used to things."

"Things?" Jacey asked.

"Oh, you think everything's the same because you've met a few British people and you speak English and watch Masterpiece Theatre on PBS, but it's not all that similar, to be honest."

She looked around. "I mean, kids in pubs, that's kind of shocking, especially with the way the parents all still smoke outside, and every other word they say is fuck."

Bex sighed and took a sip of her drink. "And everything's so *old*." She shivered, as if a cold wind had just blown through the sunny enclosed courtyard they were sitting in. "And like, you just want to go out for a couple of drinks in an ordinary place but it's all haunted this and haunted that."

Bex waved both hands, made tiny circles in the air like she was trying to conjure up a few restless souls. "Like here, for instance."

"Really?" Jacey felt a weird tug – a jab to the solar plexus, only from inside her body.

"Didn't you read the sign outside the entrance? A soldier got beaten to death back in the 1600s, and one of the grooms from the stables got blamed, even though it was obviously someone from the soldier's own regiment."

Jacey looked up for the sign, but it was obscured by a layer of ivy.

"Well, you can imagine what they ended up doing to the innocent horse guy – pretty much tortured to death – and I guess I'd have haunted the place if that's what happened to me."

Rob and Jared came through the door, stepping carefully down the brick steps, and made their way across the slippery cobbled patio.

"That's one thing you can say about places like Iowa or Minnesota," Bex whispered. "They might be flat and boring, but it's all nice and modern and there aren't any ghosts."

Jacey felt the tug again.

Bex was wrong. Ghosts were everywhere. Nana Ivy taught her that. In cities and on farms, from London and Cambridge to the tiniest village in Minnesota. The dead were the dead wherever you went, and the sort of dead were the sort of dead. But Bex didn't have a Nana Ivy, so how would she know?

Chapter 3

The taxi from Lewes station dropped them off at the top of the driveway, halfway up a steep hill between the main road and Malin House itself, just visible through a thin curtain of slender, swaying trees.

"Looks like quite the place," Rob said.

The driver took out the four huge suitcases he'd managed to wedge into the trunk.

"Just don't listen to any of the rumours," he said, as he got back into the cab. Then he rolled up the windows and drove away.

"Wonder what that meant," Jacey said.

Rob was craning his neck, staring up at the house. "What?"

"The driver said something about the house, about not listening to rumours. Didn't you hear him?"

"No." He puffed up his chest, obviously proud that he'd bagged such an important gig, and one with such an awesome property attached. "And even if I did, I wouldn't believe anything a taxi driver said. You know what they're like."

They struggled up the steep, stony part-paved path to the house, gazing upwards. Jacey could make out a high, pitched roof, and arched windows, and even from far below she could tell that the house was bigger than any she'd ever lived in or could have imagined living in. There was a little turret that was a storey taller than the rest of the house. It had tiny windows, and a pointed copper roof.

"A tower," Rob muttered, shaking his head, stopping with the luggage every few metres to catch his breath and gawk at the house. "You see that, Jace?" he said. "A fucking tower?"

When they were near the top, he turned back. Jacey was struggling to keep her heavy suitcases upright.

"What do you think?" Rob said.

She stopped. Caught her breath. Now that they were close to the house it loomed even larger; it was dark and gloomy, on the outside at least, with brown shingling on the sides. There was rust-red painting on the window trims and the small front veranda's railings were painted white. Ivy grew up the side, just like it had at the pub in London, almost covering the entire wall, clinging to the shingles like dark green fingers.

"I mean, you like it, right?"

She smiled. Of course she did.

Waiting for them at the top of the hill were the caretakers, Martin and Helen, who lived in a cottage on the other side of the driveway on the far edge of the huge lawn, just visible through a screen of trees.

Martin strode towards them and shook their hands. He was somewhere near retirement age, Jacey thought. He reminded her of her father, what she could remember, the tanned face and arms, the thick wrists, the hands that gripped tightly and were rough with doing outdoor work. Helen was slim and pretty, with smooth skin and straight blonde hair streaked through with grey, pulled back in a ponytail. She wore a light denim skirt and T-shirt and sneakers that were stained green from being worn outside.

"Here, let me," Martin said, taking the heavier of Jacey's suitcases.

"How was your journey?" Helen asked.

"Still a little jet-lagged I think," Jacey said. "But we're both OK, aren't we, honey?"

Helen looked at Rob, expecting an answer, but he was still gazing up in wonderment at the tower.

"When did you arrive in London?"

"Flight got in on Tuesday," Rob said.

"Well, it takes a few days to get acclimatised," Martin said.

They strolled along a narrow pathway that led to the veranda, and it was hard for Jacey to focus on the conversation with the house looming over them.

"We've only been to the States once," Helen said, as she climbed the steps to the veranda, and reached into the pocket of her jacket for the front door keys. "New York during the Thanksgiving holiday. Such happy memories, and people were ever so friendly."

Martin and Rob were dragging the bags up the stairs. Helen opened the door, and Jacey felt her heart thump as she stepped up and crossed to the entrance.

"You go in first, honey," Rob said. "See what you think."

Jacey stepped through the doorway. She was aware of her mouth being wide open, and as Rob clunked the suitcases across the threshold, she closed it self-consciously, and clapped her hand over her mouth to stop herself from saying something stupid.

"Impressive, isn't it?" Helen whispered.

"Wow," Rob said again, stepping into the hallway, gawking himself, and really, Jacey couldn't blame him. What else would you do in such a magnificent place as this, and one that, temporarily at least, was going to be their home?

"It's not as old as it looks," Martin said. "That disappoints a lot of our guests."

"No?"

"Late nineteenth century. 1879, I think, isn't that right, Helen? Gothic revival. The tower was tacked on even later, about 1913. It's just for decoration, sadly, there are no creaky steps to the top."

Helen nodded, stepping further into the entrance hall. She looked around the room, as if checking for something – a missed speck in her dusting of the mantelpiece, or a cobweb swinging between the crystal and gold chandelier. The veranda was comparatively small – two wicker chairs around a tiny occasional table, not much bigger than the balcony in Jacey's mother's one-bedroom apartment in the small town where they settled after the farm had been sold.

"It was a bit of a folly," Martin said, setting Rob's cases down on the black and white tiled floor.

"Like, a mistake?" Rob said.

"No, like a folly people build – maybe it's just a British thing. A fancy structure that has no real purpose, other than to show off to people how rich or how important the person who built it was."

"But this is a house," Rob said. "Obviously, it has a purpose."

"It cost a lot more than the builder could afford," Martin said.

"Oh, so that was the folly. Over-stretching himself financially."

"Indeed," Martin said.

"Indeed," Rob repeated, eyes furrowed and serious, as if *indeed* was an expression he used all the time.

Martin took the heavy luggage upstairs, one bag at a time, and Helen gave Jacey and Rob a tour of the ground floor. Through a door to the right, there was a small living room, with a TV in the corner, a sofa, a small fireplace. "Ooh," Jacey said. "Looks like a cosy place to settle in on a winter's night."

"We call it the snug," Helen said. "Americans call it a den, or sometimes a family room."

"Have families ever stayed here?"

"Not very often." Helen glanced around the room, as if she were looking for more of those invisible cobwebs. "It's a bit gloomy for children, and the families that have been booked in usually haven't stayed for the length of their exchange."

"I would have thought kids would love a place like this," Rob said. "So many nooks and crannies to hide in."

"Yes, you'd think so, but …" Helen touched one of the heavy curtains, pulled it back slightly, letting in more light. "It's not for everyone."

Through another door was the kitchen. It was much brighter than the den, with windows overlooking the wide lawn and a door to the outside. There was a large, open fireplace and a massive stove, which looked more like a furnace or a cupboard than anything to cook on – dark blue painted cast iron, with doors of different sizes, and railings, and heavy burners with lids on the top. In the middle of the kitchen stood a long oak table, with seating for eight.

"Looks like the kitchen at Hampton Court," Jacey said. "We went there last week."

"Fireplace is a bit smaller, I dare say," Helen laughed.

"Not by much," Jacey said. There were scorch marks on the inside of the chimney, and dark smudges on the ceramic floor tiles, even some smoky shading on the ceiling. Rob bent over to look up the flue. Helen craned her head slightly, too, as if she was afraid Rob would find some evidence of inadequate cleaning.

"Is this chimney open all the time?" Rob asked. "No flue or anything? Like, if we wanted a fire?"

"Not as far as I know," Helen said. She stepped back and then walked towards another door. "You'll have to talk to Martin about that, he's the expert on those types of things."

They passed quickly through a small pantry, with drawers and shelves and numbered bells on the wall. "They're to summon the butlers and maids," Helen said drily.

"This house doesn't come with servants, does it?" Jacey laughed.

"No, but the house's original owners had a cook and a nanny for their two children, and occasional staff for dinners and functions – and they could be summoned by pulling chains connected to the bells that would ring in here."

Jacey felt Rob behind her, reaching for her hand, squeezing it with amazement.

Leading off the pantry was a huge dining room with two chandeliers on the vaulted ceiling that reminded her of the ancient cathedrals they'd visited. Besides the table, covered with a thick tarpaulin, there was a large built-in sideboard, and a huge silver coffee service, the kind the church ladies used to bring out for important events back home in Minnesota, like weddings and funerals.

"Feel free to use any of the rooms," Helen said. "This next one is the main reception area. The drawing room, I suppose." She led them past another huge fireplace, more shiny wood panelling on the walls, hundreds of books in floor to ceiling shelves, windows that were darkened with dull stained glass, and furniture covered with linen sheets.

"Most guests stick to the kitchen and the snug so we've left the coverings on," Helen said, "but it's entirely up to you. This is your home now, after all."

Rob shot a glance at Jacey – his eyes widened a little like: *Our home? Can you believe this shit?*

The next door led back to the entrance and, by now, Jacey was dizzy with everything they'd seen. Gradually, she got her bearings – when she faced the stairway, the door to the nook was on her right, and the door to the drawing room was on her left. In the middle was the staircase, and at the back of the hallway, there were two smaller doors.

"Where do they lead?" she asked.

Helen stepped across the tiles to the back of the hall, glancing upwards again at the chandelier, which even when unlit, seemed to radiate light and warmth.

She opened the door on the left. "This is the broom cupboard. Cleaning supplies, hoover, a few shelves for anything you might want to store."

"And the other one?"

Helen stood beside it. She ran her fingers over the wood, but didn't open it, or even touch the handle. "That leads to the basement. We keep it locked because there's nothing there, really. The central heating boiler, some old bits of broken furniture. Martin takes care of all that, any maintenance or repairs, so just let him know if you have any problems."

By the time Helen and Martin led them upstairs, showed them to their room, and finally left them alone, Jacey and Rob were numb. The master bedroom was like the hotel suite they'd stayed in on their honeymoon. There was a huge, canopied four-poster bed, with a duvet covered in a white eyelet and embroidery, and matching vallance and pillowcases.

Through the window, Jacey could see the lawn, and beyond it the river that ran through fields and parkland before cutting towards the centre of the town, visible in the distance. Jacey went to the window, pushed back the off-white sheer curtains and watched Martin and Helen crossing the lawn to the caretaker's cottage that was hidden by trees. Martin slipped through a gap in the trees and Helen looked back at the house, up at their window.

Jacey let the curtain slip and stepped back into the room.

"Look at this, Jace." Rob smiled, like a kid, and bounced up and down on the side of the bed. "Isn't it awesome?"

"Hey, careful," Jacey said." We don't want to have to get Martin back to fix the bed before we've even had a chance to use it."

She checked the drawers, on the bedside tables and the huge heavy wooden dressers. Empty of course, ready for their things. The bookshelves were full of bestselling paperbacks, and out-of-date reference books – *Birds of the British Isles, Fodor's London, 2010*, and hardback copies of criticism and fiction by writers whose names she was vaguely aware of.

Rob got up and opened his briefcase. He took out a copy of his book and wrote an inscription. *To the residents and caretakers of Malin House.* The books seemed to be arranged in alphabetical order; he placed his in the Gs. Then he sat down again, did a few more bounces, before reaching out to Jacey, drawing her towards him.

"Seriously, Jace. Can you believe it?"

She shook her head. Any doubts she'd had – her fears of being lonely, or of Rob becoming arrogant and distant, as he had seemed to be since he got this job – evaporated. Her mother had warned her that not being able to work and being dependent on Rob could change things between them, but, so far, at least, everything was theirs to share. And she'd find her own niche once Rob got settled into his teaching. Moving to England could bring them closer together.

"I know it's not ours," she said. "Like to keep, but ..."

Rob's hands touched hers, and she lay down on the bed beside him. Soon he was touching her arms, moving his hands up to her shoulders, and across to her face. He ran a finger along the outline of her ears, across her eyes, down her nose. He touched her lips and she groaned softly, moving in even closer to him, feeling the warmth of his body, the beating of his heart.

She reached her hand under his T-shirt. The slim firm belly, the line of hair leading from below his belt up to the furry ridge of his chest. And then down again, fumbling with his belt, undoing the button of his shorts, pulling at the zip.

He was already hard, and she remembered that walk through St. James' Park, how cold he'd been towards her, and for how many months, and that tug of jealousy as she watched the couple with the baby, so relaxed and happy, the sting of resentment when they met Jared and Bex, who laughed at each other's jokes, and held hands under the table.

Well, she and Rob were here now, in that very same place: a loving, passionate couple, like the others. He was pulling her T-shirt over her head, desperate to unhook her bra, as if he couldn't wait to touch her skin, caress her breasts.

A new beginning.

Breathing in the fresh scent of the clean sheets, looking at the billowing fabric of the canopy, glancing at the mahogany mirror that was perfectly placed, so that she could see what Rob was doing, rising above her now, grabbing her ass, hiking her legs up around his shoulders.

Looking in the mirror, watching himself.

Until his eyes wandered upwards, distracted.

"What you looking at, babe?"

He shook his head, glanced at himself in the mirror again. "Nothing. Sorry."

He turned back to her and smiled. "Only you."

Chapter 4

When they went to bed later, after making dinner, eating it al fresco on the lawn, they made love again. Then again in the morning – *that made it three times in twenty-four hours*, Jacey thought. How long had it been since they'd done that? Months, at least. Maybe even years.

Afterwards, a gentle rain on the windowsill threatened to lull them back to sleep, but they dragged themselves out of bed, into the huge wetroom for a shower. By the time they'd dried off and dressed the rain had cleared and the sky was blue. There was fresh kindling in the fireplace, and a basket full of logs, but the wet lawn looked inviting with the sun shining, so they dragged the chairs from the veranda down onto the grass.

Jacey felt something warm flicker in her chest, a sensation that she recognised as happiness – the profound 'rightness' she'd felt only a few times in the past few years. The night of Rob's book launch in Minneapolis, the pride at hearing him reading one of his essays, the joy of his call-out to her, his effusive gratitude and praise. She'd felt it the days after their wedding, too, and as she waited on a wicker chair on the wide lawn of a mansion (that was the only word for it) in England, she remembered their honeymoon trip. The giddying bustle and noise of San Francisco, and then a drive up the coast to a cosy B&B outside Mendocino, set on a cliff above the sea; the sounds of waves against the rocky shore, and in the morning, the soft, soothing barking of seals.

In England, there was only birdsong, but the sweet feeling was the same. Rob brought her coffee and croissants that Helen had left in the kitchen; he kissed the top of her head while she held her journal against her knees and wrote down her feelings.

She looked beyond the fringe of trees, where a gentle slope led down to the narrow stream that ran in front of the house, on its way to the centre of town, where it would join the river that divided one side of Lewes from another. On the other side of the house was a small lawn, and the caretaker's cottage, and a gap through tall shrubs and bushes that led to another rocky path up a high, steep hill.

An auspicious start, she wrote, while she waited for Rob to fetch the butter and jam, and bring out a jug of cream.

And so it was. Blissful.

Later that day, they pulled the covers off the furniture in the drawing room and explored the rest of the upstairs.

"We're like Hansel and Gretel," she whispered breathlessly as they crept down dark hallways and gingerly opened doors into empty bedrooms. The Gothic-style windows overlooking the looming hills at the back of the house meant that those rooms were all dark; the brighter front-facing rooms had larger windows, and an open view across the lawn, over the highway and the wide parkland next to the river.

"Hansel and Gretel were brother and sister, right?" Rob squeezed her hand. "So that would make our behaviour rather incestuous, wouldn't it?"

In the last room on the dark side of the house's first storey, there was another four-poster, covered in a white dust sheet. Rob stepped inside, beckoned her to follow him to the edge of the bed.

She put her arms around his waist, hooked her finger into a belt loop of his jeans. "What behaviour would that be?" she said.

Rob leaned backwards, taking her with him, as they fell onto the bed.

"What do you think, Jacey?" Rob said, rolling to the other side of the bed, so she could lie next to him. "Could we fuck in every room of the house?"

"I don't see why not," she said, covering his mouth with hers, kissing him, feeling his tongue inside her mouth, his hardness pressed against her body. She paused for breath. "We've got almost a year, right?"

She pulled her T-shirt up, and he ran his finger along the edge of her bra, where her breasts spilled out. She expected him to reach inside with his hands, or lower his head, but instead he stopped.

He moved away from her, pulling down her T-shirt, covering her skin.

"You hear that?" he whispered.

Jacey listened. Birds tweeted in the trees outside, distant traffic whispered on a highway.

"Jesus," Rob said, jumping up, standing between the bed and the door.

"What?" she said.

He turned around, his brows furrowed in an expression of confusion and fear.

"Jesus Christ, Jacey, can't you hear it?"

He held his body stiffly, every muscle tensed.

She listened. No, she couldn't hear anything.

"Those screams, like somebody's being murdered?"

She climbed off the bed, stood next to Rob, waited for the 'Gotcha' which would probably be combined with some tickling around her belly to make her laugh even more.

"OK," she said. "That's enough."

Straightening her top, she went to the door. This was getting old. Annoying, but she didn't want to spoil the mood they'd created, so she jollied him along. "It's a good joke, darling, but it's not *that* funny …"

Rob stood still. She kissed his cheek as she passed, and he grabbed her arm, tightly, just below the elbow.

"No," he whispered. "You can't …"

There was no point trying to pull away from him – that would only turn his prank into an argument. She could already feel herself getting angry at the way this was playing out. What was the point of this performance? She thought about her feelings a few minutes ago – brimming with love and desire, wanting to have sex with him on some random bed.

Rob remained frozen to the spot, still holding her in place.

"I mean it, Rob," she said. "It's not funny. Not in an old house like this."

Finally, he relaxed. "OK," he said. "It's stopped now. Whatever it was."

She looked back at the bed. Any thoughts of making love had evaporated. She rubbed her arm where he'd squeezed it. "Can we go back downstairs?"

Rob still hadn't moved. "You really didn't hear anything, Jace? No screaming?"

"Of course not," she said, quietly, her anger subsiding "Honestly, Rob."

She opened the door and he stopped her again – a hand gesture, a look – and he stepped out into the hallway, like he was checking to make sure everything was OK.

Suddenly his fake fear was catching. The air quivered slightly.

She'd seen him like this once before, on a rickety carnival rollercoaster in some little town out in the country. He'd had some kind of panic attack on the way up the steep incline, and when they got to the top, where you could see across the fairgrounds and all the surrounding farmlands, he'd been shaking, and shouting "No, no, no" and rattling the safety bar, until their car was plunged into the darkness of the enclosed part of the ride. She'd been terrified, too – that Rob would try to jump, or that the flimsy wooden structure was going to collapse beneath them, that Rob had been having a premonition, or that his panic would set off a horrible chain of destructive events.

The Abyss. That's what the coaster had been called, and when they emerged, both of them shaken, Rob brushed the whole thing off as a joke, like he would do this time, too, when he'd played with her long enough.

Downstairs, things went quickly back to normal. She put the kettle on for coffee, though Rob decided to try tea the English way, with milk and a teaspoon of sugar. While she watched the kettle boil on one of the massive stove's burners, Jacey decided not to ask Rob about what had happened. He was still quiet, and seemed troubled, but who could tell, really?

If it had been a joke – and what else could it have been – then why didn't he own it? Why would he not acknowledge it? Tease her a little, but make it out be to be a bit of harmless fun?

He hadn't meant it cruelly, she accepted that. A joke. Hahaha, and he'd have to keep it going, even if she didn't think it was funny, because that's what guys like Rob did – the entitled, the successful – even if he himself wouldn't acknowledge being either of those things. It was straight out of the guys-who-never-grew-up playbook – pranking somebody for no real reason other than they could.

And maybe that's what this was about. A little control. A way of putting her back in her place after all the sex. See? I don't really want to fuck you in every room in the house. I was only kidding. I mean, sorry Jace, but you're not *that* hot.

She made a cup of coffee and tried to damp down her feelings of disappointment. She was building what happened into something way too big, and she couldn't let herself be distracted from what had gone so well before. She patted him on the head as she passed the kitchen table, where he'd settled with his tea and his tablet. He turned to her, smiled slightly. All normal. All good.

As she stepped outside onto the veranda, into the warm autumn sunshine, she told herself she had to let this go. Not let one of Rob's jokes, or quirks, or pranks, fuel her anxiety or lower her self-esteem. She was still happy, that was the main thing.

They were fine, the two of them, trick or no trick.

Chapter 5

Jacey's mother struggled with the iPad Rob had given her before they left for England, so she and Jacey could Zoom and Facetime.

"Mom?"

Picture off. Sound off. Sound on. Picture … picture …

Picture reversed … oh, there was her face. Back again.

"Jacey? Can you hear me?"

Her mother was sitting at the kitchen table of her senior apartment, framed by reminders of the past – faded photographs and dusty souvenirs, and a shiny ceramic plate decorated with hearts and flowers that said 'Jacey and Rob 7/17/13' in bright, swirly lettering. Something in her mother's confused and anxious expression reminded Jacey of their annual Christmas viewings of *The Wizard of Oz*, with Dorothy locked up in the witch's tower, looking at Aunty Em in the crystal ball, her aunt's image fading and swirling and reappearing for an instant, desperation and worry furrowed on her face.

"Is everything all right over there, sweetie baby?"

When was the last time her mom had called her that? High school. Back when she was going out with the guy from the local college who had tattoos and piercings and a string of convictions for various petty crimes.

"I'm fine, Mom. Honest. I'm keeping busy, like I told you."

And Jacey *was* fine, in her own way. The days were passing quickly and she didn't feel bored. She often went into Lewes to explore the town's narrow streets and secret alleys, keeping track in her journal of all the things she was discovering. Sometimes it worried her, how much time went by without her talking to anyone except Rob, but she didn't tell her mother about that.

"You haven't gone to Cambridgeshire, have you?" Her mother's voice sounded strained. "To Nana's hometown?"

"Not yet," Jacey said, feeling a twinge of guilt.

Her mother breathed out what sounded like a sigh of relief.

"Well, there's nothing there anymore, so I wouldn't bother. From Nana's time, I mean. And anything left over from the war would have been torn down years ago, like the US airbase, and Daddy's old barracks."

"Just as well that I've got so much to do, then," Jacey said.

That was a lie, of course. She was occupying herself as much as possible, but what she spent her time on wasn't exactly work, not a job in the sense that Rob's was. She could travel to Cambridge and back every day if she wanted; there were plenty of trains from Brighton, the nearest large town. There was nothing to stop her.

Her mother seemed happy to change the subject. "Yes, it's good that you're busy, honey."

"I'm even cooking a little, Mom. The English things that Nana used to make."

"Not shepherd's pie?"

"I found a recipe on the internet. A better version, I think."

"I hope so," her mother laughed. "I still remember the stink of that old mutton she used to grind up by hand. And the cabbage, boiled to within an inch of its life. My word, that was awful. Even the pigs wouldn't eat it."

Her mother stopped talking and looked away. She coughed slightly, as if something dry had got caught in her throat. Jacey noticed the worn look around her eyes, the tiny wrinkles, the dark, slightly sunken skin underneath.

"All right, Mom?"

Her mother sighed again. "Oh, I'm fine, darling. The memory of that smell! And worrying about you, of course. How are you getting along? You and Rob?"

"Oh, Rob is totally in is element."

"And he's treating you OK?"

"Of course he is, Mom. Why wouldn't he be?"

Her mother took another deep breath, as if she had more to say on the subject, but in the end she just nodded. "Good, Jacey. That's good. It's just, well …"

Finally, she wiped the worried frown from her face and smiled. She kissed the screen of the tablet and waved, ending the call after a few fumbled attempts.

Jacey put down the phone. She tried not to think about how lonely her mother sounded, how tired and anxious she looked. And those questions about her and Rob – where were they coming from?

As she bent over the deep sink and sprinkled more cleanser on the drain, something prickled on the back of her neck. A rush of heat, like a sudden bout of sunburn. Instinctively, she pulled up the back of her shirt and spread her hair behind her shoulders, covering up any patch of bare skin. She turned around, thinking someone might have come into the room – Helen offering to help her clean, Rob grabbing a book he'd left behind in his dash to get out the door on time.

No one was there, of course, but she still felt something, and she remembered the conversation with her mother about Nana Ivy. Was it Nana's ghost, watching from beyond the grave, with her piercing, burning eyes? She'd been a stern taskmaster – one of those everything-in-its-place types – and Jacey's mother had gone against that grain after Nana died, allowing the farm kitchen counter to be over-run with dirty dishes, and the floor sticky with muck brought in from outside.

Until the ghost of Nana struck, that was. It was a joke between Jacey and her mother, how Nana's ghost would come to Jacey's mom and force her to clean at the worst possible moment. On Christmas morning before opening presents. On birthdays, delaying the party. When they were meant to be getting in the car and heading somewhere for a vacation – never very far, a weekend at a rented lake cabin, a trailer on a campsite in a local state park.

But even though they joked about it, it wasn't always funny, this 'haunting'. It would upset her mother sometimes, making her so frantic that Jacey imagined Nana's ghost was actually there. And when she tried to help, her mother would shake her off, do everything by herself, as if the responsibility for keeping things clean was hers and hers alone.

Jacey started scrubbing, and the memories came, unbidden. Her mother and father, talking while they were huddled over some important papers in the farm kitchen, or out in the barn, dark and damp with the smell of horsehair and hay. Those strange episodes where her mother's words would turn into crying and shuddering, and her father would try to comfort her, but she'd push him away and say that it was *her* fault, what happened, nobody else's.

What had her mother been talking about, Jacey once again wondered, rubbing the stone surfaces harder and harder. Ancient history, whatever it was.

Me, her mother would say.

I'm the one who's to blame. Me. *Me.*

Chapter 6

"What's that you're writing, Jace?"

She'd taken to having her morning coffee outside on the lawn, when the weather was warm enough, and filling a few pages in her writing journal. She hadn't seen Rob come out of the house, but when she looked up, he was smiling, as if he was genuinely interested, and the morning sun was shining on his short dark hair, the greyish flecks making him look even more boyish, somehow. He'd ditched the button-down preppy look for a faded Guinness T-shirt, khaki shorts and white Adidas. Her adorable husband. Handsome. Intelligent.

"Just some travel notes." She closed the book – a cheap lined notebook she'd bought at a newsstand at the station in London while they'd waited for the train down to the South Coast. To disguise its true contents (stupid, she thought, as she did it – I mean who cared, really? And anyway, wasn't it her business and nobody else's?) she'd carved the words *Travel Journal* on the front with a purple gel pen she found in one of the drawers in the little TV room – the snug as Helen called it. "Almost caught up with everything we did in London."

"Sounds cool. I'd love to read it sometime."

"Well, I might put some of this online, add a few pictures and call it a blog. You could definitely read it then."

Like that. Flippant, as if whatever she was doing was no big deal.

A shadow covered Rob's face, a shadow that told her she might be inching a bit too closely to his turf – the writing part, at least. He stepped closer, as if he could somehow see through the cover of her closed book.

"A blog?"

"Yeah. Like, a year in the life of an academic's partner."

"Really?"

She shrugged. She'd just thought of that. A handy, throwaway idea to detract him from what was really inside her notebook.

"That's OK with you, isn't it?"

"I guess. I mean, nobody really reads them anymore, do they?"

He was on his way to work. Not a teaching day – his academic timetable wasn't up and running yet – but a seminar for new lecturers. He'd bristled at the name of the event. He wasn't called 'Professor' here like he was in the USA, because Professor was an honorary title, not a job description. Here he was a senior lecturer. What did that sound like? Some retiree from a nursing home, wheeled in to teach English Appreciation to guys on football scholarships.

He took out his phone, checked the time. "I need to get to the station." He bent over, kissed her head. "See you later. Tonight."

She watched him go, and when she was sure he wasn't going to pop back to pick up something he'd left behind, she took the notebook out again, peeked at the morning's writing. It wasn't bad, even if she said so herself. She'd written a description of Rob's face, finding just the right metaphors for the colour of his eyes and the way his lips curled up when he smiled..

She also tried to capture the sounds outside the bedroom window as she'd lie half awake. The trees swaying and rustling in the breeze, the whooshing sound that she took to be the river, only it was probably just traffic on the main highway.

These observations weren't for a travel blog, of course. They were going to go into a story that she'd been thinking about ever since Rob told her that he wanted to do a year's exchange in England and reminded her that her grandmother had come from some village near Cambridge, leaving her home to live on a farm in Minnesota as a G.I. bride in the Second World War.

It would make a good novel, wouldn't it? A woman from the back of beyond – the English fens, whatever they were – moving to the ass end of nowhere on the other side of the world? From one closed, almost cloistered, world to another.

She tried to imagine what Nana Ivy had been like as a young woman. She'd seemed stern and old even in her wedding picture, taken when she was only eighteen. How could a woman who looked like that have made such a huge leap for love – following a man she hardly knew to a new life in a country she must have known little about, as if she was desperate to make an escape?

But looks could be deceiving, and anyway, Nana Ivy would look much better on the cover of Jacey's book. There'd be a sepia print of a pretty, if somewhat plain woman, with a kind gentle face, and she'd be standing in the doorway of a little house that was nothing like the crumbling hovel in the gloomy village where Nana Ivy had grown up. Jacey's book cover picture would be a pretty thatched cottage with climbing roses curving around the doorway and leaded windows.

So she wasn't exactly lying to Rob, when he asked; she just wasn't telling him she was doing what he would call 'real writing'. The kind he didn't have time for anymore, now that he was stuck on the treadmill of academia, and now that he was having to support both himself and a wife.

And of course, she hadn't had time either, back in the USA. She'd had a demanding job as a development officer for a regional arts centre. It involved plenty of writing, like Rob's job did, but it was mostly coming up with grant proposals to large corporate funders and writing begging letters to local companies and well-off individuals. Rob referred to the writing that she managed to squeeze into the margins of her life – the poems, the aborted attempts at short stories – as a hobby, so that's how she thought of it, too. And as long as she talked about what she was doing in those dismissive terms, he wouldn't feel threatened, even if he did find out what she was really up to.

She read through what she'd written the previous day and finished her coffee. She couldn't stay out here all morning, even though she wished she could. She'd already told Rob she was going into Lewes to do some shopping and check out the town a little more, so she packed her bag up and went inside, keeping the front door open, wedging it with a heavy book so it wouldn't slam shut.

It was better that way, because the fact was she didn't like being in the house on her own. It wasn't the dark corridor that led to their bedroom or the empty rooms she didn't dare look into, or even the sense she'd had before, in the kitchen, of being watched. It was something she couldn't put into words, but she felt as if the house didn't like her very much. That it was judging her, finding her unworthy, because she wasn't an academic or researcher, something important like that.

With the door still open, she went through to the den and into the kitchen, where the sunlight was strong through the south-facing windows and she could see the little copse of trees in front of Helen and Martin's cottage; in winter after the leaves had fallen she'd be able to see through it, and know they were home, house lights glowing in the darkness, their silhouettes against the closed curtains.

She rinsed her cup in the sink, checked the fridge, made a list of the things they needed. Butter, and the vegan equivalent for Rob. Milk – cow and oat. They were low on bread, too, and the lettuce was looking tired and limp.

She emptied her backpack in the kitchen, but kept a pen, her wallet, the notebook. She thought about taking her sweatshirt – it could get colder later, while she was in town – but it was hanging in the closet upstairs, and she didn't want to go back up there.

Thinking about it made her shudder – that long hallway, dark as soon as you got to the top of the stairs. Those empty rooms, like hollow tombs, with the doors half open, the few bits of furniture covered with discoloured white sheets.

She tightened the straps on her backpack – that in itself seemed to offer her warmth and protection, and it gave her confidence as she went back through the den into the hallway, ready to leave.

And then she felt it – the air moving, a slight hollowing that stopped her in her tracks.

She hadn't felt it since that day in London when they'd met Jared and Bex at the haunted pub. What had brought it on here? Was it thinking about Nana Ivy again? Remembering the pictures of the old Cambridgeshire cottage?

Next came a sound – not wailing or screaming, the noises Rob had teased her about—but the ringing of tiny bells, tinkling gently, like indoor wind chimes.

She held her breath. Maybe that would stop the sound, as if her breathing was causing a disruption, increasing the airflow, like the butterfly effect.

Again. Tinkling. Slightly louder.

There was nothing sinister about what she was hearing – it was a pretty, musical sound – so why was her heart pounding? She checked the front door, made sure it was still open, proving to herself that she wasn't trapped inside. Outside, the sun was blazing on the lawn, and the damp grass shimmered in the sunlight.

But the tiny bells didn't stop. Would not, although she was willing them to, holding her breath, squeezing her eyes shut, as if sheer mental willpower could overcome them.

She relaxed her body, tried to clear her mind, but the sound continued. She looked up at the chandeliers, hoping an imperceptible breeze from the doorway was making them sway back and forth. Total stillness, and the bells kept ringing.

She looked outside again. The sunshine. The blue sky.

No change. She should go into the kitchen. Check the serving pantry. The servant's bells – there must be a window open. There was no other explanation, unless there were windchimes hidden in an undiscovered cupboard or closet.

She listened carefully – where was the sound coming from? Upstairs? One of the rooms at the back of the house? Why was it so hard to figure out? Was the noise even *in* the house? Maybe Helen or Martin were ringing bells, signalling to each other.

She plugged her ears, but the sound didn't change, and over the tinkling she heard a voice saying, "Leave now."

Only it didn't seem like someone talking to her, and it didn't feel like it was coming from inside her head.

She swallowed. The ringing continued, but she had no idea if the sounds were even real – maybe this was tinnitus. She'd heard of that. An inner ear infection, some kind of imbalance.

The voice again. Hers – it had to be. "Go, now."

She locked the door behind her, and when she got out to the lawn she saw Helen, dressed in the same clothing she'd had on the day Jacey and Rob arrived – grass-stained sneakers, a full skirt made of light denim, and a T-shirt. She was at the edge of the lawn, close to the path leading to the driveway, spraying the rose bushes with something from a plastic bottle.

Jacey approached her, trying to smile, forcing herself not to look back at the house to see if she could figure out the source of the invisible bell-ringers.

"Heading into town?" Helen asked. She looked up for a second, but carried on with what she was doing, gently spritzing the leaves of a yellow-tipped pink rose that was beginning to lose its petals.

"That's the plan," Jacey said. "A bit of shopping and maybe coffee in a café. Pretty exciting."

"I'm sure it is." Helen laughed.

Jacey felt relaxed with Helen. She was motherly and kind, and the way she sighed when she laughed seemed normal – she got Jacey's little joke – and that was what Jacey needed now that she was on her own so much of the time. "These flowers must be hard work for you," Jacey said.

Helen straightened her back, put down her spray bottle and the bucket containing all her other gardening tools. "They're very old-fashioned varieties that are planted here," she said, "so they take a bit of minding, but it's very rewarding when they're in bloom."

"I haven't exactly got green fingers," Jacey said, "but maybe you could teach me a thing or two, when you have the time. Especially if they're, like, historical. Rob would probably be interested, too."

"Gladly," Helen said. She looked up at the house, as if she was expecting to see something.

I should tell her what I heard, Jacey thought. Make light of it, obviously, not act frightened, just curious. *What could that tinkling sound be*, I wonder? Maybe Helen would have an explanation. Martin might have gone inside the house to fix something. Maybe his tool kit was full of spare light bulbs that would be knocking together and that's what made the noise.

"You might need a jumper," Helen said. She must have noticed the blank look on Jacey's face. "A cardigan or sweater?" She looked at Jacey's bare shoulders. "It can get cold in the late afternoon."

Jacey shivered. She felt stupid and exposed. Too dumb to know what a jumper was in England – Rob must have told her that in one of his many mansplaining sessions – and too ashamed to admit the reason she didn't want to go back into the house to get one, was because she was scared.

"I'll be fine," she said. "Where I grew up winters were so freezing, I hardly feel the cold unless I'm caught in an ice storm."

"Well, that's good, then," Helen said. She looked up at the house again. Could Helen hear the bells, too? Did she know what they were?

"Time to go," the voice/not voice inside Jacey's head said.

She gave a little wave, readjusted her backpack again, and trundled down towards the driveway. Despite Helen's kind smiles and reassurance, Jacey was glad to get away from her, and the encroaching shadows of Malin House.

Chapter 7

"No," Jacey said, smiling at the woman at the café table opposite, who'd just struck up a conversation. "No children."

The woman – she was much older than Jacey, mid-fifties or thereabouts, with short greying hair and a crooked fringe that she probably cut herself – stirred sugar into her coffee and winked.

"Not yet anyway, right, dear?"

Jacey shrugged and went back to her writing. Not easy, with the low-level hum of conversation and the strong smell of stewed coffee and an aroma that reminded her of the food served up in her school cafeteria. The café was old-fashioned, but not in a retro or vintage way. There were cracked vinyl tiles on the floor, with grimy dirt in the gaps between. The walls were covered with darkened veneer panelling and there were plates with pictures of Princess Diana and some smiling old woman in a tiara called the Queen Mum.

Jacey put her pen down when the waitress brought her cup of coffee and a tiny mug of what looked like cream.

"So, are you on holiday?"

Stupid of Jacey to have stopped writing. Now the woman wasn't going to let her go.

"Vacation, I mean – I heard an accent."

"No, my husband has a job here."

"American?"

Jacey smiled politely and answered with another vague "mmmm". She turned back to the notebook. She didn't want to be rude, but she wasn't in the mood for all the questions.

"Writing about your new life here in Lewes?"

Jacey shook her head. "No, nothing like that."

She put her head down, started writing again but the woman wasn't going to be put off that easily.

"So you're a novelist? A poet? How exciting!"

"Not really," Jacey said. "Just …"

The woman was looking at her expectantly, grey eyes widening, brightening behind thick wire varifocals.

Jacey shrugged. "You know."

"Well, you've certainly ended up in the right place, then."

The woman got up and came over to Jacey's table. "Mind if I join you?"

Before Jacey could answer, she'd sat across from her, chair scraping across the floor as she pulled it to the table.

"This town is full of writers, actually. Poets, playwrights, you name it."

The woman opened the heavy canvas delivery bag that was slung across her chest and took out a sheet of paper. "I'm posting these around town, but I can spare one for you."

The paper said "Lewes Writing Group. New Members welcome. Wednesday nights, 6.30 PM. The Downsman Pub."

"The pub is up by the castle," she said. "Why don't you come along? Everybody would just love you, I know they would."

Jacey looked at the paper, folded it neatly and placed it in her journal. "I'll think about it. Thanks."

"You should definitely pop by. Like I said, this place is crawling with writers – I mean published authors, not just delusional scribblers. One of our poets was shortlisted for the National Poetry Award last year, and we've got a Carnegie nominee and Mandy Bryon – you heard of her? She was on the Costa longlist five years ago."

"Sounds impressive." Jacey had no idea who those people or what those awards were.

"So you'll come along on Wednesday?" the woman said and then laughed. "Oh, I'm Madlyn, by the way. OK, my real name's Margaret but no way was I going to shorten it to Maggie – you're too young to remember Mrs. Thatcher, aren't you? Anyway, Madlyn sounds more, I don't know, mysterious. Don't you think?"

Her husky laugh reminded Jacey of one of the bartenders at a little student bar where she sometimes met up with her old college friends. She imagined spending afternoons on the Malin House lawn with this Madlyn—and other writer friends of hers—quaffing a few glasses of prosecco, or downing a bottle of Sambuca, one shot at the time. And then Rob coming back from work with his briefcase full of student essays and his face all red and scrunched together with disapproval.

"And what's your name?"

Jacey's heart sank. Firstly, she didn't really want to get to know this woman and secondly, telling her name would mean a long, drawn-out conversation about its origins, just like it had with Rob, and with virtually everyone she'd met since. Nobody was happy with it; everyone had something to say.

"My name's Jacey," she said. She held the woman's clear-eyed gaze, as if daring her to make some kind of comment.

But the woman just smiled again. "Well, I'm pleased to meet you, Jacey," she said. "I certainly hope we'll meet again."

"Yes," Jacey said. "I'll think about the club."

Madlyn stood up, held out her hand. "Do more than think about it," she said. "We'd be delighted to see you." She waved at the cashier behind the till and lumbered to the door.

"You probably wouldn't think so," Madlyn said, smiling again, "but I'm sure we've got loads in common."

The bell above the door rang, and Jacey was reminded of the strange sounds she'd heard at Malin House.

"In fact, Jacey," Madlyn said, "I know we do."

Chapter 8

One month into their stay, the end of September, and things were tense. The autumn was closing in on them – the days were so much shorter here than at home – and nothing had turned out to be quite what they'd been promised.

The noises, those strange tinkling bells, had stopped; that was one good thing. And Jacey didn't feel quite so unsettled in the house now that she'd moved some clothes downstairs – her jacket, a sweatshirt, and an extra pair of sneakers – and put them in the small closet in the den. She'd taken a few toiletries down, too – toothbrush, moisturiser – in case she needed to freshen up during the day. There was a half-bath off the kitchen – Helen called it a cloakroom – with a sink and toilet and shelf space for a few items.

She was pleased with what she was writing – her observations of British life, as limited as those things were so far – and with the meals she was cooking, and the way that she was keeping the kitchen cleaner than she'd ever managed anywhere else.

But Rob was disappointed and dismayed by the way things were going for him. His university post would mostly be teaching freshmen – Rob called them 'First Years' – and he felt he was back to square one, professionally, teaching students who were barely out of high school. Not what he'd been led to believe.

And they'd had to pay a 'surcharge' on their healthcare, which left Rob apoplectic with rage. Before they left the US he'd gone on and on about the National Health Service and how it was free at the point of use but now, it turned out, it was free at the point of use to everybody except university professors – sorry, lecturers – on exchange programmes, and their spouses.

Most of all, the whole 'lecturer' thing still grated. Rob thought his book at least would have awarded him a title of greater respect. He was assured he'd be given a temporary professorship on the back of it here in the UK, but he wasn't part of their system, so therefore … regrettably … yes, of course, he could rightly refer to himself as Doctor Gibson, but Professor? No. Sorry. Just not how things worked.

The humiliations kept piling up – such as struggling to get the car they'd been promised and then it turning out to be a standard transmission – a stick shift – that meant every time they dared venture out Rob was honked and yelled at, and drivers flashed their headlights when they drove behind him.

"What does that mean?" Jacey asked one afternoon as they were driving from the campus to a local hiking area up in the hills – *Downs*, Rob reminded her, *here in Sussex they were called the Downs*.

"What?" he asked, when he finally got into the left lane and was able to relax a few minutes before having to press down on the clutch and shift gears again.

"The other car flashing? Do you know what that's about?"

He glanced over at her, a quick shot of contempt. As if anyone with half a brain would have been able to figure out that it was a compliment to his genius driving. Why was she even bothering to ask?

Rob loved the house, though.

He'd walk from the entrance to the drawing room to the dining room, and through into the kitchen and den. Then back to the entrance hall and up the stairs, and he'd linger on the landing and look at the chandelier, and then he'd go back down the stairs and do the whole loop again.

He took the sheets off the furniture in the drawing room and began retreating there after dinner, lighting the fire, like he was camping out. He never told Jacey she wasn't allowed in during the evening, but it became understood. By him; by her.

And he kept out of 'her' den. An unspoken trade-off, a bit of equality, even though she wanted him on the sofa beside her, the two of them cuddling up in the evening, watching movies, all that weird British TV, otherwise what was the point of them being here together?

Sometimes she could smell smoke from the drawing room – cigars, not cigarettes or weed. And she heard him speaking. At least she thought she did. If she crept from the den into the kitchen and opened the door to the servants' waiting room, she could hear talking, sometimes, and laughter. Voices that she couldn't make out. Women. Maybe it was the radio or a podcast. Maybe it was a phone call home – he had a mother, too, after all. Or Zoom chats with old friends who he probably missed terribly. Or maybe it was just another sound that wasn't real, like the bells; a figment of her overblown imagination that would drive her mad if she wasn't more careful.

There was a break in the week before Rob's teaching term began, so they took advantage of the warm weather and travelled to London to see their friends Jared and Bex.

"Have you heard much from them lately?" Jacey asked.

Rob was staring out of the train window, watching the trackside shrubbery that was decorated with bits of torn plastic supermarket bags, like modern art Christmas trees.

"Honey?"

Rob shook his head, as if he'd just been woken from a nap. "No," he said, taking a deep breath. "I haven't seen them, since, um … like, the day we met at the Grenadier?"

"Well, nice they got in touch again."

"Yeah."

Rob smiled at her, and let her take his hand, before looking out the window again. He was wearing black jeans and a navy university hoodie. He'd grown a scraggly little beard – stubble, really, that was flecked with bits of grey like his hair – but he looked cooler with it, sexy, and she thought about that first day in the house, how he'd been so overcome with lust and how their lovemaking had an urgency that she hadn't felt in months, and sadly, hadn't felt again.

He pulled his hand away. It was like he could read her mind. As if he knew she'd been thinking about sex with him, and his pulling away was a signal for her to not get her hopes up, that what had happened when they first got to the house was an aberration. It was back to normal now. Once, twice a month, maybe, if he wasn't tired, if he didn't have too much work on his plate. Back to the loneliness of lying beside a body that she desired, but was too timid and anxious to touch.

"Where are we going?" she asked brightly, trying to keep the disappointment from her voice.

"A place Jared recommended. Another one of their haunted pubs. Somewhere in the back end of Mayfair."

Rob led the way through the train station to the Underground, and down the escalators that plumbed the depths of the city. Jacey stood in front of him, conscious of his presence on the step behind her, wishing he would touch her shoulders, or lean over and kiss her head. He guided her onto the Victoria line platform and held her hand as they got off the train at Green Park station, but he dropped it as soon as they were safely on the platform.

From there, it was a winding route across a four-lane road – Piccadilly, Rob said it was – and into a warren of narrow streets that ran higgledy-piggledy behind the main road, away from Green Park, with names that lasted for a block and then shifted direction slightly and changed into something else, Half Moon Street, Curzon Street, and then a quick turning into a tiny road that led to a square with a tree and a red telephone box, and old street lights that looked like the Victorian gas lamps she'd seen pictures of.

"Wow," she said, wanting to stop and take it all in, but knowing that Rob would be annoyed that they looked like tourists. "How did you manage to find this place without looking at your phone?"

"It's not as out of the way as it looks."

Jacey laughed. "Really? It's like the maze at Hampton Court. I wouldn't be able to find my way back to the Underground station if you paid me a hundred bucks."

Jacey must have said the 'hundred bucks' part of her sentence a bit too loudly because she noticed Rob flinch.

"Yeah, well, I looked at the map before we set off this morning, so …"

And that was that; no more discussion.

Bex and Jared were already at their table. The pub was dark and it took Jacey a few seconds for her eyes to adjust, but the plunge into darkness didn't faze Rob. He seemed to know exactly where Bex and Jared would be sitting and he left Jacey behind, floundering in confusion, getting stuck between a beefy man who was coming out of the men's toilet and a nimble-footed waitress gliding through the kitchen's swing doors.

By the time Jacey got to the table, Rob had taken a seat beside Jared.

"Hey."

Jared stood up, gave her a quick air kiss; from Bex she got a wave. It was not considered cool to give hugs and kisses, with memories of Covid still persistent.

"Did you want to find a place outside?" Bex said. "It just felt a little cold today."

Jacey looked at Rob, waiting for him to answer. These were his friends, after all, that made it his prerogative. But he had his phone out and was looking at something, and Jacey sat down opposite Bex at the other end of the table from him.

"This is fine," Jacey said. "Really."

Rob put his phone away. "Oh, sorry," he said. "Something from work. Didn't mean to space out."

He looked at the phone again – the screen was blank as far as Jacey could see. He turned it off and stuffed it into his back pocket. Then he moved his chair slightly closer to Jared, while Bex leaned across the table towards Jacey.

"So, how's life in the haunted house?"

Jacey looked at Rob. This was his area of expertise. Going on about follies and neo-Gothic architecture, and why it was so prevalent at the time the house was built, but he seemed to be studiously ignoring the women. "It's not really haunted," she said, "and it's not even that old, at least not by British standards."

"Oh, I'm disappointed to hear that. Rob gave us the wrong impression entirely."

There was something in Bex's voice that Jacey didn't like. It was as if she was admonishing Rob, but why would she do that? Besides, she hardly knew him. It had been years since they'd worked together, even before he'd met Jacey.

"Sorry?" Rob and Jared looked up.

"What's this you're talking about?" Jared asked.

"Bex asked about where we're staying," Jacey said. "About how it was, living in a haunted house, and I said it wasn't haunted, and Bex said Rob had told you guys the opposite."

"Oh." Jared looked confused. "Is that right? You guys are living in a haunted house? Must have missed that conversation. If I'd known, we'd have been down there in a heartbeat."

A waitress came to the table with plastic-coated menus. Jacey took one, but when she tried to look at it her eyes glazed over and the print was just a blur. She coughed a few times. It was as if something was stuck in the back of her throat. She thought of her mother – their latest phone call, when her voice seemed to tighten and she struggled to speak.

Rob squinted at the menu. "I hear the fish and chips are excellent here," he said.

No one answered him. What could they say – how would they know?

Suddenly, it was like all the air had been sucked out of the room, and the other customers had vanished. Jacey felt the hollowing – familiar by now – but why had it come on so fast? So strong? She balled her hands into fists and held them between her legs, squeezing her thighs as tightly as she could to keep herself together. No keening or swaying. Just be still. That's the way.

When the waitress came back, Rob smiled. Charming as always, to pretty young women at least. Earlier, when she'd brought the menu, it was obvious that she'd come from another country, and Rob asked her about this.

"Poland," she said.

"Oh, that's amazing," Rob said. How long have you been here in England?

"Before Brexit," she said. "Many years now."

"And you're planning to stay?"

"I'm a citizen. Yes." She sighed. She's had this conversation before, Jacey thought, and not always with people who were as nice to her as Rob was being.

"Well, that's just great," Rob gushed. "Seriously. Really happy for you."

The waitress sighed warily. "Yes. Me too. Your order?"

Rob didn't say anything about the fish, or ask any more questions. He ordered a cheeseburger, Bex had a salad and Jared ordered lasagne.

"I'll have the fish and chips," Jacey said. She smiled at the waitress. "My husband was saying that they're meant to be delicious."

"They are good," the waitress said. She looked down at her little iPad and clicked on an item. She smiled over at Rob. "Your husband is very clever."

"So what, you think I'm banging that waitress?"

Jacey didn't answer. She'd managed to bag the window seat on the way back, wresting Rob from his usual prize position, and on the whole journey they'd hardly spoken a word to each other. They were nearly home and the trees along the tracks were getting darker and darker; the sky above was almost black by the time they pulled into Lewes station.

"I'm really tired," Jacey said. "It was a long trip, just for lunch, don't you think?"

"Well, no, the pub was nice and it was good to see our friends."

Jacey laughed. "Our friends."

"What's that supposed to mean?"

When they got off the train Jacey went through the ticket barrier first for a change, and Rob got trapped behind her. He had to wait for the guard to let him through, but Jacey kept going without him, taking a left onto the street outside, and rushing past the taxi rank, and through the tunnel that ran under the tracks. As she got to the other side, and started up the hill again, she heard Rob's voice, calling after her.

"Jacey! Jace! Will you please wait up?"

Jacey would not. She wanted to run, but the hill was getting steeper and she was quickly winded. How had she got so out of shape? Rob was behind her, panting, pounding his feet on the pavement, finally catching up with her.

A hand on her upper arm.

"Come on, Jacey, what's the matter?"

Squeezing hard. Forcing her to stop.

"Nothing," she said.

"Oh, don't pull that one, you've been in a bad mood from the minute we walked into the Sheaf."

"The Sheaf?"

"The Wheatsheaf. That's the name of the pub."

"So why did you call it the Sheaf?"

"That's what people call it."

She felt the anger rise up inside her, threatening to boil over into a direct accusation.

"What people?" she shouted. "Who calls it that?"

Rob looked at her like she was crazy. "I don't know. People. Locals."

"Locals," she growled. "Any locals in particular?"

Rob let go of her arm and pulled himself up straighter. Jacey stepped back, keeping her distance, but didn't run away.

"What are you insinuating?" Rob said.

Jacey laughed. *Insinuating*. This was like the re-run of some stupid TV movie. Something she and her mom would have watched when she was in high school. Big-shouldered women with huge 1980s hairdos, spouting soap opera dialogue.

"Nothing," she said. "I'm just tired of you having to be the expert on everything. One step ahead of me. Like knowing exactly where the pub is, and what the 'locals' supposedly call it, and having inside knowledge of what's the best food on the menu, having to be so fucking charming and clever all the time, and …"

"And what?"

She remembered what Bex said about the house being haunted, about Rob telling them about it, but she couldn't mention that now. Because it would lead to more questions. About what he was doing when he woke up at night, wandering around the house that she was scared to even breathe in. About the way he was hiding from her, locking himself in the drawing room. Shutting her out.

"Talking to other women when I don't know about it."

"What other women?"

She shook her head. She wasn't going to voice her fears, not now. She wasn't going to give him anything specific he could confirm or deny; she'd already said too much.

"For your information, I know dozens of women here, Jacey," he said. "Colleagues. Students. And, yeah, a few waitresses here and there, and no, you don't always know when I'm talking to them – because how the hell could you, unless you're a fucking spy?"

She backed away from him, her shoulders slumped, her posture slackening, sick with fear about what he was going to say next, not wanting to hear his excuses. As she turned around and ran towards the tunnel, she listened for the sound of him shouting after her, to stop. To wait, so he could explain. Like they do on TV, in the movies, so it all ends with a rushing into arms and a torrent of apologies, and a torrid kiss and an endless night of making long, languorous love.

But Rob didn't shout.

She stumbled through the tunnel, sobbing and choking on the damp air. She hurried up the path to the driveway, and across the lawn, panicked and alone. As she approached the house she looked up at the dark windows, the door like an angry mouth, and she wondered what she'd done to make it hate her so much.

Chapter 9

Jacey struggled to keep up on the rocky, uneven path.

They were pretending things were normal for the afternoon. Just a nice millennial couple, borderline hipsters in knee-high rubber rainboots – Rob called them wellies and told her a long boring story about why they were called that – out for a Sunday walk in Brighton's Stanmer Park, in the South Downs foothills, along with dozens of other families and couples.

That was a good sign, wasn't it? That they could at least fake being reasonably content?

But even as they trudged along, Rob wouldn't let things go. The pub meet in London with Jared and Bex had been a source of bickering since it happened, and it was all down to her, apparently. "You drank too much, that was the problem," Rob said. "You got all paranoid and weird."

"I had two lousy beers," she answered, breathless and angry. "Jared was the weird one, remember? Getting so drunk you almost had to carry him to the taxi?"

The park was beautiful on an autumn day like this, with the trees changing colour and the sound of dried leaves crunching under their feet, and the nip of autumn cold in the air. Jacey and Rob missed the first path and had to clamber up the side of the hill to find the hiking trail. Rob took her hand and hauled her up. She stumbled slightly when she got to the top and he had to hold her for a moment to keep her steady. She felt his hands, strong on her back, but he must have felt them too, because as soon as she was stable, he pulled them away and the argument continued.

"The way you got upset over nothing, that was the problem," Rob said. "On the way home, what was that about?"

And he was off again, not waiting for an answer. She watched him stride away, take out his phone, check the time. She half expected him to make a call before she caught up with him. *Yeah, she's with me. No, I couldn't ditch her, could I? I mean, how would that look? She's my wife, after all, I can't just walk away.*

After a few seconds, he turned around and shrugged, throwing out his arms, a gesture of impatience and annoyance.

"Come on, honey. Keep up."

She savoured the 'honey' and scampered after him like a puppy. She wished there'd been other people around, to witness what he said. That single term of endearment, that worthless crumb validating her relationship, her marriage, her life.

She was a few feet behind him – he still hadn't slowed down enough for her to catch up with him – when she heard the sound.

Bells. Glassy, like gentle chimes. Here, in the woods, where bells just weren't possible, couldn't be explained away. She stopped to listen, and Rob increased the distance between them. The sound continued, and just like in the house she couldn't figure out where it was coming from: above her, on the higher part of the hill, in front of her, near where Rob was trudging on ahead, below her, in the open parkland at the bottom of the woods, or nowhere. Everywhere. Inside her head. Random noises.

Tinnitus. She'd looked it up on the internet after the last time. She needed to go to the doctor. They were registered to an on-campus general practitioner, and she wouldn't need to tell Rob. She could just go. By herself.

She shouted after him, "Hey. I'm still here, you know."

She lightened her voice as she spoke, tried to add a slight trill of unvoiced laughter, to make it all seem positive. She wasn't bitching at him. Or being sarcastic – it was a joke. A bit of fun. Hahaha. See how relaxed and carefree I can be?

But the trick hadn't fooled him and when she finally caught up with him he was scowling, and the bells were still making their unrelenting jangle.

"Sorry," Rob said, but his eyes belied his words. He wasn't even trying to seem cheerful or happy anymore. He looked miserable, emotionally dead, and the thought of why he felt that way made Jacey's stomach churn.

He'd been happy in London, at that pub, flirting with the waitress, engaging in banter with Bex, talking about the latest football – that's what he called soccer now – scores with Jared. But when they got on the train home again, when he was alone with her …

She put her hands up to her ears. Maybe if the ringing stopped, these other, unwelcome thoughts would go away, too. Maybe she could take a deep breath, and relish the damp woody scent of wet leaves, and moist soil and crisp air that hadn't warmed because the sun couldn't break through the thick canopy of brittle-leafed trees.

"You OK?" Rob's voice was deep, echoey, as if he was speaking through a tunnel. The hollowing was back, on top of the bells. Part and parcel of the same thing, maybe. A new addition to the experience. And all played out in public, where Rob would notice, and others could, too.

"I'm fine," she said. "Just dizzy. I need to sit down."

There was a bench at the side of the path, thankfully – it was rough and splintery but better than the cold damp ground. She wobbled slightly as she sat, as if the earth was shaking.

"What's the matter, honey?"

Rob's voice was gentle, tender, almost. *Honey.* She clung to the word.

"I don't know," she said. "It's my ears, I think. I can't …" She leaned over, head between her knees, as if she were actually feeling faint. It was all she could think of to do, the only normal response to the abnormality of what was happening.

"You can't what?"

She willed her back to straighten, her mouth to move. Sitting up again, shaking her head as if that would clear her fevered brain, she said, "Nothing. I'm fine."

Because Rob could never know what was happening. How would he understand what she was going through? He'd think she was weak, pathetic.

"Just hearing weird sounds."

He sat beside her, hands held together between his legs. No attempt at touching her or putting an arm around her trembling shoulders.

"Sounds?"

She waited for him to say more, for him to ask if they were sounds like he'd heard – that first day, the screams that he later claimed were just a prank.

"Like bells ringing."

"Really?"

"Yeah, weird, huh." She shook her head a few times, as if she thought she could get rid of the sounds that way. Then she tapped her head, trying to make it seem funny. Rob was watching her, but he didn't laugh. He didn't say anything – how could he?

"I think I might have tinnitus," she said. "That causes ringing supposedly."

"Oh," Rob said. He sighed, relieved. "That would explain it."

"I guess I should go to the doctor's office on campus, get an appointment, have it checked out. What do you think?"

There were rustling sounds on the trail behind them. A dog barked, suddenly appearing beside the bench, sniffing and snuffling in the leaves. It was a snappy terrier mix, the kind that would need a firm hand on the lead. A woman appeared. She was middle-aged, wearing sturdy hiking boots, and carrying herself with that kind of physical confidence that PE teachers had back in high school, needing nothing but a brisk stride and a harsh whistle to keep everyone in line.

"So sorry," the woman said. She barked an order at the dog who obeyed in an instant, and stood still at her feet, panting and tail wagging, while she clipped the lead to his collar.

Jacey glanced up again and realised who the woman was – Madlyn, who she'd met at the café in town, who'd invited her to the creative writing group. Quickly, she turned away and looked down at the ground as if she were admiring the colour variations in the grey-brown leaf mould.

"Is something the matter here?" the woman – Madlyn – asked.

"Everything's fine." Rob sounded defensive, perturbed that someone was butting into their business. "She's OK."

"She doesn't look OK," Madlyn said.

"Well she is," Rob snapped.

"Is that true, Jacey? Are you?"

Jacey's stomach twisted. Her attempt to avoid being recognised had failed. She had no choice but to play this out, act happy to see her, introduce her to Rob.

"Hey. What a surprise." Jacey smiled weakly. "No, I just got dizzy for a second – low blood pressure, I think – so I thought I'd better take a break."

"Glad to hear it, Jacey." Madlyn reached down to pet the dog who was nuzzling into her knees, grizzling for attention. "And I'm sure Bramble is, too, aren't you girl?"

Rob stepped forward. "Sorry, but my wife's being extremely rude here." He put his hand out so Madlyn could shake it. He changed his voice slightly, softening his tone, and trying to sound English. "I'm Rob. Jacey's husband."

"And I'm Madlyn. Your wife and I met at a café in town, and she promised to come along to our—"

"History class," Jacey said, her heart thumping. She forced herself to stand, to steer the conversation as best she could without letting the panic she was feeling creep into her voice. "You remember, Rob? We saw the notice in the library? At the pub on Wednesday nights?"

"Of course," Rob said.

Madlyn's eyes widened. "*History*," she repeated, "That's right." Bramble growled slightly, as if she'd been specially trained to sniff out pointless white lies. "Pleased to meet you, Rob."

"You, too," Rob said. "Really glad Jacey's got something she can get her teeth sunk into while we're here."

"Well, we're delighted to have some new blood," Madlyn said.

Rob cleared his throat. "So what's your area of interest, Madlyn?" He stood up taller, stretched his spine. "I'm a literature professor, but my field involves a considerable amount of historical context, as you are probably aware."

Madlyn tightened her grip on Bramble's lead. "I'm into local history," she said. "Specifically the area near where I grew up in rural Cambridgeshire."

The bells had gone – Jacey only just noticed – but the air was still shifting slightly.

"Wow," Rob exclaimed, sounding genuinely interested. "Cambridgeshire? Really? That's where my wife's grandmother was from."

"Is that right?" Madlyn smiled at her, raised her eyebrows, as if they were both in on some secret.

Jacey held her breath. The air was holding steady. As long as the hollowing didn't get any stronger, she'd be fine.

"So, any specific local history focus?"

Madlyn sighed, as if she was weighing up whether or not to answer the question. "The supernatural, I guess you could call it," she finally said. She looked at Jacey again. "Witches and bogeymen, that sort of thing."

Bramble was straining at the lead by now, and Madlyn was almost pulled back up the steep embankment. She smiled again, gave Jacey a wave. "See you on Wednesday, Jacey." After a few seconds of hesitation, she allowed Bramble to drag her away.

"Witches?" Rob whispered, after he was sure Madlyn was out of earshot. "That's what she calls history – bogeymen?" He shook his head. "Can't be much of a class."

"It's local history like she said. It's supposed to be for fun, you know?"

"Yeah, whatever. Long as it gives you something to do."

His dismissiveness rankled, as did his bounding up to the path without stopping to help her along. Now that he was sure she wasn't going to need an ambulance, he was free to ignore her again. He watched her struggle up the embankment and the only emotion Jacey could detect on his face was impatience. Why was this woman – his wife – constantly holding him back?

Chapter 10

It was dark by the time Jacey arrived at the pub, and the streets got narrower as she climbed the hill from what the locals referred to as the 'bottom' of the town to the area near the castle. There were streetlights, of course, but they were dim, almost useless, as if they were still gas-lit, not electric. There was no traffic in this part of town, either, and the houses she passed had already drawn their curtains and locked their doors for the night.

At the top of the street a warm glow spilled out the windows onto the pavement, like an oasis of warmth and comfort in the midst of so much gloom. A sign in the pub's entrance said, "Writer's Group, Upstairs."

Jacey followed the sound of murmuring voices, and found herself in a large room, with a small stage and chairs set up around tables or scattered singly at odd angles. At one end of the room, in front of the stage, Madlyn, as she called herself, was sitting alone at a huge oak desk.

Jacey sat near the back, on her own. There were other people present, most of them women, almost all of them, like Madlyn, older than Jacey. They reminded her of her mother somehow, despite the English accents. They looked open and friendly, even though none of them were actually reaching out and talking to her, and their laughter was gentle and reassuring.

She took out her phone and sent her mother a quick text to say she was thinking of her. *I'm out for the night*, she said. *What they call an evening class. First time on my own. So far, so good. Xx*

As she pressed send, she noticed the Messenger light was on beside Rob's name.

OK, she thought, *it was fair enough*. He had friends to talk to, co-workers. He had parents, siblings.

And she was the one who had gone out to the pub tonight, not him. He was the one at home alone, waiting for her. Besides, there was nothing wrong with him being online, nothing whatsoever, so why was her heart thumping, why was there a sick feeling of dread in the pit of her stomach?

Jacey went to the bar and stood next to a young man – younger than her, and way cooler, with blue hair and six piercings on one of his ears. He was leaning against the bar, using it as a table, scribbling something in a tattered notebook.

"Glass of dry red," she said.

"Small, medium or large?"

A wave of anxious thoughts washed over her: having to go home in the dark later on, lying to Rob about what kind of class this was, and wondering about the dot on her phone next to his name.

"Large, please."

The boy looked at her. He nodded and raised his eyebrows, indicating approval, as if ordering a 'large' marked Jacey out as some kind of rebel.

Back at her seat, she settled in and listened to one of the members reading her piece about a child who'd lost her parents in the First World War and was living as a servant in a grand country house. The poor little girl spent an awful lot of time scrubbing floors, it seemed to Jacey, though as far as detailed descriptions of chapped hands and cold flagstones went, this woman's writing was precise.

Jacey tried to focus on the woman's story, so that she could say something positive at the end. But her mind kept going back to what she'd seen on her phone. The tiny light by Rob's name. So insubstantial, so meaningless. Of course he'd been online millions of times before, she just hadn't noticed.

"And Millie cried to think that a girl like her, cosseted and pampered by her loving mummy and daddy, should end up in such an appalling place."

When the woman finished her story, she took off her glasses, put her notebook down, and glanced at her husband who gave her an approving smile.

"Well, what a brilliant start, Muriel," Madlyn said. "Thanks so much for sharing that."

There was a smattering of applause, a few murmurs of praise, and then Madlyn cleared her throat and clinked a knife against the side of her wine glass.

"Before we get onto the next bit of writing, we've got a new member in tonight who I'd like to introduce – she's come all the way from America, and her name is Jacey."

The others turned around, tight smiles on their faces; polite, but suspicious.

"Would you care to tell us a bit more about yourself, Jacey?"

The room got quieter, and Jacey felt a slight hollowing.

"Jacey?"

"Thank you. It's great to be here, and Muriel, that story was so good."

Muriel smiled demurely, and her husband took her hand and gave her a look that seemed to say, "See, honey? What did I tell you? Even the American liked it."

Everyone's eyes were still on Jacey. She took a deep breath, hoping she'd have a voice to speak with. "Well, I'm new to the area, obviously, and I'm here with my husband who's working at the university, and since I'm not allowed to have a job myself, I thought I'd start on that novel I've been taking notes on for the last five years, since it's partly set in England, because my grandmother was from here."

The crowd murmured their approval. Being part English seemed to warm them to her.

Madlyn smiled at her encouragingly. "And her nana was from a village in Cambridgeshire, my old stomping ground, isn't that right?"

"Yes," Jacey said. "She met my grandfather at an American air force base during the war…"

The air hollowed out even more, stifling her voice. She took a deep breath, hoping it would pass quickly.

Madlyn broke the unsettling silence.

"What was the name of the place, Jacey? Do you remember?"

Jacey cleared her throat, rasped out the words: "It was called Stanton."

The hollowing got heavier. No one moved, not even Madlyn. Jacey looked from face to face, and it was as if the lighting had changed, too, because the faces staring back at her were grey and pallid. Still as statues. It was impossible to know how long things stayed that way. A few seconds? A minute? Then, from the bar, came the sound of broken glass, and a harshly hissed "Shit" from the boy with the blue hair, and laughter from Madlyn, as the others in the room were called back to life.

Madlyn raised her voice in order to be heard.

"Stanton," she shouted. "That's where my ancestors come from, too."

Jacey walked back from the pub with another one of the writers, who accompanied her as far as the park before the tunnel and wished her a cheerful good night before rushing off on her own way home. There was a full moon, which meant that the tree branches, even the benches and the shrubs along the edge of the field had an otherworldly sheen, but at least Jacey could see properly: the sounds of the traffic on the highway made her feel like she wasn't completely alone, and the light from the tunnel underneath the road was warm and yellow.

And there, at the end of it, someone was standing. Instinctively, she held her bag closer to her chest, and rummaged inside it for her house keys. She looked around to see if there was anyone in the area who could hear her if she shouted for help, but then she realised that the person at the end of the tunnel was just a child, too small and too young to be any kind of threat.

She let out a sigh of relief. Silly of her to have been so scared. It was a little boy, hardly old enough to be in school, not even here in England where they start out as toddlers according to Rob. He was wearing baggy shorts and a striped T-shirt, and kicking a rubber ball against the wall of the tunnel – she heard the gentle *thunk*, and then the echo.

"Hello?" Jacey called out as she approached him.

The boy didn't move. Had he heard her? What was he doing, out by himself so late at night, not wearing a coat or even a sweatshirt? She crept closer, so as not to startle him, and smiled, thinking he'd be scared of her otherwise, but he didn't seem to take any notice. She took her eye off him for a second, turning around to see if anyone else was nearby – his parents or family members – and when she looked again, the boy was gone.

She rushed to the end of the tunnel and saw a shadow disappearing into the woods in front of Malin House. That couldn't have been the boy, though – it was just her eyes playing tricks. There weren't any other houses nearby, only Helen and Martin's cottage. It was possible he was staying with them – a visiting grandson – but they didn't strike her as the types who would allow a child to play outside in the dark, on his own.

She took another look.

"Hello?"

Nothing. Nobody. Weird.

She raced down the path through the woods, her heart pounding, even though she had no idea why she was so rattled, just by seeing some kid. It was stupid to be scared. How could a little boy hurt her? But there was something about the way he looked – so pale, his skin blue with cold, and the way he didn't flinch or move when she shouted out to him.

The way he suddenly vanished.

When she got to the top of the driveway, she saw lights on at Helen and Martin's, which turned off when she crossed the lawn, as if they'd been waiting up. Inside the big house – that's how she thought of it now, not quite a prison, but a gloomy and mysterious fortress – the chandelier was burning in the hallway, visible through the door's stained-glass panel, although every other window was dark.

Up on the veranda, fumbling with the key, she looked around, one last time.

There was nobody behind her. No pale, homeless child had followed her up the hill. Of course not, silly.

Then, in through the front door, across the hall, straight up the stairs without thinking, and along the dark landing without drawing a breath; with her eyes half closed, she opened the bedroom door and locked it behind her.

She slipped out of her clothes and crawled in beside Rob, pulling the covers up, listening to the sound of her husband's snoring and snorting, happy for a moment that she wasn't alone, and for a few blissful minutes, before she fell asleep, she felt safe.

Chapter 11

In the sunny morning kitchen, Rob looked up from his phone.

"Well how was it? Your first big night out on the town."

She felt the sting of sarcasm in Rob's voice. Her heart was pumping defensively: what could she say to shield herself from his contempt?

"It was fine, honey. Good."

"And were the locals friendly?"

"Yes," she said. "Everybody was nice."

She flinched inwardly at her choice of words. Rob had started saying 'lovely' when what he meant was 'nice', along with other British turns of phrase, and she was just not managing the transition away from American English as smoothly as he was. Lovely, she thought. Next time, she'd say everyone was *lovely*.

"Even that Bogeywoman, or whatever she was?"

"Madlyn. Yes."

"And what was the subject matter?"

She felt like an idiot now, having said it was a history class, and not a writing group. How long would she have to keep up with this pretence? She should just tell him, admit that she'd lied, and take his ridicule and sarcasm on the chin. It was bound to come out eventually, and she'd look even more foolish than if she told him the truth now and passed her deceit off as a stupid joke.

"Very general," she said. She was in this far, and maybe it was easier to just carry on. "One woman talked about local archaeology and another person gave quite a poignant presentation about World War One and how so many local young men died or were wounded. A huge number, considering how small a town Lewes is."

Her heart was still pounding; what if he asked for more details – what kind of artefacts had been dug up in the area, for instance, or how about an exact figure on the number of soldiers who died?

But Rob wasn't interested. She could have said anything, made up any old story, it didn't matter to him. He was looking at his phone, smiling at something he was reading. She wanted to snatch the bloody thing away from him and have a look for herself, but Rob put it down without any prompting from her. Humming happily to himself, he picked up his plate, scraped the toast crumbs into the bin and rinsed the plate in the sink.

Jacey leaned over to look at the phone, wiping the table with her hands, as if cleaning an invisible spill.

The screen was dark.

"What're you doing, Jace?"

She sat back down, straight in the chair.

"Nothing. Thought I saw a coffee stain."

"I wasn't drinking coffee."

He picked up the phone and pushed it firmly into the pocket of his jeans.

"I've got a meeting in an hour and then I'm probably going to the pub after my afternoon seminar."

He said it like he was born to the job. *Meeting. Seminar. Pub.*

"Will you have dinner out, too?"

"I don't know yet."

"I mean, it's no big deal, just so I know how much to cook."

Jacey hardly recognised the voice that came out of her mouth. Reed-thin, high and wispy. *Listen to yourself*, Jacey thought. So passive and pathetic. Like in the movie *The Shining*, the wife, what was her name? Smiling and scraping and all the while Jack Nicholson was sharpening his axe.

"Probably, is the answer," Rob said, as authoritative as ever. "Just don't expect me, OK."

And he was gone, out the door, whistling to himself, without asking what she was going to do for the day, not wondering for a second how she would be spending her time, or who she was going to see.

"And when was the last time you heard this … ringing?"

The university's doctor sat behind a desk, wearing faded black jeans, battered Nikes, and a red Fred Perry polo shirt. Without the NHS lanyard around his neck, she could have mistaken him for one of those freshmen – sorry, first years – Rob was so scathing about.

The doctor looked at something on his desktop computer. Whatever it was, it couldn't be patient notes. This was her first trip to the doctor's office. *Surgery*, Rob said, *it's called a GP's surgery*.

"A few days ago."

The practice must have been more of a birth control and STD clinic judging from the posters on the wall. A picture of a penis-shaped cactus wearing sunglasses had the headline "Could it be chlamydia?"

Jacey found it funny. Laughed to herself.

The doctor glanced over his shoulder and smiled. "I guess you can get a pretty good idea what most of our consultations are dealing with. Suspected tinnitus ... makes a refreshing change."

"Unless chlamydia makes your ears ring, of course," Jacey said.

The doctor laughed. And she felt good for a second; being witty, making a British doctor (*sorry, GP*) chuckle would really have impressed Rob. Too bad he wasn't here.

She sat quietly while the doctor got on with asking questions. Did she have a job that involved loud noises? No. Had she experienced headaches, blurred vision, other visual difficulties? No. Was she on any medications? No. Had she had a head injury recently? No.

Was she under any undue stress at the moment?

She waited before answering.

The doctor sat up.

Well, was she?

She took a deep breath. Dammit.

Mrs. Gibson?

She had to be careful how she answered. "It's been quite an adjustment, living here. Being alone, with just my husband, who's pretty busy most of the time, and me not having a job."

The bells started again, right there in the doctor's off – surgery, *surgery* – and there was a hollowing with it because she couldn't hear anything *but* the bells. She was aware that the doctor – *GP you fucking moron, GP* – was saying something to her, but she couldn't hear it at all.

"So, you are experiencing a bit of stress?"

She ran her hands over the textured beading on her purse – *no, handbag, it was called a handbag here in England, you stupid piece of shit* – and stared at the floor.

"It's happening now," she said. "It's very noisy. I can't hear anything else, nothing you're saying to me. I'm sorry, Doctor."

She gripped the arms of her chair. The hollowing was making her want to dash towards the door, race out of the building and onto the campus grounds.

"Are you all right to continue, Mrs …"

The doctor's voice yanked her back into the room. *Answer him, Jacey. You can hear him, so you have to say something.*

"Yes." One word, that's all she was capable of. Like this was a courtroom, and she was a witness who'd just broken down on the stand when questioned.

"I'm fine." Two words.

The doctor took her at her word. He was young – what did he know? About her? About the hollowing – what *could* he know?

"OK, so you are having a challenging time settling in here, understandably."

He typed something into his computer.

"So besides this … bell ringing, or tinkling sound … do you hear anything else?"

She looked at him without speaking. He had brown eyes. A handsome face. Kind.

Before she could answer, the doctor said, "I guess I'm thinking of voices."

Voices.

Things were quieter now, the air was clearer, the pull of the hollowing had weakened. She looked out the slightly open window – she could hear the sounds of the world, the laughter, the shouts of students, but the view was obscured by off-white vertical blinds that swayed gently in the breeze that wafted in along with the sounds.

"Like, human voices, is that what you mean?"

The doctor looked nervous, aware that he was opening a can of worms, raising possibilities that he wasn't equipped to deal with.

"Yes. I suppose that's what I mean."

She thought about the first time she heard the ringing. There were sounds, similar to voices, telling her to leave the house. Should she tell him about that? And there were those noises from Rob's drawing room, that seemed like voices, but she couldn't be sure. Was that important?

The doctor was watching her, waiting for an answer.

"No. I don't hear voices."

"OK," he sighed, relieved. "So, would I be right then in saying that you heard ringing? And other rather vague aural disruptions?"

Jacey nodded.

"I'll give you something to help you sleep, just in case you need it."

The doctor typed into his computer, and a few seconds later a green prescription form churned out of the printer.

"And there's nothing else? No other … problems?"

She felt her face redden. Should she tell him about the hollowing? She'd call it something else, of course. A change in volume, a sense of pressure building up around her head, sometimes a hissing sound like escaping steam, sometimes an inability to move, other times that horrible pull, taking over her body …

"You're not experiencing or hearing anything that concerns you beyond what we'd associate with the tinnitus, is that correct?"

She heard the laughter of students outside the window. She heard a man's voice. Sounded like Rob's, in the midst of all those young people, but it could have been anyone.

"No," she said. "It's just the sounds."

* * *

Outside in the bright sunlight, Jacey felt like a ghost, swirling around the young people who were smiling in groups of three or four, with jeans and backpacks and hoodies and sneakers, all the girls smart, and pretty with their long, sleek hair shining in the sun and—

"Hey! Hey!"

There were footsteps behind her. "Hey, it's Lacey, isn't it?"

She thought about racing away, pretending she didn't know that Lacey meant Jacey, escaping before anyone else saw her in her baggy grey cords and faded Old Navy sweatshirt and cheap black Walmart Reeboks.

"Lacey. Hey!" The person who jogged up beside her was a young man with dyed black hair, cut short so that it bristled out of his head like an orb or a halo. Who was this? One of Rob's colleagues? A student?

She wished she had a hairbrush so she could sort out the lanky clump that was hanging down around her shoulders. Or bash it over this guy's head and make her getaway so she wouldn't have to talk to him. Why hadn't she taken a shower before she came out, worn nicer clothes, put on a little make-up?

"We met at the writer's group," the young man said. "Well, sort of met. I broke a glass remember? I said 'shit' and all the old ladies, like, totally lost theirs."

It was the boy with the blue hair, who'd been doodling at the bar, looking out of place. "I didn't recognise you. Sorry."

The boy touched his hair. "Yeah, well, I like to mix things up, style-wise. Keeps people on their toes, you know. Like they can never be too sure of which one of me they're going to meet up with on any given day, if that makes sense."

"Sure," Jacey said, though it made no sense whatsoever. She put out her hand for him to shake. "And it's Jacey, by the way, not Lacey."

"Oh. Both cool names, though. Maybe you could swap around sometimes."

Jacey laughed. "Not a bad idea."

"And I'm Rael."

"Oooo – also cool."

"Well, it's certainly cooler than my dead name, that's for sure." He cringed and rolled his eyes.

"Dead name?" Jacey asked.

Rael raised his eyebrows. "Yes. You know…"

Jacey felt her face redden, when she realised what Rael had been subtly trying to tell her. "Oh, God. I beg your pardon, I'm sorry for being so …"

"You're not being anything," Rael said. He was walking beside her now, and seemed totally relaxed, as if he was in the company of an old and trusted friend. "I mean, how were you to know that this totally butch specimen of unadulterated masculinity was once a mild-mannered little girl called …"

He touched Jacey's shoulder, leaned in and whispered: "… Ruthie."

Rael laughed. Jacey liked that he was joking with her, and that he'd trusted her with the information that he was trans, that he let it drop into the conversation casually, even though she was so slow on the uptake. She was still a little wary, though; of so much information so soon, a throwback from her small-town childhood of keeping things hidden, but Rael didn't stop sharing. He was on his way to the station, too, so he walked along with Jacey, telling her the story of his life, talking non-stop so that all Jacey needed to do was nod sympathetically, and say "um-hum."

He took a breather while he stopped to roll a cigarette and fought to get it lit. And then he was off again, telling Jacey how he'd always suspected he was a man, but he'd been born and raised in some rural backwater, where such things weren't ever talked about, or understood. He'd struggled until his teens and then when he told his mother he wanted to transition, she "totally lost the plot."

"Is losing the plot a bad thing?" Jacey asked.

"Oh yes, Ms. Jacey. Very bad."

Ms. Jacey. He'd already given her a nickname; she liked that, too.

"I mean, she freaked. Like totally panicked. And it wasn't 'losing a daughter' or anything like that. I have two straight cis sisters and they are more than likely to pop out the requisite number of grandkids between them. And Mum knew how miserable I was."

"Maybe she was afraid of all the transphobes," Jacey said.

"No. It was something else. My mum is really supportive, and I thought she'd be a proper ally, but she couldn't deal with it in the end; and so she got rid of me like, *there's the door,* and pretty much forced me to move away to Brighton."

Despite his flippant tone, and the breathless speed of his words, Jacey could hear the hurt in Rael's voice, the sting of betrayal. "But wasn't moving to Brighton a good thing?" she asked, hopefully. "Isn't it meant to be a safer place to be trans? More inclusive?"

They stopped to let a group of students pass by – boys and girls, terribly young-looking, who were staring at Rael and smirking.

"Well, yeah, that's what it's famous for, but …"

Rael gave the students a little wave, but they carried on giggling and sneering. He took a drag of his cigarette, waited until they moved further down the path, as if he was worried they might come back. When they were finally out of sight, he shook his head and took another intake of breath. "Anyway," he said, "my mum wouldn't have known much about the Brighton LGBTQ+ scene."

Rael flicked his cigarette butt onto the road.

"It was something else," he said. "Something about being a boy."

"I don't understand."

"It was dangerous, that's what she said. Being a boy was a bad thing, and she wanted me as far away from the village as possible. Everything's fine between us now, but I never did get what she was on about."

They said goodbye at the station. "See you next time you go to the writer's group," Rael said. "You made a big impression, you know, with your ancestors being from the same place as Madlyn."

"Really?"

"After you left she couldn't stop talking about it. She said she knew all about your grandmother, the one who left."

"She did?"

"And she was very cagey when people asked her for details. It was quite the story, she said, but she wouldn't tell us any more."

Just as she got on the train a message from Rob pinged into her phone. *I'll be late tonight. Don't wait up.* He ended the text with a big red heart and an x, so that was better than nothing.

And he'd warned her he might go to the pub, and this message just confirmed it, so she couldn't really get angry. Not his fault that the job had perks, was it? Not his fault she'd be spending another night on her own.

But that conversation with Rael had unsettled her somehow. As she walked out of the station and trudged across the park towards Malin House, she felt exposed and vulnerable, as if people were watching her, as if they knew things about her that she didn't know herself. Things to do with Rob. Their marriage. Things to do with her family, crazy as that seemed.

The Perfect Couple

She remembered feeling this way when she was a little girl, every time she and her mother would leave the farm and drive into the local town to do shopping or run errands. The stares at the grocery store, the whispers in the café, that she knew were something to do with them. And now she felt it again, dozens of years later, thousands of miles away, as if some shame or stigma was following her still.

Chapter 12

What woke her up in the middle of the night, Jacey couldn't tell.

Rob was beside her in bed. She could see the shape of his body under the duvet, rising and falling with each raspy breath. She smelled alcohol on his body, whisky seeping through his pores. What time had he got in?

She leaned into him, rested her hand on his hip as he breathed out a sigh. Her body tightened. She braced herself for the sound of a name, whispered in the dark. That pretty waitress at the pub they visited with Jared and Bex. What would her name be? Orsha or Petra. Or Anya. She looked like an Anya, that one. Soft blonde-brown hair. Gentle eyes.

Anya.

No. The poor young woman was just doing her job, being nice to the customers. Rob had always been like that – flirty, sometimes too much so. She knew that when she married him. It was part of what had attracted her to him, that other women found him cute and charming, too.

He turned towards her in his sleep. He was snoring gently, his chest rising, his slim, smooth shoulders creeping out of the heavy duvet and his feet sticking out at the bottom. When he slept he looked so handsome; all the tension was gone from his eyes, and his mouth was relaxed to the point he appeared to be half-smiling, the way her old dog Thora used to look when she was curled up in front of the oil fire stove in the farmhouse kitchen, tail wagging, dreaming about running across a huge field and catching a ball or a stick.

Sometimes when she woke up before Rob – she always seemed to these days, hours before, sometimes long before sunrise – she'd touch him, a gentle brush with an index finger, never intending to wake him, just happy to spend time alone with a face that looked kind and patient and loving to her. A face – still remembered, still cherished – that would disappear as soon as he opened his eyes.

She turned away from him again, tried to let her mind wander away from thoughts of waitresses, or meeting Rael at the university, just by chance, and hearing bizarre stories about Nana Ivy from total strangers. What the hell was that all about?

As she closed her eyes, she breathed in deeply, trying to conjure up memories, like Thora's jumping and playing on the farm, and the calves in the barn during the spring; the smell of all the animals; the tangy sweetness of the sileage they fed on; the gentle sway of tails in the milk house as if the machines that were attached to cows' swollen udders were giving them pleasure, not pain, relieving the pressure in a soothing motion.

Her father appearing in the upper half of the stable doorway, wearing a grease-spattered green wool cap, pulled down to his eyes to keep him warm.

Calling her name. Again and again. *Jacey! Jacey!* Angry and harsh. But that couldn't be him, because he never raised his voice to her.

He was always kind, letting her mother do the scolding. He just chuckled and winked and gently teased.

Jacey! Jacey!

Hazy half-sleep and then awake with a jolt.

Jacey!

As if there was someone in the room, shouting at her, but of course there wasn't. She'd fallen asleep again and was dreaming.

Conscious of Rob's breathing, of his body beside her, wishing she dared cuddle into him, or that he would turn towards her and reach out like he used to, cradling her in a safe, loving embrace.

The minutes ticked on. She didn't dare close her eyes in case that dream voice rose against her again. If she could get up, climb out of bed, if she had the courage to go downstairs to the kitchen and make herself a cup of herbal tea, that would be better than tossing and turning all night. But that would mean venturing out into the hallway, and how could she? With the darkness, and those shadows that lurked in every corner, even by day.

She'd have to try to sleep again. She remembered the pills the doctor had prescribed in case the tinnitus kept her awake. Not much good to her now, a piece of paper with a scrawled signature crumpled up in the bottom of her purse. She'd go to the drugstore – *the chemist* – tomorrow, have the medication on hand at all times, in case she needed it, like tonight.

She closed her eyes again, hoping for happy places and sounds and smells to seep into her semi-consciousness. Those Hereford calves, chestnut brown fur, off-white faces, stumbling onto their feet, reaching their tiny heads to their mother's bellies for warmth, for milk.

It was no use. She was wide awake. She wanted to reach over for

Rob's phone to check the time, but didn't want to wake him, so she slipped out of her side of the bed and walked over to his.

The phone said 03.45.

The phone also said fourteen new WhatsApp notifications.

She reached for it on the table – her stomach twisting with the dread of what she might see – but before she could pick it up, strange noises began, like a warning for her to stop. They were quiet at first, a sound like rusty gears that won't mesh, metal teeth grinding together

She shivered; the room was getting colder. And the sounds grew louder, becoming like groans of pain, as if somebody in the house was dying. She hopped back into bed, pulled the covers up to her neck, shook Rob's shoulder.

"Honey?"

Rob grunted, turning away from her.

"Honey, there's a noise."

Another grunt.

"You need to wake up, Rob."

"I'm awake."

"There's a noise, you need to listen."

"I am." His voice was muffled by his face scrunched into the pillow.

"Well, you said you heard noises before."

"I can't hear anything now, Jacey."

"You can, just listen." She could hear her voice tighten, pitch itself higher as her fear and tension rose.

Rob sat up halfway, propped on his left elbow. "I fucking can't, OK? Now let me go back to sleep."

"It sounds like it's coming from the basement."

"It's not, Jacey."

"How do you know?"

"Because there's nothing there that would make that kind of sound."

"How do you know? We're not supposed to go down there."

He rolled over, flat on his back. He pulled the covers up and turned away.

"It was a joke, remember? I already told you. Those noises I said I heard? Maybe it was a stupid thing to do, trying to be funny, so I guess I'm sorry, but I don't want to talk about it now. One of us has to work tomorrow, you know? We're not both able to do nothing all day except clean floors or sit around in cafés bothering people."

She inched away from him, feeling the air between them shift. Not the hollowing this time. Something else.

"What are you talking about?"

"That woman we ran into at Stanmer Park."

"I wasn't bothering her – she invited me to her class."

"Whatever, Jace. I've got five more hours of sleep ahead of me. And I don't want to spend it talking to you about some pointless bullshit."

He turned over onto his stomach, pulled the pillow over his ears.

Jacey listened, more angry than afraid now.

The noises were real. She knew it. She wasn't imagining anything; Rob could fuck right off.

If only she had the courage to go downstairs herself. She'd find out that it was harmless – the furnace about to blow a gasket, or another one of Rob's tricks. A tape of some scary sounds. Halloween was coming up; it made sense in a way. Rob could laugh it off, tell

Bex and Jared about his amazing prank and how his stupid wife fell for it.

She crept to the door, opened it. See how brave she was? See?

She craned her neck to see into the hallway.

There. Her heart shuddered, and she fought the urge to scream. A flash of something, a bright yellow blur, like headlights through a window – but there were no windows on this side of the hallway, and of course there was no car.

A flashlight?

Was someone in the house? Maybe Martin left something in the basement, a tool he needed, a hammer, a drill. Maybe he'd come back for it now, at night, so he wouldn't bother them by day.

She listened for footsteps. A recognisable voice.

Nothing, but the dull grinding from somewhere, below, above, outside her body, inside her head, she just couldn't tell.

No. It was tinnitus. That was all. An inner-ear disorder, and the light was her eyes adjusting to the darkness, some kind of sympathetic nerve twitch helping her focus. Or a migraine without the headache part. They could be terrifying things, she'd heard that, could make you imagine you were dying or going crazy.

She blinked a few times.

There. No more lights. Back to the darkness.

The grinding stopped, and the groans turned into soft cries, barely audible, like a child whimpering, or a kitten mewling for its mother.

And then. A *feeling*. Not just the air shifting around her, not just the hollowing.

She stepped into the hallway, holding tight to the door handle, ready to rush back inside if anybody or anything got too near.

Something was on the landing.

She couldn't be sure of the colour because it was still so dark, but it was small and round, a toy of some kind, with painted letters on it.

At the top of the stairs, like it was waiting for her.

A child's rubber ball.

ABC.

Chapter 13

A bell above the door rang when she opened it, and it tinged again a few times before the door slammed itself shut.

A man in jeans and bomber jacket was standing at the counter of the cab office's narrow waiting area – two padded vinyl chairs, and a low table full of grubby takeaway menus. He was leaning over, looking for something on the other side of the barrier.

"Got 'em," he said, straightening up, clutching a brace of keys on a ring. "You have a good evening, Lou."

Behind the counter, a woman – Louise was on her name badge – about the same age as Jacey's mum, late 50s Jacey figured—held up her hand to wave him off, and the bells rang again as the man nudged past Jacey and went back outside.

The sounds – the reminder of what she'd been hearing, and what she'd seen last night at the top of the stairs – made her flinch. She tried not to think about the ball that had miraculously disappeared by the time she woke up in the morning. If it had ever actually been there, of course. If she hadn't been hallucinating; if she wasn't going completely insane.

A call came through the switchboard's speaker and Louise chatted with a woman who was hoping to get a cab to the airport the following morning.

"Traffic at that time will be murder. 'time's your flight?"

Jacey wasn't sure if she should stand and wait, or if the etiquette was to sit down until she was called. Louise glanced at her and waved as if to say "Hang on, be with you in a second."

Jacey leaned against the counter. She wasn't dizzy exactly, but she was waiting for something – the hollowing, the bells – to start up as soon as she was able to talk to the dispatcher and tell her where she and Rob had been dropped off.

Malin House. *Don't listen to what anybody says.*

She looked at the walls, grey and bare except a frayed, faded calendar from three years before, and an empty cardboard brochure holder for a literary festival that had been held last summer.

"What can I do for you, love?" Louise said.

"I've got a receipt here from a few weeks ago."

"Sorry, love, but I'm not able to doctor anything. You want to fleece the taxman that's your prerogative but leave me out of it."

She looked ready to take another call.

"No, I wanted to track down the driver."

Louise looked even more suspicious. "Look, all our drivers are properly vetted. Enhanced police checks, the lot. Not every company in town—"

"No, it's nothing like that. I just wanted to talk to a driver about something he said."

Louise held her hand up while another call came in, and then heaved herself out of the chair and lumbered over to the counter. "Let me have a look at that."

She picked up a logbook that was stashed under the counter, ran her fingers over the entries until she found the right numbers. She let out a little sigh and gently closed the book.

"Sorry, love, but whatever it was you wanted to talk about, you're out of luck."

"Oh," Jacey said. "Doesn't the driver work here anymore?"

"No, he doesn't, I'm afraid."

"Well, is there any way I could get in touch with him? Did he move to another company?"

"He didn't move anywhere. And he left no number."

"Oh, I see." What was going on here?

"Because he died."

"What?"

"Ron. The driver. Dropped dead while he was out having a pint with some of his mates. Heart attack, love, just keeled over."

"Oh, that's terrible."

"Well, probably not a bad way to go, but he was only sixty-five. Not much of an age, these days."

Jacey felt staggered. "He just drove us home from the station a few weeks ago."

"Tell me about it." Louise looked past Jacey to the open doorway, as if she still expected Ron to be coming in for a shift. "So, what did you want to know? Anything I can help you with?"

"No, just something he said, something I'm not really sure I even heard right, but it's OK. Not important."

Jacey was already backing away from the counter. The news about the driver had rattled her; she didn't know what to think. She hadn't known the man at all, could hardly remember what he looked like, so why was she so unsettled by the fact that he was dead?

"You sure there's nothing you want to ask me? Sounds like you're not originally from around here, so if you have any questions about the local landscape … ?"

Louise took out a packet of cigarettes from a side drawer of her desk and lit one up.

"Sorry about this, but seeing as I'm the only one working here … talking about Ron has kind of upset me."

"Oh, sorry …"

"It's not your fault. My filthy habit. Was Ron's too. Never used to smoke in the office when he was around. We'd go out the back and have a smoke there. Kind of our ritual. Soon as he got off his shift at seven a.m. Only he'd have two or three to my one, so I guess that's what got him."

"I'm really sorry for the loss of your friend."

The lady took a drag on her cigarette. "So, where did he drop you?"

"Malin House."

Louise grunted slightly. It was half a laugh. "Oh, the old Malin curse, is that what you wanted to ask him about?"

"No, not exactly."

"A lot of silly stories surrounding that place."

"That's what he said. *Don't believe the rumours.*"

"Well, he was right, love. Is that what you wanted to ask? About what the rumours were?"

Jacey nodded.

"Well, I'm going to tell you the same thing he did."

She coughed a few times, and took another puff. "Don't listen to them. OK?"

"But what are they?"

"Doesn't matter," she said. "Don't listen."
She waved her hand, getting rid of the smoke.
"Not if you have to live there."

Chapter 14

She was sitting on the small veranda, where she'd plugged her laptop into an extension cable Martin procured for her a day earlier, so she could keep it charged while she worked outside.

But it was cold now, at the end of the day, even with the woollen blanket she'd taken from the back of the sofa in the little den wrapped around her shoulders. It was getting dark, too. Over the tops of trees, she could see blue skies but the sun was well below the horizon.

She closed the laptop, carrying it in front of her like a tray, dragging behind the charger and extension lead, and began her night-time ritual, the special one she devised for times like tonight. Rob had messaged her in the morning after he left. *Brighton pub after work with Glasgow profs. Not sure what time I'll be back. Late probably.*

Late definitely, Jacey thought.

She flicked on the switch for the chandelier in the hallway, but kept the veranda light burning, too. She looked up the stairs at the shiny dark wood. Since she'd seen the toy ball, or whatever it was on the landing, she looked even more carefully, in case something else had been deposited there.

Today, nothing. And there'd been nothing on the landing the

morning after she'd seen the ball either – who'd got rid of it? It was real; she definitely saw it, she wasn't going mad or delusional, so where had it gone? Had Rob taken it?

She should have asked him in the morning, but he'd been in a hurry, as usual, and he'd hardly looked at her when she said "good morning," and set a cup of coffee on the table in front of him. Trying to be helpful, doing her best, supporting him in his work, but he was so bleary-eyed after his late night that he didn't even say thanks.

She checked the basement door: locked. She put her head to the door and listened – there was no grinding, no sounds that someone could imagine were screams. She crept across the hallway and into the den, locking the door behind her. She set her laptop on the low coffee table between the sofa and the TV stand and turned on the floor lamp.

Then she went into the kitchen and flicked on the overhead light. She stepped into the food larder at the back of the kitchen, and through to the tiny, enclosed porch that was full of cracked rubber boots and moth-eaten jackets and umbrellas with rusted ribs and mouldy fabric. She checked the porch door that led to the side lawn and locked the larder, too.

On the other side of the kitchen was the serving pantry, where the old servant bells were suspended on the wall, above the shaded windows, coiled like sleeping bats with long bronze tails. She reached up and touched one of the clappers, letting it go and listening to the muffled sound it made as it tinged against the bell. This wasn't the high, delicate pitch she'd heard – or imagined she'd heard – that time in the kitchen, or during their walk at Stanmer Park. She checked each window behind the shade and tried to lift them, one by one, but they'd been painted shut and hadn't been opened for a very long time.

She kept the lights on, before creeping back into the kitchen, closing the door, and turning the key in the lock. Stupid, she knew that. As if the light would make a difference, as if locks could stifle the sound.

Finally, everything was shut up tight. She was isolated in two cosy rooms. There was the little bathroom at the back of the kitchen, and so she really didn't need anything else. She had food and water, she had a blanket, she had her laptop, a TV, food, something to cook it with, and a sofa to sleep on.

Kitchen and den. That great big house, and she only felt safe in two of the rooms.

And when Rob got home, she could easily pretend she'd fallen asleep watching TV, and had forgotten to unlock the door. She never turned it off when she was alone. Kept it on one of the BBC channels that played historical documentaries about kings or queens she didn't know or care anything about. They were quiet programmes, though, so easy to sleep through when she got tired.

She made a cheese and mushroom omelette and poured herself a glass of the Italian wine that she loved, and was so much cheaper here. Back in the den she put down her plate and wine glass and looked for the remote control. There it was – stuck between the sofa cushions as usual – but when she pulled it out she found something else, too. A slip of paper. A train ticket.

Rob hadn't gone to the station and then found out it was missing, had he? She imagined him going to the booking office, demanding a replacement, acting all superior and entitled. Or maybe he'd just hop on the train, assuming he could charm his way into not having to pay again, play the scatty academic, or lapse into the confused American tourist – she'd seen him do that once or twice, when he'd made some mistake with a ticket machine, assuming the rules only applied to idiots, to everyone but him.

But this wasn't a ticket. It was just a receipt for a ticket that cost £24.50.

Southern Railway. Day return. Lewes to London.

London? Rob never said anything about going to London.

Jacey took a bite of her omelette and then set down the plate.

The food wasn't right. There was a sharp, metallic taste, as if the butter she'd fried it in had turned rancid.

London. The print was small, and Jacey had to squint to see the date. 29th September. Departure time 17.00.

Today. Five o'clock, straight after work when he was supposed to be going to Brighton with a professor from somewhere else. Manchester. Scotland. She couldn't remember exactly what he'd said.

This didn't make sense. Why would he have a ticket for London when he was only going into Brighton?

She cut into the omelette again, held up the soggy yellow triangle and sniffed it. It definitely smelled rotten – had the eggs gone bad, too? She put down the fork, pushed the plate to the side of the table.

Her stomach churned; she couldn't eat any more.

She carried the plate back into the kitchen, scraped the food into the bin, set the plate in the sink, and picked up her phone.

Rob had probably texted her, told her about the mistake. The meeting was in London – silly of him not to mention it, so many details to be getting on top of, what had he been thinking. Don't wait up, he'd say. It'll be late by the time I get back.

Nighty night.

There were no messages, from Rob or anyone else.

But so what, she thought. So what if he didn't text. He was at a meeting. It's not like meetings weren't part of his job. And London wasn't that far away from Lewes. An hour or so on the train.

The rotten egg turned over in her stomach.

She washed the plate and the things she'd used for cooking. For a second, she felt dizzy, and held the side of the big stone sink. A minute later and she was fine. She could walk across the floor, no trouble, and the whooshing sound in her ears wasn't too much either. There were no bells or groans or the crying of someone in pain. There was no hollowing, or fear.

Just the dread; the feeling that something was terribly wrong.

Back in the den she settled herself in. On the TV a blonde woman was narrating a documentary about one of Henry VIII's wives. God, weren't the Brits sick of that man by now? Didn't they know everything there was to know about the fat, murdering bastard and his stupid wives who couldn't figure out what the hell was going to happen to them?

She took a sip of wine, but it tasted sour, like vinegar, so she spat it back into the glass.

She turned down the sound of the TV, so that it was quiet enough not to get distracted by the presenter's irritatingly sweet voice, but loud enough to drown out the sounds of any creaking floorboards or groaning doors or grinding metal, or any high-pitched bells, that she knew weren't real but still tormented her.

Sun streamed through the open windows, and a cool autumn breeze rushed in with the warm light. It was morning, and she was alone in bed, completely dressed, underneath the covers.

How had she got here? Why were her memories blurred, and her thoughts heavy and incoherent?

And where was Rob?

His side of the bed was indented, the covers that side rumpled up, sheets pulled out, as if he'd had a lousy night's sleep, and had tossed and turned and gone somewhere else to sleep. The clothes he'd worn the day before – new jeans and long-sleeved T-shirt and fresh-out-of-the-box Nikes that he insisted on calling *trainers* – were placed on a chair, expertly folded, with her jeans and sweater resting on top of them.

He'd made it home from London, obviously, and somehow managed to put her to bed, without her becoming awake enough to remember. She sat up. Her head was hazy, as if she'd drunk more than half a glass of wine. What the hell was wrong with her? She remembered last night, curling up on the couch in the little den, that woman on the TV leering at her, judging her, too, for not being clever, for not being as cute and pixie-like as she was. Jacey remembered sitting up straighter, practising at sucking in her cheeks, seeing if she could somehow twinkle her eyes like that, too.

She climbed out of bed, patted down the creases, and tucked in the sheets and the bottom end of the duvet, even though Rob assured her that nobody in England ever did such a thing. She washed at the sink in the bathroom, using a washcloth (*face flannel*, Rob insisted) and put on fresh clothes and brown, slouchy boots, not as expensive as the Uggs. Her mom bought them for her at Target, but they were just as comfortable, really …

God, the way her brain worked. Like everything had to be justified, an explanation given for why she did what she did or moved the way she did, or thought her thoughts. Nobody can hear inside your head, she wanted to scream at herself. Nobody gives a shit about your fucking boots, especially when you are only just thinking about them, not having an actual conversation.

The voice in her head was weird again. Not hers. Not a real voice. Not even intrusive thoughts.

Nothing. Nobody.

She listened for actual sounds, like Rob in the kitchen making her breakfast, or Martin in the basement – he sometimes rattled things down there, God only knew what. Moving the coffins around, Rob had said once when they heard the sound late at night, and, securely in Rob's arms, with the bedroom door locked, she had laughed at the idea. The chill it gave her was exciting, not scary. A weird sort of turn-on.

Not so funny now, was it? With nobody's arms around her, no husband keeping her safe. Not making her horny, was it?

She ran a brush through her hair and left it down. The woman on the TV history show wore her hair short and straight, with two little barrettes on either side. *That would never work on me*, Jacey thought. She opened the middle drawer of the dressing table, found some styling product and scrunched it through her hair.

Good, she thought, when she'd worked it all through and tossed her head. Total rock chick badassness. She pouted her lips. Nice and plump.

She crept to the door, opened it, looked out into the hallway. She could hear Rob's voice, coming from further down the hall, that dark corridor where he'd heard – or so he claimed – the terrifying sound. But who would he be talking to this early in the morning?

She crept down the hallway. Silently, on tip-toe so he couldn't hear her creeping up towards the door to the room, opened just a crack.

Spying. Admit it, Jacey. Listening in, and the feeling of dread was so overpowering that she had to lean into the wall to keep from falling over.

Yes, that was his voice, barely audible, but there was no one else in the room. He must be on the phone. Someone from work. Who else would it be? Or from back home. What time was it there? She tried to think. It was late – middle of the night. It could still be someone from home. His parents, or his brother in Minneapolis.

"I know," he said.

Know what? What did Rob know?

"And I feel the same way, honestly, I do."

She wanted to scream. About what? About whom?

"OK," he said, and somehow Jacey sensed that the call was coming to an end. "Uh-huh, OK, yeah," all that stuff and then finally, he said. "Yeah. Me, too."

Me, too.

Jacey knew what that was shorthand for.

I love you too, only you couldn't say it out loud because you were in the same house as your wife, and even if she was still asleep those words had a way of getting louder in such still and suffocating air, and travelling further along the hallway than they normally would, and seeping through the walls, and—

Footsteps. A throat being cleared.

Jacey crept back to the bedroom with her eyes peeled on the door that Rob was about to emerge through. But she was faster than he was and she got to their room – *their* room, hers and her *husband's*, their *bed*room – before him. She went to the dressing table, took the brush out of the drawer, held it up to her hair, and watched in the mirror until the door opened, and Rob saw her.

"Hey," he said. He hadn't come into the room, but he got in the first word anyway, of course. "What happened last night?"

"What do you mean?"

"I came home and you were asleep downstairs. Looked like you'd made quite a dent in that bottle of Pinot."

He was in the doorway, leaning nonchalantly.

"No." She shook her head. "I hardly had any."

Rob raised his eyebrows. "Whatever you say."

"But how did you get me up the stairs? I don't remember a thing."

"See what I mean?" He laughed and smiled, mocking her.

"Well, it wasn't much fun, sitting there on my own again, so even if I had drunk half the bottle, nobody could blame me."

He came to her, put his arm around her waist, ruffled her hair. "I guess it's not fair, huh?"

Why was he behaving like this? So nice – sorry, *lovely* – all of a sudden. His kindness was making her angry. If she didn't get her emotions under control she'd end up screaming accusations at him, or pulling the ticket receipt for yesterday's train trip out of her pocket, and stuffing it down his throat.

She took a deep breath. Managed a weak smile.

"So where *were* you?"

"Huh?"

"Last night." She thought about that TV presenter; tried to sound as sweet and girly as she was. "I don't mean the meeting, I mean later."

His face turned pale. He didn't answer, but he smiled and made a sort of half-grunt, half sigh.

"When I woke up, you weren't in bed."

"Oh," he said, and the sigh got bigger until it was a huge heaving sign of relief. "I got you up the stairs, by some miracle, and then I couldn't bloody get to sleep, so I went back downstairs."

Bloody. Just listen to him, she thought.

"Yeah, I wondered at first," Jacey said. Voice still calm; charming, she hoped. "Since you weren't here. You know, like did you even come home?"

"Of course I did," Rob sputtered. "What time did you fall asleep?"

He was covering his tracks. Checking to make sure their stories matched.

"Not sure. It was late though. I know what I was watching. That history programme about Henry VIII, with the presenter you have such a crush on."

He laughed nervously, his face reddening. "Oh, honey, don't be ridiculous, I don't have a—"

"Anyway, towards the end of that. Henry was about to have Catherine Howard's head chopped off."

"Well, we did stay for an extra drink or two last night. I blame that new guy from Glasgow. Glasses of single malt whisky at the end of the night and then the taxi rank by the station was closed so I had to walk all the way back."

His face was red from talking but his voice was shrinking and the space between them was getting wider, and she could feel the hollowing of the air and the pull towards something as she grabbed the brush and fought the urge to hurl it at him.

"I won't be doing that again," Rob said.

She could hardly hear him, but his face was sweaty and shining, as if his lies were bubbling inside him like lava and he was about to explode. She put the brush down again, stuck her hand into the pocket of her jeans and fingered the crumpled ticket receipt for his journey to London.

She took a deep breath. Would she be able to speak?

"I hope not," she said. "I don't like being in this house on my own."

When he was gone, and he was gone quickly, without saying anything else, stumbling through the doorway and into the hallway like a disturbed burglar, she went to the bed and sat down.

The lies – the blatant, fucking, piece-of-shit cheating-bastard lies – were making her dizzy and sick. And her admission – *I don't like being here on my own* – filled her with another kind of dread.

She should have kept her mouth shut, not told him the truth. Saying it made her vulnerable. Weak.

Speaking her fears made everything real.

Chapter 15

By late October, the academic year was in full swing and the weather was more autumnal. If the shades of the trees weren't as vivid and garish as those back home, they were still pretty: the woods on the hills behind Lewes were dappled with yellow and orange, and the air was crisper, the skies a more vibrant blue. Jacey bought a pair of hiking boots at a garden centre that sold outdoor wear as well as plants and shrubs. Helen pronounced her boots to be sufficiently 'stout' and helped her prepare them for the wet winter months by applying a spray of silicone that would keep them dry and make them easier to clean.

Every day, after cleaning the kitchen and the den, Jacey would write at the kitchen table for an hour or two and then put on her new boots and go for a walk. She rarely went to town on these walks, but hiked up narrow cut-throughs to the top of the hill behind the house, where the marked paths were stony and firm. Martin explained that the hills were full of chalk, like the White Cliffs of Dover, and that meant the paths rarely got too muddy or boggy no matter how much rain fell.

Jacey liked this routine. There were separate paths – one that led along a ridge, and then into a thicket of spindly trees – not quite enough to be called woods, much less a forest. In the other direction the path was straight across the top of the hill, with only bits of gorse and thistle, and tufty grass that the thick-wooled sheep seemed to keep mown.

When she was up on the hill, whatever direction she took, Jacey forgot about the things that were happening down in the house, between her and Rob. It wasn't that they didn't matter anymore, but the fresh air and the steady pace of her walking made the tensions and stresses seem farther away, and other things seemed clearer, less oppressive. So, maybe things weren't perfect right now – how could they be, when she and Rob were adjusting to life in a new and sometimes strange country? – but they were better.

As Jacey walked, strode and clambered, intrusive thoughts about other things – strange sights, impossible noises – disappeared, too. She looked up – something her mother always told her to do – and saw the persistent thick steel-grey clouds that looked like they could be bringing rain, but very rarely did. Those clouds seemed solid, made of fabric – a giant canopy covering the sky, protecting the earth from the sun's harsh rays.

"You're getting to be quite a hillwalker," Helen said one afternoon when Jacey came back down the hill and cut across the lawn, slightly out of breath, but invigorated and energetic. "Maybe you should join the local rambling club. Make some new friends while you're here."

"Yes," she'd said, smiling. She didn't tell Helen that she'd already turned her back on the chance to make new friends – she hadn't returned to the creative writing club. Madlyn saying she was from the same village as Nana Ivy had unnerved her. Something in the way she said it, as if some mysterious connection was binding them together, and in the way the hollowing had intensified when she'd spoken those words.

Lewes was such an odd place – the dark alleys, the spot on an ordinary sidewalk – *pavement!* – marking the place where Protestant martyrs had been burned at the stake during Bloody Mary's purges – so would a group of hikers be any different than the people who lived in town? No. They'd be worse. At the writing club she'd been able to sneak away, get home quickly. If she'd wanted she could have taken a taxi. But on a hilltop? Faced with prying questions and strange coincidences, where could she escape?

The clouds were thickening, but Jacey had already turned back towards home. Another pasture to cut through, a few more stiles, and she'd be back on the main track that led to the café and the car park on one side, and to the path down the hill on the other.

It had rained heavily in the past few days, so the field was soggy and there were muddy puddles beside the solid chalk surfaces. But her boots stayed dry, and her jacket kept out the wind, and as she plodded along she was imagining a hot cup of tea when she got home, milky and sweet, and she was hoping that Rob hadn't finished off the batch of oatmeal cookies she'd baked over the weekend.

She was getting closer to the Malin House path, and the faint hum of traffic on the main road to Brighton was just about audible when she strained to listen. She climbed the last stile, carefully leaning against one of the posts to avoid the barbed wire that was looped around it, keeping an eye on her feet to keep her balance.

She straightened up, ready for the last leg home, and noticed something on the path in front of her. A little boy was kicking something – a stone or small rock – along the chalky ground, clumsily shuffling his feet. He was wearing a T-shirt and shorts and canvas shoes – in this weather, up here on the cold, windy downs.

It was the same boy she'd seen before, outside the tunnel, but what was he doing here? During the daytime? Shouldn't he be in school? And on his own, with the wrong clothes for the time of year. He must be freezing, the poor thing.

"Hey!" Jacey shouted.

The boy kept his head down.

"Hey, are you all right?"

The boy didn't stop kicking long enough to answer. It was a stupid question, Jacey thought. Obviously he was all right – minding his own business, nothing to do with her, really, but …

Maybe he was home-schooled. There were plenty of those people in Lewes, she imagined, ones who thought they could do as good a job as the professionals. This boy's parents were probably just over-relaxed. Maybe they let him play outside at night, and wander the hills by day.

But he looked so cold.

She looked behind her. Was anyone else around, any other adults who looked like they could be his parents?

No.

And when she turned back to the path, the boy was gone.

She listened for the sounds of his mother or father, or brother and sister, somebody calling him to join the family group, or shouting angrily at him for running off, but there was nothing like that. The boy had simply disappeared. She looked in the copse of trees that ran from the path down the hill. Was he hiding in there? Had he run off because she'd frightened him? Or was he waiting for her to follow him into the woods so he could jump out, play a trick on her, scare her to death.

"Hello?" she said.

She stepped off the path, towards the line of trees.

Suddenly, she felt heat on her neck, and it was like eyes were behind her, watching.

She turned around again. Nobody. She looked at the café in the far distance, a squat, tiny shape, but anyone there would be too far away to even notice her.

She took a deep breath. No one else was around at all, and her isolation was making her nervous. The boy couldn't have just vanished into thin air, yet it appeared that he had.

At least there wasn't any hollowing. There were no strange sounds, or tinkling bells. Just birds singing and the breeze rustling the branches on the trees.

She had no choice but to move on, even though the thought of the boy, so poorly dressed for this weather, made her nervous, as if she was abandoning him, like she'd find out later that he'd died up here, of exposure or hypothermia.

She shouted out again. "Hello? Little boy? Are you OK? Wherever you are?"

It sounded so stupid. Of course he was OK, not that he could hear her; the weather wasn't that bad, there were just sharp gusts of wind and a sudden chill when the sun went behind a cloud. Besides, he couldn't be very far from his home; it's not like they were out in the wilderness.

She picked up her pace, keeping watch on the line of trees for any sign of the boy, but he was gone, on his way back to his family, and safety.

She focused on her walking, and when she got to the path that led down the hill, she crept down in tiny steps, careful not to lose her footing and tumble all the way to the bottom. Soon, she could see

Malin House, and the lawn, and Helen in the garden, on her knees, planting bulbs.

Helen was all smiles when she greeted her.

"And now, a hot bath in that lovely en suite?" she chirped. "Nothing like a good long soak after a strenuous hike."

Jacey smiled. She was getting good at hiding her feelings, her fear. Going up to the bathroom would mean being upstairs on her own. No, a quick wash up in the cloakroom next to the kitchen would have to do.

She went into the house through the back porch, straight into the kitchen, and it was as if her anxiety had crept in behind her. So many unanswerable questions. Did Helen pity her? Did her walking – her rambling – seem like an odd thing to do? And was it? She was staying out longer and longer, now that the nights came closing in by late afternoon. There were so many things she didn't like about being on her own in the house: the mysterious sounds, the hollowing and the bells, the things that appeared at the top of the stairs …

Rob's laptop was on the table, his briefcase beside it. For once he'd got home before her. She listened for sounds and heard something from one of the other rooms.

She crept out to the hallway.

"Rob?"

No answer. The sounds were in the background, a humming throb.

"Rob, are you at home?"

She took a step closer to the drawing room door, and the sound became more distinct. Laughter, that's what she heard; but it was a woman's voice, definitely not Rob's.

She held her breath. What was this? Was he with someone?

She inched closer, and it became clear.

Rob was on the phone. Or in a Zoom meeting. That was all. Talking to someone who was on speaker.

Except the woman – whoever she was – wasn't saying anything. She was merely laughing at whatever Rob said. A high, girly giggle, that went on and on and on, piercing the silence of the house, stabbing at Jacey's head like a knife, digging into her heart.

Chapter 16

As the train rumbled along the tracks towards London – they were headed for another pub lunch with Bex and Jared – Jacey read the latest from her mother, a long string of messages that had been waiting on her phone when she woke up in the morning.

Her mother was worried. She'd had a strange dream, she said, and she didn't normally have dreams. And it made her think of Jacey. Was everything all right over there?

Jacey was tempted to ignore the rest of the texts. She had that power; she could simply delete them all and not respond. She didn't have to sit up like an obedient puppy every time her mother got in touch.

But of course she responded. A good daughter, as always. *What was the dream, Mom?*

Her mother's reply came straight away.

Stupid really. Nothing happened, nothing scary or dangerous. Don't know why it made me feel so jittery when I woke up.

Rob was leaning against the window, eyes closed, pretending to be asleep.

After all, it was only sounds.

Jacey sat still, glad that Rob had his headphones in, as if without them he'd be able to hear her heart, pounding with dread.

And not even bad sounds, her mother said.

Jacey looked out the window, put her phone on the table in front of her, screen down, switched it to silent, while she looked in her bag for something to read. She flicked through her book, her eyes not falling on any actual words or sentences, just watching the blurred shapes swirling on the paper.

When they were almost in London, she picked up her phone and checked the rest of the messages.

They were pretty sounds, her mother had written.

Nice, tinkling bells.

When the train pulled into the station, Jacey could see through the window the huge glass monstrousness of the Shard, London's newest famous landmark. Pointed, obviously, with a serrated tip at the very top of it. And the entire structure covered in glass. What would happen if the building shattered? Had anyone ever thought of that? Raining knives on London's streets? Jacey cringed at the thought of it, her skin prickling, her muscles flinching as if she could feel the needle-sharp edges cutting her into ribbons of sinew and blood.

Maybe that was what the sound of bells meant, she thought. A premonition of disaster. Rob took her by the arm and dragged her off the train, hustling her down the escalators onto the massive concourse. She wasn't in the mood to dawdle, either: the sooner they were away from the station, and out of the shadow of the Shard, the better. The pavements were crowded – there was a hospital nearby, and patients seemed to have escaped onto the street in various stages of dishevelled undress. A man in flipflops and sweatpants, and with a grubby T-shirt torn to shreds pushed aside a woman in pyjama bottoms and some kind of kimono.

They turned into a narrow courtyard and stood in front of the pub. It was a warm day for October, and the sun was streaming through a gap in the surrounding office blocks onto a large cobblestoned courtyard full of noisy forty-something males, nursing pint glasses of beer on picnic tables, or standing in small groups. The pub was one of the oldest in London, a coaching inn that according to Rob had been mentioned in both Dickens and Shakespeare. Was such a thing even possible? Of course, if Rob said it was so, it had to be.

Bex and Jared were standing under the pub sign, oblivious to Jacey and Rob's arrival. One look told Jacey something wasn't right. Jared's face was red, Bex's eyes were puffy, as if she'd been crying.

"Looks like we've come at a bad time," Jacey whispered.

"Don't mind them," Rob snapped. "They're always arguing like that. Jared can be a real bastard at times."

"He can?" Jacey asked, but she wasn't sure if it was the inside-her-head voice, or the outside one. Rob was already striding over to the others, smiling like a politician, putting his hand out for Jared, hugging Bex. As she tried to twist out of Rob's embrace, Bex looked towards Jacey – what was that expression on her face? Embarrassment?

And then, the hollowing came. Of course. Jacey could hardly leave Malin House now without some sort of episode. She stayed still, not daring to move from the spot where she'd planted her feet. She looked away from Rob's over-exuberant greetings and gazed up at the pub's shuttered upper windows. She counted out the seconds. One, two, three ... it was only a little hollowing. She could still hear Rob's voice, laughing at something Jared said, the hubbub of the other people in the pub courtyard.

Five, six, seven.

And the sun was still shining, so that was good. There was no sudden darkening of the sky.

Eight, nine, ten.

As long as there were no bells – and there weren't – it didn't really matter. On its own, the hollowing was fine. She just had to stay quiet, not try to lose her balance or shout over the noise.

"Jacey! What's the matter?" It was Jared's voice, not Rob's, but she heard Rob answer for her. "She gets like this sometimes. Kinda spaced out, looking like she's seen a ghost or something."

She took a step towards them, raised her hand, smiled and waved.

Later, after they'd had lunch and a few pints, Bex went to the bathroom – sorry, Rob, the toilet, or the bog, or the WC – and Rob went to the bar to order a final drink. Jacey had never really spent time on her own with Jared, and he smiled shyly. "So how's it going?"

"Yeah," Jacey said. "Fine."

"Takes some getting used to, doesn't it, this place?" Jared's voice was kind and calm; it invited trust and confidence. "And I'm not just talking about the fact that all the pubs are haunted."

"Yeah, I remember Bex saying that. Like, how you think everything will be the same, but it's not."

"No. I still believe it, after being here a year. Everything about England confuses me." He smiled. "Not just the way the roads are laid out."

He glanced at the bar. The amber-coloured ceiling lights had been turned on, creating a warm glow that showed through the open doorway. Rob was chatting with the barmaid; she laughed at something he'd said.

"And you," Jared said. "Are you all right?"

Her laughter was unconvincing. "Of course. Why wouldn't I be?"

"Just when I saw you coming in – yeah I know, me and Bex were having one of our little 'moments' … you know what she's like …"

Jacey didn't know what Bex was like, so she said nothing.

"Stubborn as hell, but you, I don't know, when you were standing there you looked terrified."

"Well, I wasn't."

She wished Rob would get back with their drinks, or Bex would come down from the bathroom. She didn't want a conversation with Jared about what had stopped her – the anxiety attack, or however she'd have to explain the hollowing to him.

"So, how long have you and Rob been together?"

"Almost ten years. Married for seven."

Great, she thought. *Back on safer territory.*

"And it's all going good?"

"Yes," she said. "Of course."

Not that it was any business of his. Why was he even asking?

"And nothing's ever been …" Jared glanced over at the bar. "I mean, Rob's never been …"

"What?"

"I don't know. Weird."

"In what way?"

"You've seen the way he flirts with Bex."

What could she say? Bex. Her heart pounded. The last time they met. The other pub. Not the Polish waitress – *Bex*. How had she not picked up on that?

"And, well …"

Rob was paying for his pint, throwing one last smile back at the barmaid.

"Look, I probably shouldn't say anything, but I knew Rob's old girlfriend back when we were in college. Trudy?"

Trudy. She'd heard the name. Rob never really talked about her, though. She'd seen a picture in a shoe box full of old mementos, asked him who she was. Trudy had reddish hair and bright blue eyes. A cute girl, art major. Went on to become a successful designer, Rob said. Shoes, or hats. Moved to California, that was all he knew.

"We were buddies, me and Trudy. This was before I met Bex. It was nothing romantic, we were just really good friends."

Rob was walking away from the bar, balancing the pints and wine glasses on a round drinks tray.

"So, anyway, she told me stuff about him."

Soon, Rob would be close enough to hear what Jared was saying.

"I mean, about what he was like."

On the way home, Rob didn't even try to break down her silence.

He had his headphones on, as usual, and was moving his head back and forth in time to the music. But she felt the distance as a void inside her chest. Not like the hollowing, but as if her heart was gone, and all her feelings. Her husband was just a person sitting across from her, a stranger, a random man who looked like someone who'd once been in love with her.

What would happen if she took his hand? Would he swat it away? Make his shame and disgust with her obvious? Did she even *want* to touch him after what Jared said?

"Hey, Jace?"

He turned to her, finally, and took his headphones off.

"Was something up with Jared today?" he asked.

"What do you mean?"

"Well, Bex looked so miserable, and I saw the two of you talking while I was at the bar."

The carriage shook and rattled, a sharp swerve along the tracks.

Rob took her hand. "And that fight they were having when we got to the pub. I just wondered if he said anything to you."

She shook her head, remembering her conversation with Jared, wishing she had the courage to mention it.

"What were you guys talking about, anyway?"

"Nothing." She shrugged. "Just stuff about how we're settling in, and asking if I liked it here and …"

A teenage boy sitting in the back of the carriage let out a shriek. Jacey had seen him and his friends when they swaggered up and down the aisle. They couldn't have been more than fourteen or fifteen, but they were drinking cans of beer, laughing raucously.

Rob pulled his hand away from her, disgusted, as if she'd been the one who bought those kids the beer. "Does every other word they say have to be *fuck*?" he tutted, turning away from her again.

He said it quietly, so nobody heard him, and he kept muttering, but Jacey couldn't make out the words. It wasn't because of the train noise or the fact that Rob was facing away from her, looking out the window again with his headphones on. It wasn't even the hollowing; it was the random thoughts, filling her brain.

Somebody named Trudy. Rob's girlfriend that he never talked about. Weird that Jared had mentioned her tonight, so many years later. Had something bad happened to her? Back then, in the past?

Why bring it up now?

Jacey looked at her husband. Foot tapping along to the music, head nodding, body shifting slightly, a silent, carefree dance.

Cold. That's all Rob was, not deliberately cruel. Insensitive, and short-tempered sometimes, but that was because he was so busy, because he had so many things to negotiate here in a new country with a new, demanding job, and systems and procedures he wasn't quite sure of yet. She couldn't blame him for that.

She looked at the boys again. One had opened his jacket, was showing something off to his friend. What was it? A weapon?

"Rob?" she whispered.

Rob didn't hear her. He'd retreated further into his music. He'd slumped in the seat, nestling his head into the gap next to the window.

She looked at the boys again and one of them caught her glance and smiled. He said something to his friend, and then they both laughed. It was like they knew how frightened she was, and how little Rob cared. The boy facing the opposite direction – a fat red-headed boy with freckles – put two fingers on each side of his lips, spread them apart, and stuck out his tongue at her, flicking it back and forth.

She pretended not to see, not to understand what it meant. She took Rob's hand, waited for him to squeeze it, waited some more.

There was no hollowing, but she'd never felt more invisible. More alone.

And she thought of what Jared said about the man beside her. *What he was like.*

Chapter 17

On a sunny, crisp day, while hiking up the hill behind Malin House, Jacey noticed that she wasn't breathless and her legs didn't ache after ten minutes of climbing. She remembered what Helen had said about becoming an expert hillwalker and felt a warm glow of pride in her chest. She was succeeding at something, improving herself. If only she could talk to Rob about it, share this sense of achievement.

But of course, he'd just pooh-pooh things, like he always did. When she told him how much she enjoyed walking on the downs, he just said, "Well, what's the point in that, if you're not going to stick with it."

"I am," she said. "I'm really liking it."

"Well, what about the history class? You enjoyed that, didn't you?"

"Yes."

"Then why haven't you gone back?"

She shook her head.

He put his hands out again, in that gesture that showed his impatience and incomprehension.

"I can't explain it," she said. "It felt … awkward."

"Well, who was that down to?"

"Me," she said. "Of course, darling. All my fault."

It had been at breakfast; he'd been on his phone, so he hadn't even registered the angry sarcasm in her voice. He just shrugged, brushing away her inadequacy, her inability to rise to the challenges that moving to England had presented to them. She imagined him reflecting on his own resilience, on getting around the limitations of his job, settling in more confidently to the driving, using the time to make new friends and socialise – why couldn't she grab this amazing opportunity and run with it?

But she was here now, again, at the top of the hill, striding back towards the hill path that led back down to Malin House, home after a long, bracing hike, in which she didn't hear any bells or experience any hollowing. She was just feeling healthy, and strong and—

Footsteps crunched on the path behind her.

She turned around, expecting it to be a strange little boy again, cold and lost, but it was just a dog, and she soon felt the familiar sensation of an excitable creature behind her, sniffing her legs, then bounding around to the front of her and putting his paws up on her jeans.

"Bella! Get down!"

Bella was some kind of poodle cross, bouncy and energetic. As Jacey kept walking, the dog trotted along beside her. She stopped, so its owners could catch up.

"Well, hello again!" A man's voice rang out. "Our American friend."

While Bella nipped at her ankles, a couple, similar to so many she saw hiking on the downs, white and sixty-something, with sleek grey hair and slim athletic builds, strode towards her.

"Hi," she said. Who were these people?

"You don't remember us, do you?"

The man put Bella back on the lead.

"The writing group. My wife read her story, and you said some very kind words about it."

"Muriel," Jacey sputtered. "Oh, course. I'm sorry I didn't recognise you, out here in all this bright light."

"I know," Muriel laughed. "And of course, we pensioners all look the same."

Jacey felt her face redden. "No, no that's not what I …"

Muriel let out a whoop of laughter. "Oh, don't worry, I'm only joking. We recognised you because you're new."

"And a very glamorous and mysterious American," her husband added.

"Now I know you're kidding," Jacey joked.

"Not at all," Muriel's husband said. "It was really great to see somebody fresh and exciting turn up for a change."

Muriel lifted Bella up into her arms and let the dog nuzzle under her shoulder. "We're disappointed you haven't been back," she said. "I hope we didn't scare you away."

The man cleared his throat. "By 'we' she means Madlyn, our illustrious leader, of course …"

"Nobody scared me away," Jacey said. "I've just been …"

"Too busy writing?" Muriel asked. Her blue eyes twinkled. She obviously meant it; she seemed to be brimming with enthusiasm and kindness.

"No. Other things," Jacey said. "But I'll definitely come back sometime. I really liked your story."

"Thank you, darling, that is so lovely of you to say."

Muriel let Bella down, unhooked her lead and let her scamper before them on the path.

"But why don't we go get a cup of tea. The café is just up ahead. I need the loo, Bella needs a drink, and John needs …"

"A rest. You might as well go and say it," John laughed. "These two girls are running me ragged. Come on, let's all get to the tea shop before it closes. I won't say I'll race you, because there's no way in hell I'd ever win."

The café windows were steamed, and the floors were wet and a little muddy from where people had tracked in dirt from their heavy – *stout*, as Helen would say – boots. A boy made a few rounds with his mop, but the whoosh of dirty water only thinned out the sludge. John waited at the counter for their drinks and Muriel and Jacey sat at a table near the door; Bella yapped excitedly every time it opened and new customers arrived.

"So, Malin House," Muriel said. "What's it like living there?"

Jacey smiled. "It's big," she said. "A lot to keep clean, I guess, although we don't use all the rooms. But it's definitely nicer than any place I've ever lived before."

"No, I mean, what's it, *like*." Muriel glanced over her shoulder as if she was worried somebody might be listening in. She whispered: "Living in a haunted house."

Jacey held her breath. Another chance, she thought. To tell the truth about what she'd experienced, about how she felt, but she carried on with her denial – these people were strangers, after all – and her bravado.

"Oh, that's just a stupid rumour. It's not really haunted."

"Well, maybe the ghosts are a bit timid with you, but that's not what other people have experienced."

Jacey remembered the conversation with the taxi driver, and the woman at the cab stand. What had they said? *Don't listen.*

John was having a long chat with a man behind the counter. She wished he'd hurry with their teas. John seemed like a sensible man; he wouldn't want to sit around and talk about ghosts or hauntings.

"Honestly, there's been nothing to report," Jacey said. "It's a little gloomy. I'm not 100% happy about being on my own there at night, if my husband has a meeting, but I always know that Helen and Martin are nearby if something goes wrong, even when Rob's not home."

"Well, I wouldn't like it. I mean, the list of people who've run away from the place screaming is as long as your arm, isn't it, John?"

John arrived with the teas. He set the mugs down, took the tray back to the counter and said something to the man who'd served him.

The man at the counter looked at Jacey and waved. Jacey's face reddened. They were talking about Malin House. They were talking about *her*.

"You know you shouldn't be telling this poor girl tales," John said, when he was back at the table. "You'll only scare her."

"I'm not scared," Jacey said.

"Well, you should be," Muriel said.

John put his hand on Muriel's, a slightly admonishing gesture. "I mean it, sweetheart. You're getting to be as bad as Madlyn."

Muriel pulled her hand away. "I'm not," she said. "But you weren't the one talking to people, were you? That poor Australian woman a while back? Her husband taught at the university, too. Remember her?"

"Darling, please. Give it a rest."

Muriel ignored her husband. At her feet, Bella growled.

"At first it was noises," Muriel said.

Jacey said nothing, but her heart was beating so strongly she wondered if Muriel and John could hear it.

"Banging and pounding at night, like a building site, the poor girl told me."

"If it kept her awake," John said, "of course it drove her round the bend. Doesn't have anything to do with …"

"But that wasn't the worst of it," Muriel said.

"Here we go." John looked away from his wife and his jaw clenched.

"She soon started seeing things."

"What kind of things," Jacey asked.

"She could never be certain. Shapes. Lights and shadows, she said. Nothing she could make out clearly."

John sighed. "There. You said it, honey. Nothing but shadows."

"We met at the café in town," Muriel said. "She was always on her own. I'd seen her around the place a few times, looking a bit lost, so I felt sorry for her, and we struck up a conversation, you know. Like *we* are. And she told me how unhappy she was and how her husband was up to no good – at least that's what she suspected."

"Poor thing," Jacey said.

"I told her she should go home to her family. Australia, wherever."

John was shaking her head and *tsk*ing. Jacey knew she should ignore what Muriel was saying, that it was nothing more than gossip, but she couldn't help herself.

"Whatever happened to her?" she asked. "Do you know?"

"Oh, yes," Muriel said. "Though it wasn't very nice."

Jacey's stomach flipped. She felt the colour draining from her face, and John's and Muriel's eyes on her.

"What was it?" Jacey said. "Did she die?"

"Oh, no," Muriel said. "Nothing like that."

"She ended up in a lunatic asylum," John said. He looked at Muriel. "There? You happy now?"

"You know you can't say that, dear. Not anymore."

"Psychiatric hospital, then. Is that better? Whatever you want to call it doesn't make much difference. She was sectioned, poor girl. Put away. For God knows how long."

He looked at Jacey. "She lost it completely, I guess you could say."

"Lost it?" Jacey's voice was reduced to a whisper.

"She set the house on fire. Tried to burn it down."

Chapter 18

Jacey took the pizza out of the oven, slid it onto a heavy marble serving tray and heaved it onto the counter.

It was almost dark when she came down off the hill, and she'd totally forgotten that it was Rob's meeting night, so she had to get into the house quickly, switch on all the lights, lock herself in the den, and do something easy for her dinner.

She looked at her phone. There was a text from Muriel, as promised. *You call me any time, Jacey*, she said. *If you want to chat or meet for coffee. I'm always at home these days, when I'm not up on the hill.*

But there was no message from Rob.

She rang his number.

Straight to voicemail. She left a message.

Sorry I missed you, darling, but got waylaid on my walk. Lovely old couple I met at the history club (why was she so determined to keep up that lie? Why had she called Muriel and John 'old'? What did their age matter?) *invited me to the café for tea.*

Frozen pizza was better than cooking. No risky fire involved. No flame to tend, just a quick flick of the wrist to turn on the electric oven. Couldn't cause any damage that way, only to herself; the red-hot electric element wouldn't explode or burn, it would only sear and singe and scar her skin, if she got too close.

While the pizza cooked, she had a look around. Where had this fire started? How? There was scorching on the floor in front of the fireplace's hearth. It could have been an accident – too much kindling or a dropped touch paper – but maybe this Australian girl had been anxious, or had expressed fears about the house, so when a fire accidentally took hold in the kitchen her husband put the blame on her and had her locked up as a danger to herself and others.

That might have happened. Part of a husband's cunning plan. Maybe he was the one who'd set the place on fire, to get her sent away, so he could be rid of her, move his girlfriend in. Jacey checked her computer, googled *Malin House* and *arson*. There was a short item in the local newspaper under the headline 'Fire Breaks Out at Historic Home', and a picture of smoke billowing from the kitchen window, but nothing about how the fire started. Nothing about the woman or her husband. 'Ongoing investigation' was all the article said, and that seemed to be the end of it. Maybe this arson story was one of the Malin House rumours that the taxi driver was warning her about when he said not to listen.

Jacey poured herself a glass of wine and took her pizza into the den. The TV programme with the cute historian wasn't on. Instead of Henry VIII there was a documentary about Queen Victoria, linking her back to all the other royal families of Europe. The host was an old man with silver hair who was an expert on the subject, but he wasn't even trying to make the show interesting. The people he interviewed seemed bored, too. Queen Victoria? Nice lady? Never chopped anyone's head off or had them burned at the stake, so who gave a damn about her?

She finished the pizza, took the plate back into the kitchen, searching the window frame for signs of smoke damage. Through the window she saw that the light was on at Helen and Martin's cottage. Would it be too late to go and ask them about the fire? About the woman who supposedly started it?

9 p.m. Definitely too late. She closed the curtains.

But curiosity gnawed at her. It didn't make sense that a nice couple like Muriel and John would make up such a dramatic story, even if the newspaper couldn't print all the details without enough proof. If she could find out what happened, if she could get in touch with this woman, whoever, wherever she was, she might find some answers. *Was* there something wrong with this place? Maybe what she'd been hearing and seeing wasn't just tinnitus, after all. Maybe it wasn't migraines. Maybe it was real, and something to be actually afraid of.

At the top of the stairs, on a small writing table, there was a guest book. She'd walked past it every day, on her way downstairs, dozens of times, and never once thought to pick it up and have a look. This woman might have signed it. She might have left a clue for any future occupants, a way to get in touch with her if nothing else.

Jacey could feel the book waiting impatiently for her, willing her to bravely climb the stairs so it could reveal its secrets.

Jacey stood up and went to the door that led to the hallway.

Come on, she told herself. *You can do this.* The top of the stairs, that's all. A quick run up, grab the book, rush back down, and look through it while you snuggle up, all comfy and safe on the sofa in the den, with the doors locked behind you. Look at how you go up to the hill almost every day, even though it's spooky sometimes, when you're all alone. Look at the way you can make it through the tunnel under the road without running, even in the dark.

She put her hand on the doorknob, turned it to the right, opened the door.

This could be a test. This could be the first step in not letting her life be ruled by fear, not controlled by the hollowing or the sounds she heard, or the notion that she was living with a husband who didn't love her anymore, in a house that hated her, too.

She opened the door to the hallway. The chandelier was burning brightly. Too bright; she felt caught by the light, exposed. She reached her hand to the wall and turned it off. There. Maybe that was better. Once her eyes adjusted it wasn't completely dark. There was moonlight – a half moon at most, but something to see by, without the harsh, revealing glare. And there were no sounds; there weren't any bells.

Everything was quiet. The coast was clear.

In through the doorway she stepped, onto the tiles, and listened. Nothing. Silence.

And she wasn't even scared. Wasn't that something? There was no thumping in her chest, her breathing was steady, her head was held high.

She went to the bottom of the stairs. She looked up into the darkness. No one was there. See?

See?

But there *was* something.

There. At the top …

Moving. Shivering, as if it were alive.

Swaying at the top, and then falling, down one step, and then another, bouncing.

She shuffled back, too afraid to make any other movement.

It grew nearer, this thing that was small and round, not much bigger than her clenched fists. Down it came – bounce, bounce, bounce.

Another step back. What was it?

A ball, with letters, same as the one she'd seen before.

Landing at her feet, its painted surface like cracked old skin. Its colours pale, faded – blue, yellow, red.

A harmless toy.

ABC.

The den's wall clock chimes had disturbed her, and she woke to find Rob standing over her, swaying slightly, reeking of alcohol and cigarettes.

"You're still awake," he slurred.

She sat up, looked at the clock. "It's three in the morning."

"No, it's not." He shook his head, swayed again, needing to grab the back of the sofa for support.

"Not three," he said. He looked at the clock, squinted, nodded. "2.47. See? Not three o'clock."

Jacey couldn't tell if he was joking. "2.47, three o'clock, what's the difference."

"Big difference," Rob slurred, "thirteen fucking minutes."

He turned and went through the door. His feet shuffled on the hallway floor tiles. She heard him stumble on the steps once, twice, and a few seconds later the room to their door slammed shut.

What should she do? Join him? Make another stab at the stairway, grab the guestbook, crawl into bed for a quick peek. He was probably already fast asleep. Or should she stay down here, wait until morning? Then she could confront him with her suspicion and worries; he'd find it hard to fight back with a terrible hangover. She'd have the upper hand for once, the least foggy brain.

And after she'd shared her anxieties and worries with him, maybe there'd be no more tinnitus, or bells, or hollowings. Was that what this was all about? Anxiety. Stress.

She'd ask him about the ball, too.

After the stupid thing fell down the stairs the she'd stared for about five minutes, not daring to touch it. As if it would actually come alive, grow tentacles or fangs, gobble her up. After her heart had stopped pounding and she gathered the courage to pick it up, she'd carried it back into the den and then put it away, out of sight, in the wicker firewood basket in the kitchen, under some logs.

It was harmless enough, just a spongy rubber ball that had been coated over. There were bite marks on it, as if it had been used as a teething soother, and there were patches where the print had worn off. Rob must have been the one who put it on the landing, like he'd done before. Just for fun. A silly game.

How could he have known she'd seen a little boy kicking a ball that looked almost exactly the same? It was stupid of her to have got so frightened. To have thought of burning the ball in the fireplace, as if a worn-out toy was some cursed talisman that had to be completely destroyed.

She listened for more sounds upstairs; no, Rob was definitely asleep.

She'd stay where she was, cosy and safe. But first she got up and locked the doors on both sides of the den, the one leading to the hallway, the other to the kitchen. She checked that the windows looking out over the lawn were locked; the blinds down, the curtains drawn tight.

Pulling the blankets over her shoulders, she settled herself on the couch. She leaned behind her to flick off the table lamp when something caught her eyes, caused her heart to lurch again in terror.

There. Reflected on the television's black screen was what looked like a child's body on the arm of the sofa, legs dangling back and forth.

She clutched the blanket, drew up her legs, forced herself to look at the reflection until what she was seeing made sense.

Finally, it did.

Rob had slung his jacket over the side of the sofa. That's all it was – coat sleeves hanging down. Seeing the ball tumble down the stairs like a severed head had made her crazy with fear.

Stupid, stupid to be so afraid. Dangerous, the way her heart was pounding.

She picked up the coat, smoothed it over herself, another layer of protection from the bogeymen and the ghouls.

She slipped her hands in one of the pockets.

Inside, a scrap of paper.

She took it out.

Another train ticket.

She turned the light back on.

The ticket was for today. Lewes to London. Return journey.

Jacey's heart sank.

Coming back at three in the morning, drunk and angry.

London again. She could see that; she was holding the proof in her hand.

But where in London? And who with?

Chapter 19

The bartender – a girl who didn't look old enough to drink herself – was struggling with the wave of grey-haired writing club members who were crowding the bar, anxious to get in a drink before the class began. Jacey tried to imagine her mother's church lady friends behaving like this, but it was impossible. Jostling for position, desperately pushing their way to the front of the line, waving their plastic bank cards like weapons.

Muriel and John were among the group, and when Jacey arrived, Muriel hailed her over. "Great to see you again," Muriel said. "We were worried we'd scared you away."

There was a space created at the bar as someone got served, so John muscled to the front of the queue. "We're ordering a bottle of red," he shouted. "We'll get a glass for you."

She joined Muriel and John, and another person at the table – Rael, hair dyed back to blue, clutching a fountain pen that seemed to have leaked over his fingers and stained his nails.

"This is Rael," Muriel said.

"Hi there, Rael," Jacey shook Rael's hand.

"Just so you know," Muriel said. "Rael's trans-masculine. His pronouns are 'he' and 'him'."

Rael sighed and rolled his eyes.

"He writes poetry," Muriel said, accentuating the "he," as if congratulating herself for getting it right.

Rael picked up Muriel's hand and patted it patronisingly. "*She* knows, darling. We've already met."

"Well, I didn't know about the poetry," Jacey said.

"Consider yourself lucky." Rael muttered. "Seriously."

John picked up the wine bottle and topped up everyone's glasses. "Jacey's grandmother's from the same village in Cambridgeshire as Madlyn," he said.

"So I've heard. What was the name of the place again?"

"Stanton."

"Spooky, isn't it?" Muriel squealed.

Rael shrugged sarcastically.

"Oh, come on," John said. "You've got to admit it is a pretty big coincidence?"

After the last meeting Jacey had managed to convince herself that it wasn't such a big deal. After all, England was a small country, with a limited supply of villages, so the chances of someone being from the same place as Nana Ivy wasn't so strange, was it? But now that Rael raised the question, she realised how naïve she'd been. Of course it was weird.

"And Jacey lives in that haunted house," Muriel said.

Rael grabbed his chair, swivelled it to face Jacey. His mouth dropped, and he took in a huge gulp of air.

"No shit? Malin House?" he said. "Why didn't you say?"

"I was telling her about some of the people that lived there before," Muriel said. "Well, one of the people. The Australian girl who tried to burn the place down."

"Oh, that fire story is complete bullshit," Rael said.

"How do you know?" Muriel said. She sounded a little tetchy, not her usually warm self. She obviously wasn't happy that Rael was muscling in on her story exclusive, challenging her version of the events.

"Well, she didn't burn it down on purpose," Rael said. "Whatever happened, it wasn't Katherine's fault."

Muriel narrowed her eyes, as if Rael had said something controversial. "And what makes you such an expert?"

"I knew Katherine, too," Rael said.

Something shifted in the air, tightening around them like a thick cloak, muffling Rael's words so that Jacey struggled to hear them.

"At uni. In my first year. She took a few classes while she was here."

Jacey could have been imagining it, but it seemed that John shot Muriel a look – like a signal, or a sign that she shouldn't say any more.

Madlyn stood at the front, ready to start the meeting. Jacey took a sip of wine, breathed deeply, grateful when Madlyn tinked her glass to get everyone's attention, and the hollowing cleared.

Every hundred metres or so, Jacey and Rael stopped so he could re-light his roll-up.

The two of them left together after the meeting. Rael had brought some poetry along to read but decided at the last minute to leave it for another week, despite Muriel's encouragement. "Not the right demographic," Rael had said. "If you get my meaning."

John, who'd stayed quiet for most of the night, chortled. "Probably pornographic," he muttered.

"Bingo!" Rael squealed.

It was a dark, clear moonless night, and although the sky was studded with diamond-bright stars, the darkness felt oppressive. Some of the shops and houses were decorated for Halloween with spray-on spiderwebs and illuminated Jack-O'-Lanterns, but there was no point, Jacey thought. No cut-out spooks could make the narrow, shadowy streets of Lewes creepier to her than they already were.

She and Rael walked in silence; he stopped for another flick of the lighter and a draw on the cigarette. "Sorry," Rael muttered. "Gets boring. I know."

"It's OK," Jacey said. "Hey, I live at Malin House so I'm not in any real hurry to get back home, am I?"

A joke. That made it better.

Rael took a puff on his cigarette.

"Do *you* think the house is haunted?"

Jacey shook her head. What could she say? What did she *dare* say to someone she hardly knew, who might even be one of Rob's students. Rael could be a plant, a spy, someone Rob was using to gather evidence of her suspicions about him, or even worse, the fragile state of her mind.

"Well?" Rael clicked the lighter again.

"No," Jacey answered. "Not haunted."

"But weird, right? Like, freaky AF?"

Jacey sighed. "Maybe. I don't know."

Rael took a huge drag and blew the smoke out of the side of his mouth.

"Well, Katherine – my mate who lived there – thought it was. She heard things, she saw stuff she couldn't explain. Told me about experiences she didn't understand."

"I thought you hardly knew her," Jacey said.

"That's what I told them. You have to be really careful with that Madlyn and Muriel crew. Like, keep things close."

They were on the move again. The high street was empty. There were a few lights on above the shops, but otherwise, it was as gloomy and claustrophobic as a cave.

Rael looked around, twirling with a little flourish. "This fucking town, man."

"What's the matter?" Jacey laughed. "Don't you think it's quaint?"

"Yeah, just like that house you live in," Rael said.

Jacey took a breath. How much should she tell him? "I guess it *is* weird."

"You only guess … Jesus, what's wrong with you?"

"I try not to think about it."

"So there are no unexplainable noises or things just appearing out of nowhere …"

Jacey waited for the hollowing – now would be the time, when she was vulnerable, confronted with frightening things she couldn't understand, having to lie to someone about the terrifying reality that was her—

"Jesus Christ," Rael shrieked. "Look at that!"

Rael's outburst was loud enough to have woken anyone in the flats overlooking the streets. There, in front of them, crossing the road, was a large fox, as far as Jacey could tell, because she'd never seen one in real life – and three baby foxes.

"Are they—?"

"Vermin. Yes."

"But they're wonderful, Rael. How can you say that?"

The mother fox's fur was glowing orange under the street light, and the little foxes' undersides were reflected on the road's damp surface.

"Golden brown rats with cute, fluffy tails," Rael huffed, "but still rats."

The foxes slunk between two parked cars and then nipped behind a green bin and crept down a narrow alley.

"I've never seen a fox before. And this is the last place I expected to find a wild animal."

Rael finally gave up on his cigarette, flicking the butt into a drain in the gutter that was already full of leaves and bits of paper and plastic.

"Now that the excitement's over, let's get you home," he said.

"There's no need to, Rael. I'll be fine."

"I mean it. There's plenty of time until my train back to Brighton, so I might as well be a pal."

Rael held out his arm, crooked at the elbow, and Jacey threaded her arm through his. "Or a gentleman, even?" she said.

Rael laughed. "Don't push your luck, sister."

It felt good, the laughing. And with Rael, Jacey felt she could be herself again. Not walking on eggshells, not so scared of saying the wrong thing like she was with Rob. They went over the bridge that crossed the railroad tracks and cut across the parkland that led them to the tunnel.

"Here we go," Jacey said, taking a deep breath.

"There's nothing wrong with the tunnel, is there?"

"I don't know."

She and Rael slowed down. "Oh my God," Rael said, eyes wide, jumping slightly, like a kid about to be told a scary story, and anticipating the thrill. "What?"

"A couple of weeks ago I saw something weird."

"Tell me. Tell me."

Should she tell him? Did she dare?

"It was probably nothing."

"Oh, that's what Katherine used to say, all the time. I got so sick of it."

"OK," Jacey said. "A little boy. Kicking a ball against the tunnel wall."

Rael laughed. "You're right. That *is* nothing."

"I know, but then I saw him again a few days later. On the hill. And dressed the same, like with shorts and a flimsy T-shirt and not wearing a coat."

They were at the mouth of the tunnel. Rael shrugged. "Still not impressed."

"But he was too young to be out on his own, at night … and even up on the hill, and then …"

Rael let go of her arm, took her by both arms.

"You can tell me, Jacey," he said.

"A few nights ago, when I was home alone, and Rob – my husband – was out late, doing God knows what with God knows who, I was about to go upstairs to get something, and when I got to the bottom of the staircase I looked up and there, at the top—"

"The boy was standing there? Oh my God!"

"No," Jacey said. "It wasn't the boy. It was just a ball, but it was exactly like *his* ball, and something made it move, and go down the steps, bouncing down like somebody's head and …"

Suddenly, Rael let go of Jacey's right hand and dragged her along by her left arm, pulling her through the tunnel, screaming at the top of his lungs.

"FUUUUUUUUUUCK!"

And when they got to the other side, they were breathless and laughing.

"A ball," Rael said. "Really, Ms. Jacey? Is that the best you can do?"

Jacey smiled. She liked the way Rael called her 'Ms. Jacey'. And she liked the way he thought that what she saw was nothing to be frightened of.

"You must think I'm stupid for being so scared," Jacey said when they got to the house. "Like, I'm overreacting."

"No." Rael shook his head. "It is fucking weird, and after hearing so many stories about that house from Katherine, I don't think you're stupid at all. I'd be scared of that place, too. In fact, I'd get the hell out if I were you. I'd run away, as fast as I could."

Rael kissed both cheeks and watched her go through the front door, waving as she closed it behind her. He promised he'd wait until she got safely upstairs, and turned the light on in her bedroom, and she knew if she looked down from the window, he'd be there.

When she was in bed – safe, lights on for a few seconds so she wouldn't wake Rob – he texted.

Good girl, the message said, and she felt strangely proud of herself, that she'd gone upstairs by herself in the dark, as if that was a major achievement.

Brave Ms. Jacey, to stay another night in that horrible house!

Chapter 20

When Jacey came into the kitchen the next morning, Rob didn't react. There was no 'good morning, honey', no 'Hey, Jace'. He carried on with eating his breakfast and whatever he was doing on his laptop, not even glancing in her direction.

He was dressed for work – a blue shirt and red tie under a dark grey crew neck sweater. His hair was curling over his collar. *Just look at him*, Jacey thought. Her handsome young husband. It almost hurt, how much she still loved him, and how little he cared.

A few seconds later, still without looking away from the screen, he said, "What time did you get in last night?"

He sounded like somebody's old-fashioned father, talking to a rebellious teen. "Just after eleven, why?"

"Oh? My phone said eleven twenty."

Jacey held her breath. She went to the cupboard above the sink, took out the coffee, placed the cafetière on the counter and switched on the electric kettle. Was he mocking her for mis-stating the time after he'd gone to London without telling her? Was this a joke?

"We left the pub at about eleven."

Rob sighed and closed the lid on his laptop. He took a sip of tea, a bite of toast. "We?"

"Yes, we."

Anger tugged at her stomach. But now was not the time to say what she was thinking – *how fucking dare you after what you did, going to London, saying it was Brighton, getting home at almost three in the morning, and acting like I was in the wrong for calling you out.*

"Someone escorted me back through the tunnel."

"And your escort. Was it a man? A woman?"

Why was he even asking her? He didn't give a damn. She thought he'd be happy that she'd made the effort to go out for a change.

"A man," she said. "If you must know."

Rob was looking weird. Eyes scrunched up, mouth twisted. But it couldn't be jealousy. It had to be something else.

"So you've met somebody there."

"Yes. I've met a few people. Most of them women, the vast majority over sixty-five. But one of them is a transgender boy of about twenty-one – gay, too, I think – who kindly walked me home."

Her heart was pounding. The hypocrisy of Rob's attitude was overwhelming. And she hated herself for mentioning that Rael was trans. What did that matter? What business was it of Rob's?

"Well, I could say things about what you do," she whined, "but I don't, because I respect your privacy, OK?"

Jacey couldn't read his face because there was no expression in it at all. His lips were pressed together, creasing slightly at the sides. Was he still angry with her? Was he actually jealous of Rael?

Rob shook his head. "Turn this back on me, why don't you?"

"And I don't want to get into a fight over things that probably mean nothing."

"Like what?"

Like train journeys to London, she thought. Now would be the perfect time spring her knowledge on him, to go upstairs, find the tickets, shove them into his sanctimonious—

"Right then," Rob said. "I'm off. Got a ten o'clock lecture."

Just like that. Before Jacey could do or say anything else. Without bothering to finish his tea or the rest of his toast.

"Not all of us have limitless leisure time on our hands."

He pronounced it the British way – *lezhure* – of course.

"We can talk tonight then," she said.

"Yeah. Sure."

That was all. Two words.

As soon as the front door slammed, the house seemed to groan, shifting on its foundation slightly, as if some engine had turned over in the basement and was idling there until Rob's return. The dreadful silence was as bad as the hollowing, Jacey thought. The loneliness of being with someone whose feelings were gone was breaking her heart.

The morning's silence did not last long.

Minutes after Rob left, there was a knock on the door. A loud, impatient, rat-a-tat. When Jacey opened it, she saw Madlyn from the writer's club, wearing heavy boots and carrying a pointed walking stick.

"Hello!" Madlyn chirped, stepping through the door and into the hallway, while her dog, Bramble, ran in a crazy circle, sliding on the tiles.

"We were going for a walk up the hill and I saw a man that I knew had to be American – the clothes and the way he was talking on the phone – and so I assumed he was your husband. And I saw Helen on the driveway down below – we all know her and Martin in the town – and she said yes, there was a nice American girl who lived in the house, so I thought, why not drop in?"

Madlyn finally took a breath and made a clicking sound that brought Bramble to her side.

"Rude to have barged in like this, I suppose," she said. "But I wouldn't say no to a coffee if there's one going. Now that we're here."

Madlyn seemed to know the layout of the place. Bramble trotted behind her as she went through the den to the kitchen. She sat down at the table and looked around the room, the same way Helen had on their first day, as if she were searching for something out of place, or dirty. Jacey took out the cafetière, gave it a rinse under the sink, and boiled the kettle again.

"So how do you like living here?" Madlyn asked, smoothing back her hair that was hanging in lanky strands on either side of her sweatshirt's lowered hood.

"It's great."

"Must be fantastic for a writer."

"It's quiet, that's for sure."

"Especially if you're into the horror genre."

Jacey measured the coffee out, poured in the water, watched the grounds swirl in the darkening water. What was she supposed to say to Madlyn? She hadn't invited her over; she didn't want to even think about the house, much less talk about it. And, as for the writing, she had no idea what she was into. Words on paper, that's all it was so far, and pretty hopeless words at that.

"Are you? Like working on ghost stories?"

Jacey shook her head uncommittedly and shrugged. Why was Madlyn asking these questions. Why was she *here?*

The coffee looked ready – Jacey was never sure.

"Do you want milk with yours?"

"Yes, and one sugar, please."

Jacey brought over a sugar bowl. Like everything in the house, it had been here when they arrived. It was old fashioned, with a dark blue and gold design, interlaced with pink peonies and yellow daffodils, and some other flowers that she couldn't recognise; Rob had spent ages looking them up on the internet, so he could know their names, so he could know *everything*.

"So." Madlyn put down her mug. "I told a little white lie earlier on. I already knew you lived here. Figured it out from a few of the things you said the other night, and when you mentioned where your grandmother was from – the same village as me – I couldn't resist stopping by and saying hello. I mean, it's such a coincidence."

"Are you saying you knew my grandmother?"

Madlyn picked up the teaspoon to add more sugar, clinking it against the side of the mug, making a sound that reminded Jacey of the tinkling bells.

"Hey, I'm old," Madlyn laughed, "but I'm not that old. She left the village – ran off to the States with your grandad to get married – in the 1940s, long before I was born."

She put the teaspoon down, set her hands on the table, as if the business part of this meeting was about to commence, now that the pleasantries, and the introductory coffee was over.

"But I knew *of* her," she said. "Everyone in town did."

"Wow," Jacey said.

"We all knew the story."

There was something in Madlyn's voice that made Jacey nervous. She felt her heart beating strongly, again … she waited for the hollowing, but it didn't come.

"About her meeting my grandfather, you mean?"

"Yes, that."

"And going to America with him."

"That, too."

"And the other stuff," Madlyn said. "About the rest of your family."

Jacey smiled vaguely, ignoring Madlyn's not very subtle attempt to lure her into asking for more details, or the heavy insinuation that something in Jacey's family history wasn't exactly straightforward. She remembered what Rael had said, how Madlyn had been hinting about some scandal, but wouldn't say what it was.

Madlyn leaned forward, very close – too close.

"You know … the Kennets."

The room was quiet. It was a normal type of silence, with birds in the trees and shrubs, and the hiss of distant traffic. Jacey glanced outside; Helen wasn't in the garden, and the car was gone. Nobody was home next door.

"The Kennets?" Jacey asked. Her throat was suddenly dry.

"That's your grandmother's name, isn't it?

"No, it was Ivy."

"Her surname, I mean."

"Her last name was Smith. Ivy Smith. Not Kennet anything or anything Kennet."

"OK." Madlyn nodded. She took a sip of her coffee. "I must have the wrong family, then."

"Obviously, since that's not the name."

Jacey glanced up at the clock. Almost eleven. Rob's lecture would be over by noon. He might be willing to meet her, to have a chat and she could explain about last night. Or better yet, she could surprise him, take him out to lunch, a spontaneous romantic gesture of the type she used to do when they were first married. And he was always doing the same, bringing flowers, and buying her chocolates, and giving her impromptu foot massages while she was lying in bed.

She picked up the empty coffee cups and put them in the sink.

"I'm sorry, but I really need to be going," she said. "I promised my husband I'd meet him for lunch, and you know how unreliable the trains can be."

"Of course," Madlyn said. "Isn't that sweet? Still acting like newlyweds."

Underneath the table Bramble shuffled and growled; sniffing out lies again. Hers and Madlyn's.

Newlyweds, Bramble must have been thinking. *As if.*

Before she left the house Jacey sent Rob a text. *Hey, honey, I'm going to have lunch at the Seacole Building today – needed a change of scene! Care to join me? Hope you can find the time. I'll text when I'm off the train.*

She said nothing about last night or their argument this morning. Play it cool. Be reasonable and sweet. Maybe he'd already forgotten.

She ran to the station, jumped on the first train. She'd have just enough time to put some make-up on, brush her hair, and figure out what she was going to say to Rob about why she'd decide to drop in on him.

Because she was his wife, wasn't that enough reason? Because she loved him and she was scared something terrible was going wrong with their marriage. Because she didn't recognise their relationship anymore: his prickly dismissiveness, the way she felt vulnerable and worthless all the time.

She strolled through the campus. Between the harsh, square brick buildings, there were soft green lawns and huge trees that had already shed most of their leaves, creating an orange and yellow carpet on the ground. The air was fresh, too, and Jacey remembered her walk with Rob in Stanmer Park. Meeting Madlyn there had seemed like a coincidence. Was it?

Of course. How could Madlyn have known where she'd be at any given time? She hadn't even been to a class then. What reason would Madlyn have had for following them? And even if it was a little weird that she'd just dropped in on her this morning, there was nothing sinister in it. Madlyn was lonely. A busybody. Eccentric. And all that stuff about her Nana Ivy being part of some sinister-sounding family was baloney, too.

She strolled over to Rob's office, in a modern brick and concrete building that looked as if it was being overcome and smothered by red-tinged Virginia creeper.

The admin assistant, Stephanie, looked up when Jacey came through to the reception area.

"Good morning." She seemed a little confused, as if she was trying to place Jacey's face.

"I'm Jacey Gibson. Rob's wife."

Stephanie's face reddened. "Oh, of course, I'm so sorry, I …"

Jacey looked behind Stephanie's desk, at the long corridor where the professors' – sorry, lecturers' – offices were.

"Is he back from his class yet?"

"Who?"

"Rob. My husband. Have you seen him around?"

"Um … no …"

"He had a lecture at ten."

"Sorry, but I haven't seen him at all today," Stephanie said, flustered. She tapped some letters on her keyboard.

"Ah, it looks as though he's cleared his timetable. Meeting in London, it says. You can have a peek at his diary if you like."

Jacey's heart pounded, but she managed to smile. "That's OK." She tried to sound upbeat, cheerful. She didn't want to let on that something was wrong – that Rob had lied to her. "Must have gotten my dates mixed up."

She hurried out of the building and crossed the lawn to Seacole House. There was no point in checking the cafeteria, but she looked anyway. Just in case he'd got her message and was so touched and overwhelmed by her gesture, that he'd made a last-minute change of plan.

Of course there was no sign of Rob.

Of course he'd fucking lied.

Of course if she checked his pockets tonight – assuming he even came home – she'd find a ticket to London or even further afield, and a receipt for a meal for two, and a number, hastily scrawled on the back of one of his business cards.

With an exotic name like Marianna. Or Orsha. Or …

As if in a daze, she wandered back to the train station, looking at everyone she passed, hoping that she'd make out his face, red and sweaty as he rushed towards the refectory, trying to catch her before she'd given up hope.

By the time she reached the station, she was exhausted, but she climbed up the steps to the other platform, the one that led to Brighton. She didn't want to go back to the big house. To the spooky sounds. The tinkling bells. The hateful silence.

To the horror and shame.

Chapter 21

Rael jumped onto the train just as the final whistle was blown. He slumped down in the seat next to Jacey, put his backpack on the floor, and let out a sigh. "So where exactly are we going, at such late notice?"

"Cambridgeshire."

"The university, you mean?"

"No. Cambridge*shire*, I mean. Stanton. The village where my grandmother was from."

Rael opened his backpack and took out two cans of pre-mixed gin and tonic. As he opened one, the drink fizzed over his hands and dripped onto the floor.

"And also where Madlyn is from," Jacey added.

"Oh, my God, I'd forgotten about that." Rael took a huge, messy slurp. "We can dig up some shit on her. There's bound to be plenty."

Besides the G&Ts, Rael's backpack was weighed down with homemade cheese sandwiches, and some greasy pastry things called sausage rolls that he'd bought at a place called Greggs. His hair was Gothic black again; freshly dyed, Jacey assumed, because the collar of his T-shirt was stained grey where he hadn't rinsed it off properly.

Jacey was glad she'd called him, and glad he'd agreed to come along.

Taking the train to Stanton was a spur-of-the-moment idea, a silly adventure borne out of panic – but after what she'd found out at the university, she didn't want to be alone with her thoughts about Rob, especially not in Malin House. It was great to have some banter with Rael and drink the bubbly gin concoction that had already gone to her head and was making her feel giddy.

The train trudged across the Sussex landscape, until it reached the sprawling suburbs of London, and cut through the heart of the city. They changed trains in Cambridge and passed the college towers and church steeples of the city, before the Cambridgeshire landscape became as flat and featureless as western Minnesota, with no hills or trees, just acres and acres of muddy, recently harvested fields.

As they pulled into another small-town station, Rael asked, "So what's this sudden road trip really in aid of, Ms. Jacey. Have there been more mysterious goings on in Malin House?"

"No," Jacey said. "I just ..."

She didn't want to tell him about Rob going AWOL. She felt her cheeks getting red at the memory of being lied to, and the humiliation she'd felt at his university office, the look of pity in the receptionist's eyes, as if she'd known the truth, as if everyone did.

"Well, it's all crap anyway," Rael said. "In my opinion."

"What is?"

"What people say about the house fire. My friend Katherine, I mean. It was just her husband – her ex-husband, I should say – who spread that arsonist bollocks around. Had her bloody arrested."

"Why would he do that?"

"He wanted rid of her, of course. Isn't that what husbands do?"

Jacey didn't answer. She sat back, looked out the window at the desolate landscape. The earth seemed to flatten into nothing as they rolled along, just a thin carpet of dirt and tufty grass, while the grey sky expanded, filling her vision.

"Anyway, they dropped the charges because there was no evidence that the fire was started on purpose. No signs of petrol or whatever it is they use. But her husband put in a report saying that she'd been seeing things before the attack, and because she had burns on her hands, they assumed she was playing with fire as a kind of self-harming ritual, and she ended up in a secure mental health unit."

"How could that happen?"

"Her own husband reported her to the police. Stylishly Victorian, don't you think?"

Jacey could only nod blankly. What did that mean? What was 'stylish' about it? There was so much about this country that she didn't understand. And nothing of what Rael said was making her feel better.

The trip from Cambridge took half an hour, and the village of Stanton was a mile's walk from the nearest station.

Jacey and Rael tramped along the gravel shoulder in silence. The slight buzz of the G&T had worn off, for Jacey at least, and she wondered if Rael was regretting his decision to tag along. He stopped several times, looked out over the churned-up fields, littered with the rotten husks of harvested cabbages.

He sighed extravagantly. "Where the actual fuck *are* we?"

They arrived in the village just as the sun disappeared behind a thick bank of ominous cloud. They strolled up and down the main high street several times. A post office, a general store, two pubs – one that looked permanently boarded up despite the signs that said "Closed due to Covid restrictions, re-opening soon." There was a disused car garage, too, and several small houses that looked lived-in – there were children's toys in the tiny front yards at least – but poorly maintained and falling down.

"Oh my God." Rael spoke out of the side of his mouth, even though there was no one around who might hear him. "I get why granny couldn't wait to get her arse out of this dump."

There were several small streets behind the main road, as well as a narrow waterway of some sort, like a miniature canal. She and Rael had seen things like this all along the journey from Cambridge. Endless rows of ditches – like the irrigation systems at home – running beside the roads, separated from them by low fences or higher grass-covered banks.

"Fucking freaky," Rael said. "I mean, where is everybody?"

They wandered around until they found Nana Ivy's old house – Jacey had kept the address on her phone. Just as it had in the pictures she'd seen as a child, 1 Oasby Road seemed to suck in the light and spew out darkness. How that was possible, Jacey couldn't say, but the tiles on the roof and the paint on the front elevations were a dull, dark grey and there was nothing in the cracked plastic window boxes, just dead brown dirt. There were torn, ragged curtains in the windows, and a battered woven mat hugged the front door. The roof tiles seemed intact, though, and there was smoke coming out of a chimney, so obviously people were living inside.

"Fucking hell," Rael said. "You want to go in and introduce yourself?"

Instinctively, Jacey stepped back. She felt the air shifting around her. "Not on your life."

"What *is* this place?" Rael made a sweeping gesture with his arm, indicating that he meant the whole village, not just this tumbledown house.

"Let's head back to the station," Jacey said. "Sorry to have dragged you along."

Before she could turn away, the hollowing strengthened. She felt something else, too, that she couldn't identify. It was more than just disorienting and dizzying; it was a churning in her stomach that made her feel sick, and liquid gurgled up in the back of her throat, as if her lungs were filling with water.

"I don't like it here," she gasped.

"Well, who fucking would?"

"I'm sorry I—"

The hollowing got stronger, and she almost lost her footing.

"I need to sit." She coughed and choked, struggled to breathe as if she were drowning on dry land.

Rael took her arm, led her to the low wall in front of Nana Ivy's house.

"No. Somewhere else."

They hobbled down the pavement, arm in arm, back to the high street and the pub, where there were a few picnic tables outside, left over from summer.

She sat down and put her head between her knees, coughing and gagging. What the hell was going on? She needed something – water, or coffee, a drink that would clear her head and empty her throat.

After she'd rested a few minutes, Rael helped her up and led her into the pub. The place was all but empty. A slim grey dog – a whippet, she thought – was curled up beside a fireplace, while a blonde woman in a pink tracksuit fed the empty grate with paper and kindling.

The dog looked up as Rael and Jacey came into the room, stretched and yawned and put his head back down again.

"We don't open till four, I'm afraid," the woman said.

"Sorry, but could my friend get a glass of water or something?" Rael asked. "She's not feeling very well."

The woman straightened up. "Of course, sit down here."

Jacey took a seat by the fireplace, and the woman had brought her a glass of water.

"Thank you so much," Jacey said.

"No bother. Do you want anything else? I'm not supposed to give out paracetamol, but who the hell is going to know?"

"Exactly," Rael looked around the empty room, eyebrows raised.

"No, I'm fine," Jacey said. "Just thirsty. We need to get going, back to the station."

"Would you like a lift?" the woman said. "I can run you there in a minute."

"I think I'm OK now. The walk would probably do me good."

The dog stood up, stretched, and yawned. He nuzzled Jacey's feet and licked her hand.

"If you're sure," the woman said. "But take a card on your way out. If you feel ill again, or you need any help, call me, OK? My name is Sally."

She motioned to the dog. "And that's Stanley. We're both here all the time."

Jacey took a card and Rael walked her out of the pub. The grey sky was already darkening, although it was only the middle of the afternoon. As they slogged back to the train station, exhausted, Jacey was grateful for Rael's presence, and his uncharacteristic silence. She didn't want to talk about what had happened in Stanton, not to him, not to anyone; she only wanted to get away from that terrible place, and never go back.

Chapter 22

As soon as Jacey arrived in Lewes, the storm began.

There had been warnings earlier, announcements at Brighton station about minding one's step due to slippery surfaces, plus some other British phrases Jacey didn't understand. Outside the Lewes taxi rank, commuters were queuing, desperate to get home before the weather got any worse, so Jacey decided to walk, trudging up the hill beside the station, huddling over to avoid the worst of the weather – the pounding rain and the wind that was rattling the lamp posts and stirring up litter and debris from the road.

The trees in the park were swaying wildly, too, and at Malin House the covers from the chairs on the veranda had been blown onto the lawn. Jacey picked them up and carried them into the house, grateful when the door was closed behind her, relieved to be inside where it was warm and dry.

According to her weather app there was more rain to come, and gale force winds off the English Channel that would get stronger as the night wore on. Yellow warning it said; be prepared for damage.

Rob wouldn't be waiting for her; she knew that before she got home. He'd gone to London, after all. Cleared the entire day, according to the receptionist, and that probably meant half the night, too.

But still, she changed into dry clothes – a nice pair of jeans and a sweater that had a bit of shape to it – and set out the good china plates and put candles on the table, making the kitchen pretty and welcoming and romantic. Maybe he'd come back early, because of the weather if nothing else. Best to be optimistic and upbeat, just like it said on the insipid how-to-save-your-marriage websites she'd been looking at recently.

Be your feminine best, the websites instructed, and let him be a masculine man. *No nagging, no complaining. Cheerful smiles all around.* Jacey knew it was baloney, a way to make money out of desperate women like herself, but somehow when she was actually watching the videos it made sense. It was something to try, anyway. What harm could it do?

She messaged Rob. *Hey. Just got back from a road trip! I'll tell you when you get back. Pizza and salad OK for dinner? Let me know your ETA and I'll have everything ready. Hope you get back before this storm gets worse.*

See how she could be? So light and breezy? Nothing about *who are you with and what are you doing*. She sat at the table, pushed aside a plate and took out her laptop. She checked her phone, too. Nothing from Rob.

She opened the wine, poured herself a glass, then decided against it. The long day was already catching up with her; she needed to stay awake and alert in case Rob decided to come home after all. She sat down at the table, wrote down what she'd done, as much as she could remember.

Just the facts. *Woke up, argued with Rob at breakfast, surprise visit from Madlyn, found out Rob lied, got on a train to Cambridgeshire and went to the town where my grandmother grew up, almost choked to death in front of Nana Ivy's house.*

She touched her throat, took a deep breath, opened her mouth wide as she breathed out.

What the hell had that been? That choking?

She took a sip of wine she'd poured, savouring the taste, the feeling as it glided down her throat, delicious. She could trust herself to swallow properly. Not forgetting how to drink, that was good.

What else could she trust? Who else?

Another sip, what the hell. Another glance at the phone; still no message from Rob.

She was so tired – of being alone, of being afraid, of trying to run away from something she didn't understand.

She called his number, left a message. "Hey. I've made dinner, but I assume you're not coming home, otherwise I would have heard from you." She could hear the pleading tone in her voice, and she took a deep breath to try to clear it. "Just … it would be good if you could call, yeah? Let me know you are OK. Thanks. OK. Bye."

She put the pizza in the oven – no point waiting – and poured another glass of wine. When it was cooked, she cut the pizza into slices, took her plate of food into the den. She turned on the television, checked her phone again – nothing – and sat down to eat.

The house seemed to shift and creak around her, making much more noise than usual. But that was because of the wind, wasn't it? Outside, a branch scratched on the den window, and the glass rattled in its frame.

She finished her wine. That was it now, no more. Rob couldn't fault her for one small glass, could he? God only knew how much he was getting through tonight, how much he was pouring down some other woman's throat.

The tree outside rapped on the window again, like someone was trying to get in. The curtains were closed, and she didn't want to open them to have a look out, but of course it was the tree. There wouldn't be anyone out there, not during a storm. Helen and Martin would ring the doorbell if they wanted to visit or call to check and see if she was home first, so would anyone else.

She got up and crept into the kitchen.

As she turned on the light, there was a knock on the back door. It seemed intentional, not just something being blown against it.

Rat. Tat. Tat.

She went to the little bathroom, washed her face and brushed her teeth. She took the sleeping pills out of the mirrored cabinet in case she needed them later. In the kitchen she poured herself a glass of water.

The back door again.

Rat. Tat. Tat. TAT.

"Hello?" she shouted, shuffling towards the little hallway. Maybe Helen needed to see her about something and had decided to take a shortcut because of the weather. Not bother with the front door, try the back?

"Helen? Martin?"

No answer, just another sharp rattle.

It was the wind – she knew that, she'd seen the yellow warning – but she wished Rob would get home, even if he was drunk, even if he had a woman on his arm, just someone else in the house so she wouldn't have to be alone.

She crept back to the den. Something was still scratching on the window there, too.

She locked both doors – to the kitchen, to the entrance hall.

After she wrapped herself in the blanket, she called Rob again, left another voicemail.

"Hey. Um ... getting really stormy and weird here. Sounds ... you know what this house is like. So, if you're on your way could you give me a call, just to let me know when you'll be back? Thanks, honey."

She felt sick at the way she grovelled to him, but she needed to talk to someone before the tapping and scraping drove her mad. Her mother? No. The worry might kill her. Friends? There were plenty back in Minnesota who she hadn't spoken to in months, but what could she say? *I've locked myself in a room in this haunted house I'm living in, and I'm on my own because Rob's having an affair and—*

No. They'd warned her about going to England, after all. They made it perfectly clear that she was making a huge mistake, accompanying Rob, without having her own work to fall back on, being so dependent on him. She could hear their voices – *didn't we tell you, Jacey, didn't we.*

Rael. Of course. He'd calm her down somehow, without being judgemental or shaming. He'd make a joke or find another way to put things into perspective. Maybe he'd come over, hop on the train from Brighton or better yet, book an Uber, get to Malin House in a flash.

But there was no answer when she called him; all she heard was a strange jumble of sounds like traffic, and muffled, distorted voices.

"Rael? Are you there?"

Just frenzied static.

And now, the whole house was shaking, as if a huge monster had it in its grip and was playing with it like a toy. The scraping against the window grew louder, more distinct, like actual knocks. She could hear the back door in the kitchen, too; the handle was being rattled on purpose, someone was definitely trying to get in.

She hunkered down on the sofa, pulled the blanket over her head, counted out the seconds in her head: *ten, eleven, twelve, how long would this go on?*

More blowing, more rattling, and the window shook so hard she thought the glass would shatter.

Thirteen, fourteen, fifteen.

And then it went quiet. *Sixteen, seventeen, eighteen.* The wind still blew outside, whistling across the top of the roof.

But the terrible knocking stopped.

Nineteen, twenty.

She pulled the blanket down and listened, relishing the silence. Breathing properly at last, calming herself down, laughing at how scared she'd been, how close she'd come to losing it completely, opening the windows, kicking wide all the doors, screaming into the darkness like some hysterical teen in a slasher movie.

And then, another sound. Not a knock, or a shake.

A kick. A bounce.

Again, only louder. And not outside, either; the storm had died down, the world was quiet.

It was coming from somewhere deep inside the house; far away, but near. The basement. Of course. The scrapes and thumps were like tiny tremors, echoing in the darkness below.

She burrowed back into her blanket cocoon, too paralysed with fear to do anything else. She listened, as the muffled sound got closer, climbing the stairs, opening the locked door that no one had a key to.

Then, on the tiles in the hall – bounce, bounce, scrape, like the ball at the top of the stairs, getting louder, closer.

Her hands shook. Her heart beat so fast, and so hard, she was sure it would explode in her chest.

A bash against the door to the den. Oh, God, so close. A kick – what else could that sound be?

Another bang, and she imagined a monster, a creature looming huge outside the door – something with fangs and claws, only dressed as a little boy, wearing a T-shirt and shorts.

She picked up her phone and called Rob, but it went straight to voicemail again and she couldn't get any words out, just a gasp and cry. She could try the police – that's what Rob would say – but what would they find? By the time they got here the boy – if that's who it was – would be gone and they'd think she was crazy. And maybe she was. The sounds, the panic, the inability to make sense of anything–

Another knock on the door. Softer. Child-like.

Oh, Christ, what could she do? Let it in? Confront whatever was out there? If it was the boy, how could he hurt her? A child?

No. She would die if she opened the door. If whatever was out there didn't kill her outright, she would collapse in terror and smash her skull open on the hard tile floor.

She could only wait for morning. For Rob to come home. For Helen and Martin to come and check the place over, and find her, dead or alive. She wouldn't open up, not for anyone, not for anything. She wouldn't leave the den, not even for the bathroom, even though she was desperate to go. She'd stay where she was, no matter what, under the blanket, clutching her phone, crying into the pillow, sobbing and shaking and …

Chapter 23

There was a bright light behind the den curtains, spilling out from between the gaps into the room.

Sunshine. Daytime.

A knock on the door from the kitchen.

"Jacey?" Rob's voice. Her heart swelled with relief.

Morning.

"What the hell are you doing?"

"Nothing," she said, trying to gather her thoughts. "Sleeping."

She looked around the den. What had happened last night? There was a half-eaten piece of pizza on the floor, next to it a pile of clothing.

Wet clothing. Panties and jeans, bundled up, stuffed in a corner. Oh, God …

Another knock. "Jesus, Jace, what's wrong with you?"

"Didn't you get my messages last night?"

"Come on, Jace. Open up."

"I rang you." She could feel the panic rising in her voice, as she remembered the terror of last night. "I must have called a dozen times."

"Yeah, well, I came home, and I just thought you were passed out in the den again and…"

He knocked harder, impatient. What was she going to do? How could she answer the door, half naked, knowing that she'd wet herself?

"I wasn't passed out, I …"

"For fuck's sake, Jace, let me in.."

She wrapped the blanket around her, tying it at the waist, and opened the door. Rob was holding a mug of coffee. He was dressed for work and his hair was still damp from his morning shower.

He took a deep breath. He knows what happened, Jacey thought. The pee, he can smell it.

"What the hell is the matter with you."

"Nothing," she said. "If you'd checked your phone …"

He looked at the pizza on the floor, wrinkled his nose in disgust at the pile of clothing, poked at it with the toe of his shoe.

"What is all this stuff?"

"Nothing."

"So are you planning to move downstairs permanently or what?"

"No."

"Our bedroom not good enough for you?"

She shook her head. "It's not that."

"Well, what is it then?"

She had to tell him now. Everything. Otherwise, who knew what would happen? The truth. That was her only option now.

"I don't like it upstairs. On my own. When you're not here."

"What the hell are you talking about?"

"I don't like this house, Rob."

"What?"

"Like I said on the phone, there were noises and I got scared and …"

"Come on Jace, we live in a fucking mansion. How can you not like it?"

"I see things. I hear them."

"What things?"

There was a knock on the front door. A real knock, not some phantom, not the wind, and then the bell rang.

"It doesn't matter," Jacey said. "It's fine." She ran her fingers through her hair. She needed to go to the little bathroom and wash and brush her hair and floss her teeth. She needed clothes – clean ones. Dry.

"It's just spooky at night. Especially when you're out all the time—"

"Come on, Jace, don't start with that."

"I'm not, it's just …"

The doorbell rang again.

"Nothing," she said. "I'll get dressed if you don't mind."

Rob drained the last of his coffee. "Whoever it is at the door, can you deal with it?"

She nodded, terrified. What was she going to do? She couldn't answer the door like this, wrapped in a blanket with no underwear on and no jeans.

"I need something to put on, though," she said.

He looked at the floor again. The wet pile. His face twisted in disgust.

"Jesus Christ, Jacey."

"I was scared, that's all. I had to go to the bathroom, but I didn't dare open the door …"

Rob was shaking his head. The doorbell went again.

"There's a pair of sweatpants in the upstairs bathroom closet. Could you bring those down, please?"

* * *

When she opened the door two police officers were standing in front of her. A man in a suit and a uniformed woman.

"Ms. Gibson?"

"Yes?"

"Jacey Gibson?"

"Yes?"

"May we come in?"

"Is something the matter?"

The woman in uniform shuffled forward, anxious to get inside. "We won't take much of your time."

"Is this from America? Is it my mother?"

Jacey's heart pounded. She'd heard – from Rob, of course, the expert on all things British – that sometimes the police inform people of deaths overseas, even if the circumstances are not suspicious.

"No, Ms. Gibson, nothing like that."

In a daze, Jacey stood back, allowing them to enter. Rob came through the den.

"What is it?"

"We need to speak to Ms. Gibson," the man said. "It won't take long."

Rob took Jacey's arm, making a show of his protectiveness.

"She's not in any trouble," the woman said, "but she might want to sit down."

"We can go into the kitchen," Jacey said.

"I'll put the kettle on." Rob sounded like someone on the English detective programmes he'd watched so often on PBS.

The man spoke. "We're here about a friend of yours, I believe. A Rael Johnson?"

"Yes? What about Rael?"

"He was injured yesterday in an incident outside Brighton station."

"What?"

"He's in the Royal Sussex, with several broken ribs and other major …"

Jacey put her face to her hand.

"Oh my God. Was he attacked? Is he all right?"

"He should make a complete recovery, but until we can speak to him, we're checking people who saw him recently. And, obviously, as you travelled to Cambridgeshire with him yesterday, according to his flatmate, that includes you."

Rob cleared his throat but he didn't say anything. The female officer looked at Rob; did she think Jacey and Rael were having an affair. Meeting behind Rob's back?

"OK," Jacey said.

"Now, we don't know what happened. Attacks on the LGBTQ+ community aren't things we see very often in Brighton anymore, but it's always a possibility."

"So, what happened? Did somebody beat him up?"

"No. It was a hit and run, coming out of Brighton station."

"Somebody deliberately ran him down? Like, drove up on the sidewalk?"

"Not quite."

"He wasn't drunk when he was with me," Jacey said. "If that's what you think. We had a couple G&Ts on the train, but it was on the way to Cambridgeshire. Nothing on the way back."

The officers looked at each other, then back at Jacey.

The woman spoke this time, a kinder tone. "Do you know anyone who would have wanted to hurt your friend?"

She shook her head. "I haven't known him very long. Just a few weeks, really."

"Nothing was said about a jealous ex, or somebody who might have had it in for him?"

Jacey shook her head again, remembering what he'd said about his mother's fears when he transitioned; about the dangers of being a boy, as if something bad could happen to him because of it.

"No mention of any particularly nasty anti-trans messages on social media? Directed at him?"

"No, but I didn't follow him on Twitter or Instagram, so maybe …"

Rob fidgeted in his chair, pushing it back away from the table so it scraped on the stone floor. The kettle on the stove whistled. Jacey held her breath, waiting for the hollowing, for the sound of bells.

"So, as far as you knew, he had no enemies, online or otherwise."

"No. But like I said, I haven't known him long. I mean, I don't even know what course he's doing at the university."

Rob got up. "You said you wanted tea?"

"I think we're almost finished here, so no thanks."

The man in the suit turned back to Jacey. "Did he give you any impression that he might be depressed?"

"No. Not at all. He was funny and he made me laugh and …"

"You can't think it was a suicide attempt?" Jacey said.

The man shook his head. "We don't know. All we've got is CCTV, but judging from the way he hurtled into the path of an oncoming vehicle, it looks like he was pushed onto the road."

"So you saw who did it?"

"We've examined the footage again and again and there appears to be no one else on the pavement."

"Oh," Jacey said. She couldn't make sense of what they were saying. Had he jumped, was he pushed, was it just a horrible accident, a few seconds of not paying attention?

"I mean, we looked at what happened from several angles and …" The woman in uniform shrugged. "Nobody's there."

Chapter 24

After the police officers left, Rob tiptoed from the hallway back into the kitchen and picked up his briefcase. He pulled his phone out of the pocket of his chinos and checked something. What, Jacey couldn't tell. A message, or text, or the time of the next train.

"You OK to be left alone, Jace?"

"What's that supposed to mean?"

His eyes were still on the phone. "Well, you pissed your pants last night, got involved in some fucking crime in Brighton—"

"I had nothing to do with what happened to Rael, and I didn't—"

"After going on a crazy spree to Cambridgeshire."

"It wasn't crazy," Jacey said. She thought about Rael, in hospital, injured. Her friend who supported her when her own husband wouldn't.

"What was it then?"

Finally, he looked at her. His face was steel, so much in control. No movement. No feeling.

"Yesterday I stopped off at the university so I could have lunch with you. A nice surprise I hoped, only you weren't there, even though it's on your calendar that you would be. Even though you told me to my face that you had a lecture at ten o'clock."

Rob didn't even blink. "Plans change in real life, Jacey."

"I felt like a complete idiot trying to find you, so I called up the one person I knew besides you, and he made time for me. And we went for a harmless day trip to the town where my grandmother is from, and the guy I went with is gay—"

"I thought you said he was trans."

"He's gay and trans, but that doesn't matter." She felt a swelling of anger rise up in her chest. "What matters is that he's seriously hurt, and you're making stupid insinuations about him that just aren't true. Just because *you* mess around—"

"I had a meeting. For work. My job. And then I had dinner. Also with a man."

"You didn't answer any of my messages—"

"Because they didn't make sense. I knew you were drunk—"

"I was scared."

"You were like some crazy person, Jacey, crying and screaming, and then I get up in the morning and I see you here, lying in a puddle of piss…"

"I wasn't drunk. I was terrified."

"Of what? Going to the bathroom? Afraid some bogeyman was going to reach out of the toilet bowl and grab you in the ass?"

As she waited for the bells to start tinkling again, or the hollowing to suck all the sound and air from the room, she stood still. Said nothing. Watched him shake his head at her and make for the door.

She was happy to see him go. For once, she was glad to be alone in the house. She needed to think, about what the police had told her, about what Rob had done yesterday, about Cambridgeshire, and the sounds she'd heard that were more than anything a storm could have caused.

The Perfect Couple

When he was gone, she washed the dishes, swept the kitchen floor, picked up her wet clothes and the blanket that probably stank of piss, too, and put them in the washing machine. There was no hot breath on her neck this time, no sense that the ghost of Nana Ivy was in the house, overseeing her work, passing judgement.

There were other things that needed to be washed, too, clothes and bedding, either in the bathroom hamper or draped across a chair in their room. She'd have to go upstairs on her own to get them. She'd have to forget about what she'd imagined last night. And besides, what could be more terrible than that? Being so afraid that she wet her pants. Finding out that her new friend had been injured, possibly very seriously, in a transphobic attack.

Well, these forces of darkness – if that's what they were – could fuck right off. So could the bells and the hollowing. And so could her husband, the cheater, the liar, the arrogant prick.

Are you OK, sweetie?

A text from Muriel. Jacey had forgotten that she'd given out her number.

She texted back. *I am.*

Quite a shock. Poor, poor Rael.

Yes.

Can I call you, sweetie? Or, better yet, come over?

Jacey looked around the kitchen. The clothes were in the washing mashing. It was clean enough for company. A quick wipe and put away of the dishes, plus a sweep of the floor would make the kitchen acceptable, and all she had to do in the den was pick up a few coffee mugs and straighten the sofa cushions and pillows. Maybe open the window to let in fresh air.

OK, she said. *Do you know where it is?*

Do I? She sent a laughing face emoticon. *Lewes' very own haunted house? Everyone does, sweetie.*

She didn't know what to say. The shock of last night — and this morning's news — had numbed her senses. And there was something she didn't like about the way Muriel sounded more excited about the house, than worried about her, or even poor Rael.

Are you in this morning?

Jacey was tempted to delete Muriel's messages and block her number. She didn't have to answer or let her come around. She didn't have to speak to anyone she didn't want to. Later on, if she saw Muriel and John rambling up on the hill she could smile politely and move on. She could move far away from being nice to everybody all the time.

But she relented. As usual. *Yes, I'm here all day.*

Great!!! We'll see you in a little while. I'll bring biscuits!! Heart, heart, smile, smile, more hearts, purple and green ones this time.

A few minutes of rushed cleaning — the kitchen, then den — and a quick ascent up the stairs to the bathroom, just in case Muriel wanted to use it, to make sure there were no beard trimmings in the sink and that Rob had put the toilet seat down and actually flushed for a change. She crept down the hallway, smoothed the duvet on their bed, checked the floor for dirty undies or socks.

It was fine. Not perfect — the frame on the mirror above the vanity table had a thin layer of dust on it that Jacey wiped off with her finger. What did that say about her housekeeping despite all her efforts?

On her way back downstairs, she saw that the guestbook wasn't on the landing table. When had it disappeared? She couldn't remember the last time she'd noticed it, not that she paid attention anymore, always being in such a hurry to get downstairs in the morning, or up to their room at night.

She opened the table's drawer – empty except for a few unused brown envelopes and a handful of metal paper clips. She went back into the bedroom, checked Rob's bedside table. There were a few papers – a bill for photocopying from the university print shop, and an order form from the campus bookstore – and underneath the pile, half-hidden, was the guestbook, with its cover of cracked brown leather and the words 'Our Cherished Guests' written in gold letters, faded, scarcely visible.

She took it out. Why had Rob moved it?

As she opened the book, something slipped from between the pages and fell onto the floor: a white envelope, with American stamps and a blue airmail sticker, and address written in an old-fashioned style of writing – the letters slanted and looping.

Her mother's handwriting.

Addressed to Rob, sent to his office at the university's English Department.

Jacey looked for a clue of what had been inside the envelope, but it was empty. Why had her mother sent something to Rob? It was nowhere near her birthday, and Christmas was months away, so it couldn't have been a card or money to buy her a present. What would her mother have written Rob a letter about, one that was obviously not intended for her daughter to see?

The air suddenly shifted and swirled around her, whooshing in her ears until a noise from outside broke through the sound haze. A car was honking its horn. A door slammed and a voice called out.

"Jacey, we're here."

She tucked the guestbook back where she'd found it and stumbled to the window. She held onto the window frame to keep her balance, as the hollowing threatened to sweep her off her feet. A couple of deep breaths, and she looked outside.

"Jacey!"

Down on the lawn, two figures, like matching obelisks, moved towards the house.

Not statues. Not ghosts or zombies, or hallucinations.

Muriel and Madlyn, gliding across the lawn, arm in arm.

Chapter 25

She made tea in the bright blue pot, and tried not to think of how impressed Rob would have been of her efforts. The way she warmed the pot with the boiling water, before adding the tea bags; the way she poured the milk into the mugs first, and the sugar at the end.

"Of course, we're sisters," Muriel said. "Didn't we say?"

"I don't think so."

"Madlyn's older than me, naturally. By a good few years."

It was obvious, now that they were side by side. The same nose, and a matching face shape, oblong and symmetrical. There were differences, though, that had made it difficult to recognise their similarities. Muriel had dark hair that was only speckled with grey, while Madlyn's close crop was silvery throughout, almost white. Muriel's manicured hands were thin, her hands bony, so that her wedding ring hung slack, only held in place by the gnarled joints. Madlyn's fingers were thick and smooth, the bare nails chewed to the quick.

"Let's get to the point, shall we?" Madlyn said. She banged a teaspoon on the side of her mug, as if she was moderating a writing club critique.

"You heard what happened to Rael last night, is that correct? You had a little visit from members of the local constabulary?"

She means the police, Jacey thought. "Yes," she said. "How did you know?"

"Mine was the last number Rael rang," Muriel said. "His phone wasn't damaged in the … well, accident, or whatever it was … so the police phoned me first. They couldn't make out the garbled message he'd left, but his texts to you were there, apparently, so you were on the list as well."

Muriel stirred her tea and calmly took a sip. Madlyn seemed agitated. She stood up, walking around the table, looked up at the ceiling, as if she was inspecting the beams.

"They did a great job on this kitchen," she said. "You can't see any of the smoke damage."

"We don't need to talk about that now, Mads."

"Don't we? Isn't that the whole point? This house? What happens to the people who live here?"

Muriel gestured for her sister to sit back down, and Madlyn did, looking glum, possibly insulted at being admonished by her younger sister.

"So, tell us about the boy."

"Well, what can I say? You probably know Rael better than—

"I don't mean him," Muriel said. "I mean the little boy you see sometimes."

The *boy*. Her heart lurched. They were here to talk about Rael, to update her on his condition – weren't they?

"What about him?" Jacey said. "I saw a little boy, out on his own, and I was concerned that he must have been cold and …"

Muriel raised her eyebrows. What was going on? How did they know about the boy she'd seen? What was it to do with them?

"Well, it's living in Malin House, you see." Muriel said. "That's why we're asking."

"And the fact that your family comes from Stanton in Cambridgeshire," Madlyn added. "And you'd just gone there to visit."

Another thing they shouldn't have known about, but somehow did.

"And your grandmother was a Kennet," Muriel said. "We can't forget that …"

"A *Smith*," Jacey said, trying to keep from shrieking. What the hell was wrong with these women? "An Ivy *Smith*. How many times have I told you?"

This time, both women raised their eyebrows and looked at each other conspiratorially.

Madlyn turned back to her. "Once," she said. "You told me – or rather, denied it – once."

She shouldn't have let them see her angry. It was like an admission of guilt, though she couldn't imagine what for.

"Sorry we've upset you," Muriel said.

"You haven't. Honestly."

It was no use. They *had* upset her, and now her voice was constricting, and her eyes were filling with tears. She felt trapped in her own home. Stuck in this kitchen. Again.

"I really have things to do," she said, but the sisters didn't move. "It's been great catching up with you, and I'm glad to hear that Rael is going to be OK, but …"

"So what did Rael mean about you being brave?" Muriel said. "The police showed us the texts. Has something happened to you as well?"

"It was a joke," Jacey said. "About living in this house; he was just being funny."

Madlyn leaned over, took her hand, widened her eyes. "We're only asking because we care."

Jacey shook her head and snatched her hand away. The strength of her anger and determination startled her. But she'd had enough now, of being told what to think, what to do. "No," she said. "You're only asking because you're nosy. Because you're bored old ladies and you're trying to stir something up out of nothing."

Suddenly the air around them thickened. Thousands of tiny bells began to ring.

Not now, Jacey thought. Not when she needed them to leave. Instinctively, she looked upwards, as if the noise had come from somewhere above her. She imagined the words being said out loud – *not now* – as if she had some sort of authority over the hollowing, as if she could make it stop by being *brave*, or being *strong*.

"Well, *that's* a coincidence, isn't it?" Madlyn said, and even through the hollowing Jacey could make out her sarcastic tone.

Madlyn winked at Jacey.

What? Jacey wanted to scream. *What?*

Madlyn smiled at her sister. "Do *you* hear noises, Muriel?"

"Oh, definitely. Not sure what they are, though. Very strange."

Jacey said nothing. She wanted Muriel and Madlyn to leave, and from now on she'd avoid them both, stay away from anywhere she might bump into them – the park, the hill, the town cafés, the pub.

Madlyn picked up their empty mugs, dropped them noisily in the sink, and turned the tap on full blast so that water sprayed all over the dishes that had been left in the drainer to dry. As she dried her hands on a tea towel, she craned her neck to get another view of the ceiling.

Finally, they shuffled out of the kitchen. In the hallway, Muriel opened the door and waited for her sister to stop gawping at the chandelier.

"I think Jacey's waiting for us to go, dear."

"But what about the boy?" Madlyn asked.

She was looking at the stairs now, lifting her head upwards as if that could help her see into the darkest corner. There was a tinkling of chandelier crystals, clinking together with the breeze that Muriel was letting in.

"Have you seen him again?"

Jacey thought about the night before. The knocking. The kicks that she was certain were his.

She shook her head.

"Well, that's good, then, isn't it?" Muriel said, cheerfully, as Madlyn took her by the arm. "Maybe he's gone now, maybe he won't come back."

Madlyn stopped in the doorway, looked back up at the stairway, squinting her eyes.

She smiled at Jacey. "Maybe," she said.

Chapter 26

Stupid things.

Another load of laundry. The hamper in the bathroom upstairs was overflowing with Rob's dirty towels and there were his shirts and sweaters thrown on the back of the armchair in their bedroom.

Anything to stop thinking about what happened to Rael. About those bloody women, nosing in about things they couldn't possibly know.

Her grandmother. The boy.

Had she told them about him? She must have. In the hilltop café that day with Muriel and John, when they were telling her about Katherine. She must have let it slip that she'd seen some strange, under-dressed child roaming around, kicking a ball. And they must have been worried about him, too, that he was cold and alone, maybe abandoned by his parents, or …

As soon as Muriel and Madlyn were gone – disappearing into the mist in front of the house like tracksuited ghouls – she picked up the laundry basket that was in the back pantry and crept through the den and into the hallway. It was time to face fears. Rob was right: the toilet wasn't going to bite her in the ass, and if she saw a rubber ball on the stairs again, so what? It didn't have teeth, either. And maybe there *was* a little boy who was able to sneak into the house somehow and who wandered around unsupervised – up on the hill, down in the tunnel. Well, if she saw him again she'd ask a few questions and make him leave. And if he refused to go, she'd call Martin for help. What was the worst a kid could do to her anyway? He was a child. She was a grown woman.

Taking a deep breath and throwing back her shoulders, she grabbed the banister, felt the smooth, polished wood on the palm of the hand, gripped it tightly. Took a step.

The darkness at the top landing seemed to thicken as she climbed the stairs.

Of course it did.

The house was haunted, after all. Jacey almost laughed. It wasn't exactly news. Everyone in Lewes seemed to have vast knowledge about the hauntings of Malin House. So, what? Had anyone actually been hurt by these ghosts, real or imagined? Even if the story Rael told her about his friend Katherine was true, even if that poor woman had been chased by tongues of fire, she didn't die, did she?

The idea that the house could hate her, or want to hurt her, seemed laughable with the light streaming in through the window and bouncing off the glass of the chandelier, and the smell of the polish Helen used to make the woodwork shine.

At the top of the stairs she scanned the hallway. Nothing. Heavy blue carpet, open doors with daylight spilling out.

And if the boy she'd seen wasn't a ghost, or even a lost child? If he was a figment of her imagination, proof that she was actually delusional, what would happen then?

She tiptoed into the bedroom, holding her breath, as if she was afraid she'd wake someone up. No one was there, though, sleeping or awake, human or ghost. She took the clothes from the back of the chair, went into the bathroom and emptied the contents of the hamper into the basket.

It was simple, she thought.

If she started getting crazier, she'd go back home and let her mother take care of her.

She'd be safe in Minnesota, in her mom's small condo, with her own room that had a peaceful view of corn fields and green distant hills. She and her mom could eat at the local café that sold twenty-five different varieties of pie and served hot lunches for the seniors at half price. They could eat there every day if they wanted to. Tuna melts. Hot gravy sandwiches. She could get fat as she liked on all those pies and not give a damn about what Rob thought.

She put the basket down and checked under the bed for more clothes. No displaced underwear, but plenty of dust that she could take care of while waiting for the wash load to finish.

And, almost buried in the powdery grey, an envelope.

She reached for it, the dust prickling her nose, making her want to sneeze.

She recognised her mother's handwriting, and the address was, once again, Rob's office at the university.

But this envelope wasn't empty. The letter inside was dated a month ago.

She wiped the grubby paper with the edge of her T-shirt. Her mother's writing was large and swirly, and the stationery was old-fashioned, too: yellow, with a border of bright blue and red tulips running along the top of the page.

With shaking hands, Jacey held up the paper.

Dear Rob,

Sorry to send another letter – but I worry about talking on the phone, in case she overhears us, or even sending emails.

I hate being so sneaky, but …

I'm still worried, especially after finding out what's been going on over there.

I don't think it's good, her spending so much time on her own, and being so far away from her real home, and her mother.

And I bet it's hard for you, having this extra burden all the time.

So, I was wondering if she should come back, at least for a while. She could stay with me until your job is finished.

I'm not going to say any more about why I'm worried, because you already know what happened. You don't need more details. Lord knows, I wish I could forget them myself.

And finally, after all that, written in tiny letters.

PS I appreciate all you've done for us.

Jacey's mind was racing, her heart pounding. What was her mom talking about? What 'happened'? And had Rob been messaging her mother, sending emails about how his wife was hearing things, losing her grip?

What's been going on over there.

But Jacey hadn't even told Rob the worst of it. Not until last night. A bit of tinnitus, that's all she said. Funny sounds in her ears. What would happen if he mentioned the visit by the police? Or pissing her pants because she was too scared to move?

This extra burden. What did that mean?

She put the envelope where she'd found it under the bed, sprinkled it with dust again, wiping the rest of the dust around to cover the outline of where she'd scraped the floor with her body.

The discovery of this letter was another thing Rob couldn't know.

The list was getting long now. The hollowing. The sound of bells. Seeing the boy. And other things, like the woman who lived here before them, and had gone mad, seemingly. Even Madlyn and Muriel and the things they said about Nana Ivy belonging to some mysterious family.

A ray of sunshine lit the bits of dust she'd churned up, so Jacey opened the window to clear the air. The sun was shining now; it had burned away the mist and cloud.

Outside on the cottage's lawn she saw Martin and Helen working in the garden, sharing some task, laughing together. Helen stopped for a second and, seeing Jacey at the window, looked up and waved. Jacey waved back, grateful for a fleeting moment of companionship.

Jacey put her hand on the window's sash, ready to pull it down again, when in the corner of her eye, she saw something. A shape. A figure.

It was the boy. Just beyond the lawn, halfway to the driveway, wearing nothing but the T-shirt and shorts she'd seen him in before. And he was kicking the ball, back and forth, from foot to foot. Nothing scary about this – he was just having fun.

The window scraped and groaned as she opened it wider so she could lean out.

"Hey," she shouted.

Helen and Martin looked up at her. "What is it, Jacey?"

"No, sorry. Not you," Jacey said. "I meant the little boy. Do you know who he is?"

"What boy?"

Jacey held out her arm and pointed. The boy seemed oblivious to the shouting and curiosity he was raising. "*That* boy."

"I don't see anyone," Helen said.

Jacey's heart pounded. The boy was only a few metres away from Helen. She must be able to see him.

"On the driveway, kicking a ball." Jacey waved her arms, as if it would make her pointing more precise.

"I don't see anyone," Helen said. "Honestly."

Jacey looked again. She blinked. Shook her head.

The boy was gone.

Martin had gone back to his weeding, but Helen was still gazing up at her. "Is everything all right, Jacey?"

"He must have gone back down the hill."

"I didn't see him, I'm afraid," Helen said.

"I was worried he'd got lost or something," Jacey said lightly. She needed to end this. Not let Helen think she was anxious or distraught. "Whoever he was."

Jacey closed the window, picked up the basket and went back downstairs. She put in the laundry, made a cup of tea, and watched as the wet socks and T-shirts spun and swirled in the washing machine's window.

Her laptop was on the kitchen table. She'd hardly used it this week, or last week for that matter. All that talk, all those plans, about writing and blogging and investigating her roots seemed like a sick joke now.

My mom must think I'm losing it, she thought. Rob must have said as much.

Helen and Martin probably do too, after what just happened.

And maybe I am.

She shook away the thought. No, it wasn't true. Whatever was happening – what she was seeing and hearing, what she feared – was explainable. There was an answer to these mysteries, she just had to find it.

She opened the laptop. She googled 'Missing child, Lewes'.

Nothing.

'Lewes child disappearance'.

No entries, except a teenage girl who'd gone away with friends for a day and didn't tell anyone before arriving home, safe and sound. Jacey wasn't sure what this proved, except that the boy wasn't the victim of a reported crime or in any immediate danger, other than catching a cold.

Then she googled 'Malin House'. She'd done it before, but maybe she'd missed something. There was a picture, an article about the man who'd built it, a few items about various people who'd lived there and then a mention of the house being bought by the university for visiting professors to live in. It had been used as a film set several times, and there were articles about that, but there was nothing about a curse, or hauntings, no other mentions of the fire than what she'd already seen.

Obviously, Malin House was not really the stuff of legends. What about the Kennets, while she was at it? What about Stanton in Cambridgeshire?

There were thousands of listings for Kennet, but none seemed to be unusual or sinister, except for a Maisy Kennet from Boston, Lincolnshire, who'd been caught stealing in the eighteenth century and broke out of the local jail and escaped before she could be hanged as a thief.

Stanton itself?

A black and white picture of the depressing main street, a few facts about population and schools and the political make-up of the local government officials.

Nothing scary there, either.

Then she remembered the letter she'd found upstairs, and carefully re-hidden, the envelope in the guest book that she'd tucked back into the drawer. How many times had her mother written to Rob? Were there other envelopes tucked away in the house? She hadn't gone into the drawing room more than once or twice since Rob turned it into his personal lair. Maybe she'd find more letters there.

She went in via the servant's room, past the row of bronze bells, conspicuous in their silence. She passed into the dining room, where everything was still shrouded in thick white sheets, and hesitated slightly before opening the door to the drawing room.

It smelled of stale smoke. Ashtrays overflowed with thick chomped-on cigar ends, and clumps of grey ash. There were empty cans of beer – Five Points, the same kind Rael had at the pub. The papers and the files and the binders were what she'd expected.

On the middle of the coffee table was a tall stack of books. Rob's bestseller – he must have had them sent over from the States. She opened one. Then another. They'd all been signed – Rob's name in thick black Sharpie. Most had dedications, too. *Daisy – great work in this term's seminars. To Joanna – PhD material if I ever saw it.*

None of the books were written out to male students. None were to any colleagues it seemed. It was the girls – *Keira, Martha, Jasmine, Olivia*. She picked up the last signed copy.

To Bex – better late than never, babe! All my love, Robbie.

Robbie? When had he ever called himself that? He'd tried 'Robert' on for size a few times, thinking it sounded more academic, made him seem more important, but he was never ever 'Robbie'. Even his mother just settled for Rob.

Bex. Babe.

All my love.

Tears stung Jacey's eyes. She sat on the sofa, let her head loll back onto the cushions, stretching her legs so they dangled loosely onto the floor. She flopped her arms down at her sides and closed her eyes.

It means nothing, Rob's inscription. He could have been talking about moving to England, or the publication of his book.

The girls' names don't mean anything either.

Everything's a joke.

And you're tired. Overtired, her mother would have said, if she wasn't busy writing strange letters to her son-in-law, the words of which rolled over and over in Jacey's mind like deadly, inescapable waves.

This *extra burden.*

I wish I could forget …

Eventually, Jacey shook the words from her head. Until she knew what they meant there was no point thinking about them. She got up and put the stack of books back in order. With her phone, she took a picture of Rob's inscription to Bex before replacing the book back at the bottom of the pile. She wouldn't say anything to Rob about this. Or her mother. Or anyone. She'd decide later whether she'd show the picture to Jared, or ask Bex to explain.

And the rest of the things that were troubling her – the disappearing boy, Rael's accident, the sense that something or somebody was trying to tip her over the edge – she'd keep those to herself, too.

Chapter 27

Rob ate his dinner quietly, other than offering a few appreciative grunts and *m-m-mms*.

"This is awesome, Jace. Thanks."

Without telling Rob the reason for it, Jacey did a repeat performance of the lovely romantic dinner for two. A more adventurous menu than frozen pizza this time: chicken with garlic sauce, ratatouille, roast potatoes with rosemary and sea salt. She went one step further and set up the formal dining room. She found huge candlesticks and cloth napkins in the serving pantry, and she made a romantic jazz playlist on Spotify to listen to while they were eating.

She'd managed to quash her anxieties long enough to go into town to buy the ingredients, and getting out of the house had done her a world of good. As she cut across the lawn, she saw Martin applying a straw mulch to a flowerbed in front of the cottage, and she'd smiled and waved at him, nonchalantly.

Not a care in the world, see?

No paranoid delusions, me. Not seeing any more invisible boys. Nothing to write home to mother about, nothing at all.

She was purposeful and positive while she visited the little stores – *shops,* she remembered, *they were called shops* – for the vegetables and the cheese and the bread. The town was pretty, too, in the late autumn sunshine, and people were friendly. There was nothing sinister or claustrophobic about the place; all the Gothic shadows had shrunk in the light, and she could see why people thought that Lewes was charming and quaint.

The dinner would be a reset of her marriage. That was the idea. Even if she'd wanted to, she couldn't go back to the USA now, not after finding out that her mother had been talking to Rob about her behind her back. But where else could she go? She had no financial independence without being able to work in England, and the money in her own account wouldn't last very long. She was stuck here for the time being, so she had to make the best of it.

For once, Rob seemed appreciative of her efforts. When she messaged him to let him know her plans – a special meal in the formal dining room – he'd texted back straight away. She didn't mention what had happened in the days before, or the arguments they'd had.

And so they drew a line under things, without agreeing any terms, or even talking it over. Rob's after-hours meetings all seemed to be cancelled, though he never said it in so many words. He just stopped going out at night. And she kept to herself while he retreated into his study to work, pretending to write at the kitchen table – and sometimes actually doing it – or catching up on the strange British programmes that she wouldn't be able to watch once they went back to America.

Bedtimes were still awkward. She'd rush up the stairs before him, keeping her eyes closed on the landing, just in case. She needed to be asleep first, so she wouldn't feel the humiliating sting of his lack of desire. When she woke up in the night and knew his warm body was beside hers, the urge to reach out and touch him was almost overwhelming. Only the fear of rejection – of a sharp swat or disgusted grunt – kept her from touching his back or thigh or sliding her fingers over the smooth skin on his chest.

The hollowing had quietened, happened less frequently; so had the sound of bells. But in spite of this relief, fear and dread still weighed Jacey down. And as the days were shortening, and the darkness fell earlier, she felt that the house, and everything in it, was being slowly smothered by a thick heavy cloth.

The view from the hospital's orthopaedics tower was stunning. Built on top of one of Brighton's hills, and fourteen storeys tall, the windows of Rael's room looked out over the ocean, the shoreline and the white chalky coastal cliffs in the distance. From this height and this distance, everything – even the garish, neon-lit rides on the pier – looked beautiful.

Jacey had kept in touch with the hospital, checking on Rael's condition, getting daily updates on the phone until one day she was told he wasclose to being discharged, and he could see visitors other than immediate family. He was able to walk and would be going home as soon as the social workers assessed his needs..

"Social workers?" Jacey asked.

"Well, occupational therapy, at least," the nurse said. "He'll need some mobility support, that sort of thing."

Jacey's heart sank. "So his injuries are permanent?"

The nurse sighed. "Oh, no, he'll be fine. The bones will heal, and any residual damage to nerves or muscle tissue can be repaired in surgery or with plenty of physio. Time is really what he needs, and the support will be temporary, thankfully."

Forewarned of what to expect, the reality of Rael's appearance wasn't too upsetting.

He waved an arm that was covered in plaster.

"Yeah, I know. I look like shit."

Rael's jaw was taped and bound, because of the dislocation, so he had to speak with his mouth almost closed. His hair seemed to be a pale brown, not the bright blue, or heavy goth black, as if being hit by a car had instantly rinsed out the colour. His eyes without liner looked tired and battered, and the bruises underneath them still showed.

There was a chair beside his bed and Jacey pulled it closer so that she could hear him.

"How did you find out what happened?" Rael asked. "I couldn't use my bloody phone."

"The police came to see me."

"Really? Like, in person?" Rael's eyes widened. "What did they say?"

"Well, that you were hit by a car, and they asked me if you'd been feeling, you know … depressed, that sort of thing."

"They think I tried to top myself," Rael said "I've seen so many psychiatrists. Making a big deal out of my transition – they all love banging on about that, as if that would be the problem, not all the crap we have to put up with."

Rael's room was a double. The elderly man in the next bed coughed in his sleep, scratched a patch of dry skin.

"I wasn't – you know, suicidal – in case you were wondering."

Jacey shook her head. "I never thought you were."

"And I wasn't drunk, but of course they have the blood tests to prove that."

"What *did* happen?"

Rael looked over at the old man and motioned for Jacey to close the curtains that separated the beds, as if the thin fabric would keep their conversation a secret.

"I don't know, but it wasn't an accident, that's for sure."

The old man let out another wheezy cough.

"I was pushed into that road. I felt the hands on my back."

Jacey's heart pounded. What Rael was saying didn't seem possible, but neither did so many other things she'd experienced in England.

"But it doesn't show up on the CCTV, so they think I'm lying. They're writing it off as a cry for attention, or undiagnosed dyspraxia, some ridiculous bollocks like that."

"Do you have any idea who could have done it?"

"Who?" Despite his jaw being taped shut, he was getting louder, more agitated. "More like *what*, you mean."

Jacey remembered what the police officer said. That Rael seemed to have been hurled into the oncoming traffic, as if by magic.

"But how—"

"I had just come from seeing Katherine in Eastbourne. It was late, I'd already had a long day with you, but …"

"Katherine?" Jacey asked. "Malin House Katherine?"

"Of course," Rael said, sighing. He took a deep breath, slowed his speech down, so that he could be sure she'd understand. "I told her about you, and what you were seeing at the house, the boy … and the noises … and I asked if that's what it was like for her, and she said *no*. Shut right up. Didn't want to talk about it. Like she was still traumatised, even after all this time."

There was a sharp knock on the door, and a nursing assistant – a young and smiley woman – wheeled in a food trolley carrying lunch for the old man. "Morning, Rael," she chirped. "You'll be my next victim. See you in a few."

She made a lot of noise, hoisting up the man, getting the squeaky trolley into place.

"Katherine tried to blame everything on her husband," Rael said, when he was sure no one else could hear.

"The fires, you mean?"

"No, for making shit up about her, so that people would think she started them deliberately. Gaslight central, making everyone believe his lies."

"But the house?"

"She refused to talk about it. It was like 'Malin what'? I knew she was lying, but she still seemed so nervous and scared of the place …"

"Do you think she'd talk to me?"

The nurse pulled back the curtain and smiled at Jacey. "You'll have to come back later I'm afraid. "After lunch Rael has got a physiotherapy session."

"OK."

"Look, I'll text you her number, and you can take it from there."

"Thanks."

"Just remember to be *very* careful afterwards."

"I will."

He held up his broken arm. "Especially if you're near traffic."

Chapter 28

The walk back to the train station took twice as long as it should have.

Jacey stuck to the edge of the pavements, as far from the road as she could, clinging to the walls of buildings for support. At the traffic lights she waited until she was absolutely sure the cars had stopped before crossing the street, and even then, she stepped cautiously off the kerb.

It was bad enough people driving on the wrong side of the road, without having to worry about some supernatural force taking over the drivers so they ploughed through the pedestrian crossing to run her down, or some invisible beings pushing her off the pavement.

She kept her eyes out for anyone following her, too. Every few steps she turned around to make sure she was alone.

Halfway to the station, she stopped at a café. She ordered a macchiato and a packet of Biscoff biscuits, and took a seat beside the window. She didn't need to hurry back to Lewes. She had time to savour her coffee, collect her thoughts.

But what were her thoughts? Did she think Rael was right? That he'd been attacked by some malevolent spirit? It sounded from what Katherine said that her husband could have been behind what happened while she was living in Malin House. Maybe not supernatural then, just human evil or greed.

As she dipped a biscuit into her coffee, her phone pinged.

It was from Rael, and the message included Katherine's number.

Maybe she should delete it, forget everything Rael had said. Things were better now, at home, thanks to all her efforts. And since she'd stopped worrying about her marriage, she wasn't as frightened. The sound of bells had stopped, she hadn't seen the boy for a while, and even Rob was behaving himself, staying in at night and working at home. Sharing meals with her, even sitting in the den sometimes, watching TV. He'd suggested a weekend away during the Christmas break, visiting some of the tourist places like Bath or the Lake District. New Year's Eve on Lake Windermere. How did that sound?

Slowly, things were inching back to normality. Even the hollowing wasn't as dramatic or persistent when it happened, which wasn't very often.

Maybe it *had* all been in her mind. Maybe she'd let the strangeness of the house, and the intensity of her loneliness lead her down paths that were just speculative and silly. Maybe she'd taken what other people – strangers, really, about whom she knew nothing – told her as the truth, when she should have been more sceptical.

What the taxi driver said, right at the start: *Don't listen to the rumours.*

She paid for her coffee and headed back to the station. She checked the departure board and watched the train from Lewes pull in. As the passengers got off, she saw someone walking carelessly, bumping into other people, putting a hand up in a weak apology but never looking up from his phone.

It was Rob.

She stepped beside a pillar, let the passengers, including Rob, sweep past without her being seen.

What was he doing?

She tried to think of his schedule for today. They'd talked about it at breakfast. Non-stop lectures and seminars he said. Not a single break. He'd kissed her on the forehead before he left the kitchen. Lovingly. Tenderly. Like he meant it.

"See you tonight," he'd said.

The train back to Lewes was waiting, the doors hissing open and then closing again; the guard was making her way down the platform, ready for one final check before blowing the whistle and waving the train safely off.

Rob was at the barriers, fumbling to find his ticket.

Jacey didn't have time to think about her decision. Without worrying about being seen now – Rob wouldn't be looking behind him for anyone – she hurried up to the barriers as he strode across the station concourse and towards the main entrance.

She followed him out, and down the road that cut under the station approach. He checked his phone a few times – directions, she thought, a map to his destination, so it couldn't be anywhere he was familiar with. He walked past the shops of the North Laine, dodging people on the narrow pavement, stepping into the road a few times to avoid the other pedestrians.

When he reached the main Lewes Road, he stopped and turned around.

Jacey stepped into a shop doorway. After a few seconds, Rob carried on, and she followed again, until he finally came to a terrace of narrow Georgian buildings, with brass name-plates next to their round arched doorways.

She waited a few seconds before walking up to the building Rob had gone into. Passing quickly, with just a glance at the door, she read: 'Fitzgerald and Sawyer, solicitors. Specialists in family law.'

Family law. What the hell did that mean?

Adoptions? Custody hearings?

Divorce.

Jacey reeled backwards, as if she'd been punched in the stomach. Dizzy and disoriented, she crossed the road in a total panic, not even waiting for the light to turn green. She wandered into the gardens of the Royal Pavilion and sat on a bench looking out over the patchy lawn and the strange, oriental domes of the palace that looked like a replica of the Taj Mahal.

Rob wanted a divorce, and he couldn't even wait until they got back to the States to get rid of her. That's why he'd been so nice recently, so appreciative of her efforts to be a good wife, so determined to stay at home and spend time with her. Lulling her into a false sense of security, making her believe that everything was OK, that he still cared about her. All the while, he was just waiting for the right time to spring it on her that their marriage was over and then—

Christ!

She took deep breaths to steady herself as her thoughts raced on.

How long had he been planning this? Weeks? Months?

If months, then why had he taken her to England with him? It would have been easy to just leave her behind. A much kinder move than dragging her to a foreign country and virtually abandoning her here.

A couple strolled past her, university students from the look of it, dressed in Converse sneakers, baggy hoodies and torn, frayed jeans. They stopped just long enough to take a selfie in front of the pavilion, kissing for the camera in front of such an iconic, romantic backdrop.

Just you wait, she wanted to shout at them. *Just you fucking wait*.

But she kept quiet as she sat, alone, on a cold, hard bench, while her husband was in a lawyer's office planning how to extricate his life from hers.

After a minute, she got up, and headed to the station. The pavements were busy, and she felt jostled and hassled. She remembered her fears while walking back from the hospital. Funny, how she wasn't scared of the traffic anymore. For a fleeting second she thought, *fine; push me in the road in front of a moving car, see if I care*. Maybe if I got hurt bad enough, my husband would feel sorry for me. Maybe he'd realise what a fool he was, and he'd stop doing whatever he was doing, cancel whatever plans he was carrying out.

At the station she queued at the ticket machine and glanced at the old-fashioned station clock. Twenty-five past one. It was only early afternoon, so there was plenty of time to go somewhere that wasn't home. She couldn't face going back to Malin House now. The things she was scared of – the sounds, the hollowing, the mysterious boy – had stopped tormenting her recently, but maybe they'd just been lulling her into a false sense of security, too, the way Rob had done. Maybe they'd all be there when she got back, lying in wait.

In ten minutes' time there was a fast train to London Bridge. In less than an hour, she could be walking around Borough Market, stop in a pub or two, go for a stroll along the river. It would be fun to have an adventure on her own, wouldn't it? She'd been to that part of London before, with Rob and Jared and Bex, and she had her phone for directions, so she wasn't likely to get lost.

She bought the ticket, boarded the train, looked out the window. The platform guard blew a whistle and the train lurched forward. She settled into her seat as the world rolled by: the back of houses, clotheslines and kids' trampolines and gardeners' wheelbarrows. Yards full of junk and beautifully mowed lawns. High banks covered in empty plastic bags and dead buddleia, soggy looking fields and muddy pastures with grazing sheep.

She let the sights wash over her, and tried not to think about what Rob was doing. Or saying. She checked her Messenger account. Rob was online. There was a light next to Bex's name too. But that was crazy. Rob had hundreds of friends; no doubt Bex did, too. It didn't mean they were talking to each other.

But the visit to the lawyer. Jacey's heart sank again. What else could that mean? Suddenly she thought about Jared. He worked somewhere near the station. Maybe she could be brave and ask if he knew what Rob was up to.

Hey, guys. I'm heading up to London. Got an appointment at the embassy and thought I'd head over to Borough Market afterwards. Late notice I know, but, if you guys are around, it would be great to catch up.

She sent the text to both Bex and Jared. It would look odd if she only got in touch with Jared; this way, neither of them would suspect anything. Besides, Jared was the one she really wanted to speak to, and if what she feared was true, she doubted Bex would have the guts to face her in person.

PS. Just me today. Rob's at work. Don't worry if you don't have time.

She watched the Messenger light by Bex's name. Rob's was still on. So was hers. Stupid to think it meant anything, but that's what she was now. Stupid with fear.

A few seconds later she got the first text.

Hey. Sorry I can't make it today but have a great afternoon. A little more notice next time and we'll definitely meet up! Bex x

Then a message from Rob. *Hi, honey. Just checking if you are going to be around for dinner tonight. It's Wednesday, so, are you going to your history class? I might stay on for a pint after work, if that's the case.*

The train was nearly in London. She could see the Shard in the distance, rising on the horizon like a scalpel-headed monster in the mist. She wasn't afraid of it anymore, though. If it collapsed on top of her, cut her to shreds, she wouldn't even care.

Her phone pinged. A message from Jared.

Great to hear from you, Jacey. Good call, making the trip to Borough Market. Love that place. Yeah, I think Bex is teaching, but I could swing by and we could have lunch or something. Should we meet at the George again? Not usually too crowded this time of day.

Be good to see you, Jacey.

Jacey didn't have much time for the market, but she bought a can of mixed mushrooms in garlic oil and dried fruit in a fancy tin box. When she got to the George the lunch crowd had thinned and she and Jared met in a dark wood-panelled part of the pub that must have been where Dickens once held court.

Jared was at a corner table in the shadows, looking at his phone, nursing a pint of beer.

"Hey. Nice surprise. How was the embassy?

"The usual hassle, you know…" She felt her face redden. Why had she told that stupid lie? Couldn't she just come up to London, on her own, for no reason?

"Well, it's good you didn't have to travel too far, anyway."

"Thanks for meeting me," Jacey said. "Sorry Bex couldn't make it."

"Yeah, well …" Jared said. "Hey, let me get you a drink. Beer? Wine?"

"A glass of white. Dry."

Jacey took a deep breath. She could relax for a moment while

Jared was away from the table. She wondered if she'd made a mistake texting him and Bex. Rob would definitely know about her trip and wonder what she was doing. And she wasn't sure if she should tell Jared about the book she'd found, how it was inscribed.

Maybe she should just ask him about Trudy, Rob's ex-girlfriend – pump him for more details about how he had treated her, and what made it 'weird'. That might explain Rob's behaviour. Maybe things weren't as bad as she feared.

"So," he said, when he sat down. "How's life in the haunted castle?"

"It's OK," Jacey said. She looked down at her glass.

"Seen any ghosts yet?"

Jacey smiled. "I'm not actually sure."

"Oh? Really?"

No. She couldn't tell him about the boy. The ball on the stairs. The sounds. He'd think she was mad, too. He'd probably tell Bex about it and Bex would tell Rob and then …

"It's a weird house. A little unnerving to be in such a big place, to be honest, but I don't really want to talk about that."

"No?" He seemed disappointed.

She laughed. "You could answer a question about Rob, though."

Jared took a swift drink of his pint. A big glug. Then he moved the glass away as if he was afraid to have it too close to him. "What I said last time about him flirting with Bex, I didn't mean any—"

"No," she said. "It's not about that."

"Oh." Jared sighed, moved his glass back in front of him.

"But, last time you talked about Trudy. Rob's old girlfriend. You said you were friends with her."

"Oh. Gotcha."

"You said Rob was 'weird' when she was with him."

"Well, I'm not sure if that was the actual word Trudy used but …"

"What did it mean? Do you remember? Whatever she said."

Jared took another swig. "I don't know if it matters now, Jacey."

"You were the one who mentioned it."

"I know, and maybe I shouldn't have. I was just sort of pissed off about the flirting, I think, and now, well, everything's fine between us – me and Bex – and what I said was stupid, really."

"Oh."

"Jealous husband stuff."

"Right."

"Not really appropriate anymore."

"It might be," Jacey said. "To me."

"Oh. Sorry." Jared looked away, clearly uncomfortable. "If things aren't going so good between you guys, I mean. Really sucks, especially with you being over here and, well, being kind of on your own in that house all the time."

"How did you know I was alone?"

"Bex must have told me."

"And how did *she* know?"

"I guess I thought you'd told her."

The air stiffened. Of course. She was stupid for thinking that the hollowing had just gone away. She took a deep breath, hoping that would keep it from intensifying. She put her hands on the table, pressed down so that she wouldn't move or sway.

"You all right, Jacey?"

"I'm fine." In her head her words were distorted, as if she were speaking under water, having to shout to make herself heard. "Just this wine. I'm not used to drinking so early in the day."

Jared took another huge gulp of beer. "Wish I could say the same."

"So tell me about Trudy. Rob's ex."

"You really want to know?"

"I think so." The air was clearer now. Jacey was stupidly proud of herself, as if she'd finally mastered the hollowing, taken control of it. "I mean, yes. I do."

"OK, though. But remember, this was a long time ago. Way back in college."

Jared drained his pint.

"Do you want another one?" Jacey asked.

"I'll save it for later. Might need it then."

Jared spoke quietly, as if he thought someone might overhear him. The hollowing had quietened, but Jacey still struggled to hear.

"It was two or three conversations, really. I'd met Rob a few times, he seemed – seems – like a good guy to me. He wanted to be a writer then."

"Still does," Jacey said, "though he doesn't talk about it much anymore."

"And he drank quite a bit. Smoked pot, too, the strong kind that can make you paranoid, if you're not careful."

Jared was making excuses for Rob, Jacey thought. The way men always stick up for each other.

"So, what did he do?"

Jared ran his finger up and down the side of his glass, etching a design on the condensation. "He pretended to see things."

"Like what?"

"People in the shadows. Strangers lurking. Predators, I don't know. It was like he was trying to scare her, so she'd need him to walk her home at night."

"And could it have been true?"

"Nobody on campus was ever attacked as far as Trudy knew. Like, it wasn't in the news or anything. She never heard anything about stalkers or random attacks from anyone else."

"That doesn't sound so bad, though. Especially if the pot was messing him up."

"And then, when she asked around, or when she questioned his version of reality, he got really angry, accused her of undermining him, of not appreciating everything he was doing to help her. Made her feel shitty for not taking him seriously."

"Oh." Jacey felt a strange sense of relief. "So, it wasn't like he abused her, or anything?"

Jared shrugged.

"She would come over to my place, really upset. Like Rob was trying to fuck her up mentally, you know? Making her feel she was stupid for not understanding the danger, and ungrateful for not appreciating his offers of help."

"So he was controlling," Jacey said.

"That's what it seemed like, but I could be wrong. Trudy could have been wrong." Jared picked up his empty glass. "I think I'm ready for that drink now. How about you?"

Jacey had hardly touched her wine. She took a sip, shook her head.

When Jared sat down with his fresh pint, he said, "Hope that story doesn't freak you out or anything."

"No," Jacey said. "At least it showed that on some level Rob cared about her. I don't think he'd want to protect me from anything, real or imagined, at this point."

Despite her determination to stay calm, Jacey's eyes filled with tears. "Anything I tell him, he just brushes it off."

"So …" Jared stopped speaking for a few seconds, weighing up his words, as if he wasn't sure that the question he was about to ask was appropriate. "There *is* something weird going on? In that house?"

"I can't really talk about it," Jacey said.

"Why not?"

"Because if it got back to Rob he might use it against me in some way."

"How?"

Should she tell Jared about Rob's secret trip to the law office? About Katherine's experiences, so like her own?

She swallowed the last of her wine. "Sorry, but it's personal, you know? And kind of embarrassing."

"What? You're living in a creepy old house with a man you say doesn't care about you and wants to undermine you. How is that embarrassing? I mean, it's not your fault."

"I know that, of course not, but …"

She thought about her mother's letter to Rob. A veiled reference to something from the past. *I wish I could forget.* But that didn't have anything to do with Malin House. How could it?

Suddenly, the room grew cold, her skin felt clammy, and for a few seconds, she struggled to breathe. This wasn't the usual hollowing – not the strange sounds or whooshing air, or even the ringing of bells. This was more frightening, like the sensation she'd felt outside Nana Ivy's house in Cambridgeshire, of drowning on dry land.

"Jacey? Are you all right?"

Jared started to stand up, but Jacey gestured with a weak wave and thumbs up, that he should sit back down. She'd swallowed wrong, that was it, and that instant feeling of needing to expel water from her lungs, was intense but short-lived.

"I'm OK," she rasped. "Just the wine went down the wrong way."

"You're sure?"

People at the bar had been watching as she sputtered and coughed. The bartender moved to the corner drinks station, keeping an eye on what was going on over at table 14.

"Yes," Jacey said. "I'm fine. Honestly."

When she got back to Lewes, it was dark, and the platform was bathed in a sickly yellow light. *So many obstacles*, she thought, as the train pulled into the station. First, there was the station itself, then the dimly lit tunnel, and the dash across the wide park that was full of night sounds and deep shadows.

Just the thought of it was exhausting. And that was before she got to Malin House to spend another night with a man who was trying to get rid of her, one way or another.

Going to the pub was a better idea. Writing club would be on tonight. There'd be plenty of people, so she didn't have to sit with John and Muriel if they were there. One of the others, a kind soul like Rael, might walk her home. She could tell people that she'd seen Rael in hospital. Share the good news of his imminent discharge.

As she left the station, another message pinged on her phone. *Hey, Jacey. Since its history class – right? – I think I'll stay on after work. There's a pub quiz later and the departmental team is down a person. Hope you don't mind me stepping in, just for tonight.*

The Downsman was less crowded than last time, or at least it seemed that way. There was a general hubbub, though: the usual queue at the bar, the stressed bartenders dealing with the disgruntled seniors who had forgotten the art of patience as they got older.

Within a minute of her setting foot in the pub, Muriel and John were at her side, fluttering like enthusiastic birds. "Jacey," Muriel chirped. "How lovely!"

"Well, yes," Jacey said. She took a step away from them. "I saw Rael at the hospital today, and he said I should come back. Keep his bar stool warm."

"And how was he?"

"Very well, considering," she said. "He can go home soon, according to the doctors."

"Oh, good for him," John said. "Isn't that exciting? Maybe he'll be back in a few weeks."

"Maybe." Jacey said. "We'll see."

At the bar she took her phone out and sent Rael a text, with a gif of witches and warlocks. *Guess where I am?*

When she got her drink, Muriel and John waved her over to their table. What had she been thinking? As soon as she sat down, she realised she'd made a mistake. Muriel and Madlyn weren't just ordinary old ladies, she knew that. They had something on her, or at least they acted that way. She glanced at the door. Maybe she should leave, before things got started. Other than John and Muriel, who would even notice she'd gone?

Too late. Madlyn tinked her glass, and Muriel and John turned their attention to the front of the room, where Madlyn was readying some papers on the table in front. As she started to speak, her voice turned into a low drone. The words got slower and slower, deeper and deeper, until the sounds that came from her throat weren't human, but mechanical. A cog grinding, refusing to slip into gear.

Everyone else was oblivious to the hollowing, of course. Madlyn's mouth was moving and her audience was listening to her, rapt. They laughed – Madlyn must have told them a joke – but all Jacey heard was the droning that got louder and louder, until the sound became physically painful to hear.

She had to leave. Now. Before her eardrums burst and started to bleed.

Muriel had been watching her sister, responding with the others, laughing in the same places, even joining in with a smattering of applause when Madlyn must have announced a competition winner from their group.

The winner – a woman Jacey's age, with long hair and bright, quirky clothes – stood up on the other side of the room and took a little bow. When she sat down, Muriel leaned into Jacey and whispered, "Isn't that lovely?"

Muriel's voice had cut through the droning. Despite the pain in her ears, despite what Jacey assumed was complete deafness, she could perfectly hear Muriel's whispered words.

"Things are not always as they seem, are they?"

Jacey nodded. Smiled slightly. Pushed her chair back.

She didn't need to explain to anyone that she was leaving or tell them why. She shuffled to the hallway, stumbled down the stairs. There was a bathroom on the landing. Mixed gender, just a single toilet and tiny sink.

She grappled with the door, and managed to close it behind her, and turn the lock.

Silence.

A total absence of sound. She put her hand to her ears, checked them in the mirror. There was no blood. She closed the toilet lid, sat down, head in hands. What the hell was happening to her?

A few seconds later, she heard tapping on the door, and felt a flood of relief. She could still hear!

"Hello? Anyone in there?"

Jacey stood up, turned the water on in the sink.

"Be out in a minute."

She checked her phone. There was a text from Rael. She hadn't heard it in the midst of the droning from the hollowing, or whatever it was.

Seriously, babe? Hanging out with those women? Is that wise?

She texted back. *It's fucking weird tonight, tbh.*

There was another knock on the door. "Jacey?"

Muriel's voice.

Another text. *There were things I should have told you. Seriously, Ms J, you shouldn't be there. Nowhere near them. Get the fuck out.*

She had no choice but to open the door, but as she reached out her hand, steeling herself, she felt something in her throat. The liquid again, the water, making her cough and sputter, building up in her lungs, making it hard to breathe.

When she finally felt normal again, steady enough to leave, Muriel was outside the door, waiting.

"You feel like you're drowning, don't you?" she said.

"No, I just—"

She tried to move past, but Muriel wouldn't budge. "There's no use denying it, Jacey. It's the curse of the Kennets – strikes in every generation."

"I'm not a Kennet."

"Drowned in the fens they were. All the boys. A few of the girls."

"Like I said …"

"You can feel what it's like, can't you?"

"No." She pushed Muriel out of the way, so that the older woman stumbled backwards, reaching her hands out, grabbing the little railing to avoid falling over.

"That'll be the curse," she said. "It can get you any time."

She took a taxi back to Malin House, not daring to risk seeing anything that would trigger another horrible choking attack. Rob was already at home, making a cup of tea, frying bacon for a sandwich, appearing at first glance to be sober and calm. It was only after he started to speak that Jacey realised he was drunk.

He put up his hands and said, "Don't say anything, OK?"

"OK."

"Come on, Jace. Don't be like that."

"What?"

"So fucking nice."

"All right," she whispered. "I won't."

It made her sick, the way she sounded. So compliant, so weak. Why didn't she tell him she knew all about what he was up to, what a bastard he was? And she remembered the wife from *The Shining* again – what was her name? Always smiling and trying to make things right.

So fucking nice, just like Rob said.

But Jacey backed out of the room, slowly, silently. She wished she could curl up on the sofa in the den, lock herself in her little cocoon, the only place she felt safe, but that would only lead to more conversations, later on if not tonight. And the way Rob was – a little aggressive, very, very defensive – the best thing she could do was just say goodnight and leave.

By the time he came upstairs, she'd fallen asleep. She'd put herself in the recovery position, and let her head hang slightly off the edge of bed. Better for her airways, in case the choking happened again, some protection from whatever it was that was attacking her breathing, filling her lungs up with fluid that she hadn't drunk.

She had nightmares, the vivid kind she hadn't had since she was a child. Vivid. Water-filled. Endless irrigation ditches like she and Rael had seen in Cambridgeshire, with narrow muddy dykes between them. She was running from something, and slipping into the water, and she knew that although the water looked shallow, she would not make it out alive. There'd be quicksand or sinkholes or unseen currents that would drag her under, sweep her body away.

She woke up with a start, coughing, but not drowning. Not in any actual danger, though her heart was pounding and she shuddered with fear.

Chapter 29

Don't act like you're out of control, because you're not.

Stay calm. No crying or shivering, and if the hollowing comes, or any other sounds, just ignore them.

The university doctor listened to her heartbeat, had her breathe in and out so he could check her lungs.

"Everything sounds clear at the moment."

He typed some words on his computer keyboard, while Jacey fought the urge to lean over and read what was on the screen.

But she had to behave herself. Act like a normal, sane person, with a normal, sane problem.

"So," the doctor said, "your lungs appear to be clear of any fluid, but you've been experiencing some alarming symptoms, is that how you would describe it?"

"Yes. Choking. But not on food, and sort of..."

She put her fingers to her throat. "A feeling like I'm going to drown, that's the only way I can describe it."

"And is this related to swallowing? You know, liquids going down the wrong tube?"

She shook her head. "It comes without drinking or swallowing. Like, from inside my body, not from anything I've done."

"And otherwise, you are well?"

She was tempted to shrug. Make a vague gesture, let him read between the lines, but she simply said, "Yes. I'm fine."

"And the noises you heard the last time I saw you – the tinnitus?"

"Better," she said. "Not so often, not so loud or disturbing."

"But not gone completely?"

"No."

"I see."

He looked up at his screen. "Did you try the tablets I gave you?"

"I haven't used them for sleeping," she said. "I haven't needed to."

"That's good. Lack of sleep can certainly raise one's anxiety levels."

"I'm not anxious, doctor. I'm a little worried – curious, I guess – about my symptoms, but not otherwise."

"So am I, to be honest with you," the doctor said. "It's not reflux, or hiatus hernia, not without the burning in the back of the throat, so giving you something for acid build-up might be pointless."

He took his hands off the computer.

"I see you live at Malin House," he said.

She nodded. There was no point in lying. It was there on her medical record.

"Spooky place."

"Is it?" She was tired of this conversation. Malin House. All the time. Having to explain herself, as if Malin House was her fault, as if she was responsible for the things that happened to people there.

"Well, it has that reputation, anyway."

The doctor seemed to be waiting for her to say something else, acknowledge the horrors of living in a haunted house, so he could put her symptoms down as being stress or anxiety related, or worse, signs of paranoid psychosis.

Well, she wouldn't play along with it.

"Oh," she said. "I didn't realise."

"Really?"

"I'm not surprised people might think that," she said. "I mean, it's so old, and there are a lot of weird noises."

"Such as?"

"The usual. Creaking floorboards, wind through the gaps around the windows."

"The bells you were hearing. Were they coming from Malin House, do you think?"

What was he doing? Trying to trap her into some kind of admission? Trying to get her to fall apart?

"No. I checked, in fact, thinking there was a window open in the servant's pantry, and setting off the bells, but it wasn't that. Or anything else in the house."

She smiled. "Just in my head. Random sounds, maybe some sort of blockage picked up after the flights. I've always been affected by changes in air pressure. My husband mentioned that was a possibility."

"I see," the doctor said. "Well, I've never heard of a transatlantic flight causing tinnitus, but it's a pretty unpredictable condition. And this other thing. This feeling like you're drowning, do you think that could have been caused by the flight, too?"

She shook her head.

"Well, all I can offer you is a two-week course of treatment for reflux. It may be that the fluids that are backing into your throat aren't as acidic as we'd normally expect to find."

He printed off the prescription.

"And come back when you've finished with them. We'll see how you're getting on, and if we need to try another avenue of treatment."

"Such as?"

He smiled vaguely. "We'll talk about it then."

Chapter 30

Even though the encroaching winter was dark and damp, Jacey tried to keep Malin House warm and cosy. She never lit the open fireplace in the kitchen, but Martin had shown her how the range worked, and that meant keeping it stoked up with coal or firewood, so that it was like both an oven and a furnace. On her last trip to the shops she bought yeast and bread flour. She wasn't venturing out as much, not with the incessant rain falling in heavy sheets, and the ferocious winds that seemed like new variants of the hollowing, seeping in through the gaps in the old windows, and swooping in under the doors.

She wasn't afraid of the house anymore, at least. The knocks and noises didn't set her off into a panic. She was happy to spend time in every room – upstairs, downstairs, even in the basement, when Martin came to tinker with the boiler.

Nothing evil down there. She'd seen it for herself, checked out all the damp, dark corners.

As for Rob, he never mentioned his trip to the law office. He didn't talk about them taking a holiday break either, and neither did she. Staying away from him was the best way to handle things, she decided. If he forgot he had a wife, maybe he'd forget to file for divorce. If he thought she'd disappeared on her own, maybe he'd stop trying to get rid of her.

Sometimes she looked through Rob's things – wrong, she knew that on one level, but on another level she didn't care. It was her house, too, wasn't it? She was still his wife; she had rights. She looked through his lecture notes – nothing shocking, no 'All work and no play' written out in the margins hundreds of times. When he was out, and he seemed to be out every day now, she'd settle in for the day in 'his' drawing room, ignoring the lingering smell of tobacco and alcohol, pulling out a book from the shelves, settling down on his sofa and reading. Whatever the book was, it didn't matter. Whether she understood a word of some ancient biology textbook or not, she was improving herself, by osmosis if nothing else.

One afternoon she reached for a novel by a writer she'd never heard of, published in London in 1828. It looked like all the others, brown and shiny with gold lettering on the leather spine. But as she pulled it off the shelf something was stuck to its back cover. A piece of paper. Another empty envelope, sent from the USA to Rob at his office, addressed in her mother's handwriting.

The book may have been ancient, but the envelope wasn't. It had been postmarked two weeks earlier. Hot off the press, so where was the letter?

Jacey leafed through the book, haphazardly at first, then carefully, page by page.

Nothing.

She reached for the book that was next to the novel and did the same thing. Nothing. She looked around the tall shelves – were there any clues? Any books at an odd angle? Were there any with bits of paper that stuck out – a placemark for Rob, so that he could go back and re-read the letter whenever he wanted?

She tried a likely-looking volume – nothing. She pulled out another. Again, nothing but pages and pages of incomprehensible words.

Next, she pulled at random. Maybe that was the best way to go, hoping that instinct would guide her to the missing letter. She closed her eyes, reached out her hand. Two books fell out, but there wasn't a letter in either of them.

She kept trying, leafing through pages, faster and faster, book after book. At first, she put the books back as neatly as she could, but after a while she just set them on the coffee table or dropped them on the floor. By the time she realised it was getting dark, and that Rob would be coming home soon, there were dozens of books spread out across the room, helter-skelter, a big mess all over the place.

Her hands were shaking. She was exhausted, frightened of what was going to happen when Rob came into his private sanctuary and found out what she'd done, but she was unable to stop herself.

One more. Then she'd pick everything up, put it all back.

Reaching blindly, she pulled out a book and opened its covers. As she fanned the pages, out it flew, a folded letter in yellow paper, floating down to the floor like a pair of angel's wings.

From her mother. The floral border, the girly writing. Dated two weeks ago.

Dear Rob,

You want the whole story? I've already told you what you needed to know.

We had several family traumas when Jacey was little, one worse than the others. I told you about this at your wedding, if not the whole truth of what happened. Think back to everything I've said before, Rob. Figure it out. You're an intelligent man.

I need to know that I can still rely on you, Rob. That you won't let this tragedy – so long ago – ruin the rest of my daughter's life.

Panic pounded in Jacey's chest and swilled through her blood. The mess in the drawing room wasn't important anymore, the books could stay where they were – who cared about what Rob might think. Her mother's words were all that mattered – why was she saying those things to Rob? There was no trauma, other than losing her father and, eventually, the farm – why would she lie?

Jacey went into the kitchen and through to the porch where her outdoor things were hanging on hooks. The adrenaline rush – the need to run away, to get out of the house – was overwhelming. She put on her hiking boots, bundled on layers of T-shirts and sweatshirts and scarves, and ran outside, through the back door, not bothering to lock it behind her. Without looking back, she climbed the hill behind the house and didn't stop for breath until she reached the top. Behind her, the lights of the town were already being turned on, though it wasn't even four o'clock yet. The wind picked up, whipping her hair and stinging her face. Her normal route was towards the café, where she could stop in for a coffee if she wanted, or use the bathroom.

But there was a chance she might see someone there who knew her, who recognised her despite the cocooning layers, and she didn't want that. The other path was rockier, more slippery in the rain, and with deep trenches of mud forming on either side, but it was safer. She strode off, higher up the hill, undeterred by the rain and wind, not stopping to look behind her or over at the lights of the town.

She reached a turning. There was a sign, a blue painted arrow on a flat wooden pole.

A fence led into a farmer's field. She'd never hiked that way before. Where would it take her? To the other side of the hill? Would she be able to see the distant sea from there? They weren't far away from it, five miles or so.

She climbed the wooden stile, trudged through the mud.

Her skin was getting wet, as the rain soaked through her layers of clothing.

But that didn't matter. There was something approximating a path, and the most important thing was that she wasn't at home. She was away from Malin House. From Rob. From the letter she'd found. Her mother's words.

Trauma. Tragedy.

The lies.

She marched on, until her legs were numb with the cold and the wet and the exertion, and finally, the hills beyond the field dipped and the clouds lifted, and she caught a glimpse of the sea in the far distance, a grey shimmering blanket, with a sliver of low orange sun, quivering on the edge of her vision.

It would be dark sooner than she thought. She'd never been on the downs after sunset. What would happen if she got lost up here? How far would the temperature drop? She'd heard stories on the news: inexperienced hikers trapped on a mountainside, rescue teams sent to find them, and carrying them down, just moments from death.

But this wasn't a mountain, and it wasn't that cold.

The rain would not turn to snow.

She wouldn't die.

She stood for a moment, listening to her heartbeat, watching the sun sink into the sea and change colour. Orange. Red. Purple, reflected on the dull grey water.

The stillness calmed her; focussing on the colours was soothing.

It was time to go back. Face whatever it was that was waiting for her. Clean up the book mess she'd made in Rob's room. Talk to her mother. Find out the truth.

She trudged back to the stile and climbed over. She followed the path towards home. She looked over at the town lights, twinkling in the distance, and in front of her, the bright café window, like a far-away beacon.

Suddenly, the wind dropped.

Like the ocean drawing away from shore before a tsunami, the world became silent.

And then she heard a sound. Not the hollowing. Not the bells.

The scuffling of feet.

She looked behind her. Nothing, no one.

She heard it again. Shuffling, and then a kick. It was in front of her, or so it seemed. Somewhere on the path, but why couldn't she see anything?

She had to move. Forwards, despite her fear, despite knowing that here, on the hill, she was alone with whatever was making that sound. There would be no mountain rescue on its way. There would be no Rob, for better or worse.

She shook herself, then strode ahead, counting the steps as she did. One, two, three, four.

It was coming towards her, through the mist and rain.

Five, six, seven.

A figure.

Eight, nine, ten.

The boy.

His pale, slender shape seemed to shift in the foggy air as she got closer to him.

He was wearing the same clothes, but they were soaking wet, and his hair was stuck to his head, and water was dripping down his face.

So he was real. He *had* to be. A ghost couldn't get rained on.

"Hey," she shouted. "Are you OK?"

He stopped moving, brought his arms up, held his body as if trying to get warm.

"I can help you down the hill," Jacey said. "We can call your parents from my house."

The boy didn't speak. She took a few steps closer. He was definitely real; she could tell that now. His shorts were dirty, his shoes caked in mud.

"Oh, you poor thing," she said.

And then she remembered. "Are you looking for your ball?"

No answer.

The boy turned around.

"No," Jacey shouted. "You need to go the other way. Towards the downhill path. The way you came, I'll go with you."

But the boy didn't answer her and he started moving again, turning away from her, and heading out across the open downs, where it was colder in the wind, and the paths were muddy and slippery, easy to stray from.

"Hey," she shouted. "It's getting dark."

She ran after him, but it was no use. After a few metres, she couldn't even see him in the thickening mist.

"Hey! You need to come with me!"

No answer.

No time to wait.

She had to hurry home and raise the alarm. The boy was real; she knew it now, and she'd been stupid not to believe it before. Whatever he was doing out here on his own, in this weather, wearing those clothes, she was witnessing an appalling case of neglect – parents taking no care with the safety of their child.

She ran as fast as she could, hurrying to the hillside path, careful not to fall as she headed downwards, half walking, half climbing, virtually skidding like a sled part of the way. At the bottom of the hill there were lights on in Helen and Martin's cottage. A beacon – yes, as bright as could be.

Looming behind it, dark and menacing, was Malin House. And there, on the path in front of her, caught in the reflection of the yard light at the edge of the lawn, was the boy's rubber ball.

Shimmering.

Moving, it seemed, as if it had just come down the hill, and was waiting for her.

She left it where it was. The boy could find it later. Nobody else would take it.

As she crossed the lawn she fought the urge to shout for help. She'd have to remain calm, call the police as soon as she got home. Not get hysterical. Not shout the place down. Not let Rob, or anyone else, think she was hallucinating or making things up.

Through the back door, into the kitchen.

There was Rob, home from work, calm and cool. A glass of wine in his hand, watching her as she came in, as if she was some wild animal who'd wandered in by mistake.

"Jesus Christ, Jacey."

"Call the police," she said, trying not to let the panic rise in her voice.

"What?"

"Now. We need to call the police, or an ambulance, I'm not sure."

"What's happened?"

He looked worried, but not scared, more confused and wary and not trusting her or what she was saying.

"The boy," she said.

"What boy?"

"The boy I've seen … you know."

"No, I don't."

"In the tunnel. Up on the hill."

"I don't know what you're talking about."

Oh, Jesus. Jacey thought. She'd never told him. She'd never dared.

"I've been seeing this random kid. Like a toddler. All over the place. Down by the tunnel under the freeway, standing on our driveway and he's always wearing the same thing, and he's not dressed for winter, only summer, and he has this ball, and he kicks it, and the ball was in the house once, only I thought it was you playing a trick, but I think he's in—"

"Jacey, stop."

"The police," she screamed. "We've got to call them."

"Jacey calm down."

"He could die up there, Rob. It's so cold."

Rob didn't say any more. He went to her, pulled her hood away from her face, unwrapped her scarf.

"This boy," he said. "What does he look like?"

Jacey stepped back. She could take her own coat off, thank you very much. She took a breath, tried to keep control over her pounding heart, her surging fear.

"I told you. Summer clothes. Blondish hair. Red and green striped T-shirt. Always the same, with khaki shorts and flimsy shoes"

Rob's face went pale. "Jesus."

"But he wasn't wearing a coat, Rob. He'll freeze to death up there if we don't do something."

"And what do you think we should do?"

"I told you already. Call the police. Try to find him."

Rob went to the sink. Filled up the kettle for tea.

"There was no boy, Jacey."

"There was. I fucking saw him."

"Seriously, Jacey, you just *think* you saw someone."

"No."

"He doesn't exist, Jacey."

"How can you say that?" Rob came towards her again and she pushed him away. "You don't know anything about—"

"Seriously, Jace …"

"I bet you think I'm imagining things, but I'm not. I've seen him. I think he's been in the house—"

"That's not true."

"Maybe he sneaked in to get out of the cold."

"No, Jacey. It hasn't been here. What you think you saw, it wasn't real."

She wanted to spit in Rob's face.

"It, Rob? *It?*"

But Rob kept shaking his head, looking at her like she was crazy. Why wouldn't he believe her? Why wouldn't he understand?

"He's a boy, Rob. A lost little boy. And he's up there all on his own and …"

She got closer to him, but he kept shaking his head, and giving her that look, like *you stupid bitch*, so she curled up her fists and thumped him on the chest. Once, twice. Again. Not hard, not so it would hurt him, just so he'd listen to her, so he'd believe. But it was all a joke to Rob; he grinned non-stop, laughing in her face, flicking away the swats at his chest as if they were nothing.

Afterwards.

Rob was at the table, Jacey was in the doorway to the den, feeling safer being closer to her sanctuary, the cosy sofa, the heavy curtains.

"Sorry, Rob. It was frustration, that was all, I didn't mean to—"

"You need to see a doctor."

"I am seeing a doctor. At the walk-in on campus."

"I mean another doctor. A different one."

"Like a psychiatrist, is that what you mean?"

"Well, maybe, I mean, if you are seeing things that aren't there."

"I already told you. I'm not seeing things. It's you, you're the problem, you are the one who lies and gaslights, and hides things from me."

His face was calm. No flicker of anger, or shock. A slight jutting forward of his chin, that was all. "I'm not hiding anything, Jacey."

"Those letters from my mother." She gripped the door frame.

"What letters?"

"The one I found under the bed, addressed to you at work, and the other one, in the books. Addressed to you. Not to me."

"I can explain that, Jacey, if you let me."

But she would not let him. She dug her fingernails into the wood.

"That's what you want, isn't it?" she shouted, as it came washing over her – the anger, not the hollowing – and her plans to stay calm, to not give him any reason to doubt her sanity or to think she wasn't coping, all of them evaporated.

"To get rid of me! Lock me up somewhere!"

"Jacey, stop this."

"So you can see your girlfriend whenever you want."

She ran towards him again, but he grabbed her by the wrists, held her still.

"I KNOW ABOUT YOU AND BEX," she screamed. "I SAW WHAT YOU WROTE TO HER IN YOUR FUCKING BOOK."

And then, while Rob watched her with horror and disgust, came the hollowing. The bad, bad hollowing, where she coughed and sputtered, and the even worse hollowing where she wanted to hit him again, do something violent and hurtful. And the worst of all hollowing, where she saw things that she didn't want to see, like dirt, and cold, and a boy in a field, and rain and mud.

Chapter 31

It was inside her now. Not in the air, or in her ears, tinkling or whooshing like a mighty wind.

It had emptied her. She was nothing. A silence.

A void.

That's what it was now, what she was, had been for five days after the screaming and hitting, up in their room, her room, sleeping alone, with Rob camped out on the sofa in the drawing room. His throne room. His precious books.

His secret letters.

She slept most of the time, only getting up for a few hours a day, when Rob was gone, living his life as before, going to the university, coming back she didn't know when. She didn't care when.

She would hear him on the phone, his voice from downstairs, laughing sometimes, the sound tinkling like the bells she used to hear.

After a week, when she got back to what Rob called 'herself', he drove her to the psychiatrist. It was someone connected to the university so it wasn't going to cost very much. Rob made sure she knew that. Maybe he meant it in a reassuring way, in case she felt guilty about being such a burden, such a drain on his salary. Or maybe

Rob told her so she'd be careful what she said. No badmouthing her husband, no tarnishing his good name.

On the way into Brighton the roads and pavements were shiny, wet with recent rain, and the litter in the gutters flowed down like you'd see in a flood – only plastic bags instead of floating cars, and food wrappers instead of houses. *A disaster in miniature*, Jacey thought, imagining tiny figures riding on those candy wrappers, clinging desperately to the crinkly plastic boats.

"You sure you're OK to go in on your own?" Rob said.

Jacey nodded.

In the waiting room a kind, motherly looking receptionist asked her if she wanted a coffee.

Jacey nodded. "White. One sugar."

Listen to me, she thought. Ordering coffee like an English person. Knowing what to say. Aren't I bloody clever? Even thinking like a Brit. Rob would be so proud.

A door opened at the end of a narrow hallway.

"Jacey?" the receptionist said. "He's ready for you."

The psychiatrist's room was small, with a large comfy chair in one corner, and a table beside it with a bottle of water and a box of tissues in a ceramic holder. From a narrow window there was a view of the ocean, just behind the old-fashioned street lights and green painted railings that ran along the prom.

"I'm Dr David Andrews. You can call me David." He shook her hand. Jacey was caught by his eyes. Soft blue, like the sea behind him.

"Take a seat and let's get started," he said. His voice was gentle, too, and from the sound of it he wasn't English. Scottish maybe. Irish or Welsh. Rob would know, she could ask him.

"Tell me about why you chose to see me today."

Jacey's seat faced away from the window. Instead of the sea, she looked at the box of tissues. Was she supposed to cry? Was that part of the deal?

"I didn't choose," she said. "My husband did."

"Well, why did you agree to come in? You did agree, didn't you?"

Jacey nodded. She needed to be careful, to think before she spoke.

"Take your time," David said.

"I've had some strange experiences and feelings since I got to England, and they are starting to bother me and my husband is worried."

"Do you want to tell me about these feelings?"

"I don't really know how to describe them. I mean, I'm not hallucinating or anything, I know I'm not."

When David looked at her his eyes were still kind, but they were slightly furrowed, as if he was wondering what path this consultation was going to take. He seemed more alert – scared that she was going to say or do something completely gaga, have a melt-down, freak out and start trashing the place.

"What do you see?"

"I mostly feel things. Like a hollowing out of the air and the sound goes funny, and sometimes I hear bells when I know there aren't any bells ringing. That's why I went to the doctor on campus. He said I probably had tinnitus."

"Is that what you think?"

Jacey shrugged. Behind her she could hear seagulls, angrily squawking outside the window. Not as pretty as tinkling bells, but real at least.

"That would be a pretty straightforward cause of the sounds, wouldn't it?"

"Yes."

"So why *are* you here?"

"I told you. My husband made me come."

David seemed genuinely taken aback. "What do you mean by that?"

"I got really upset about some things, and frightened, and he said I should see a psychiatrist because my reactions weren't exactly rational."

"He said that?"

"Yes."

"Those were his exact words?"

"'Maybe it's stress,' is what he said. 'Maybe you're having extreme anxiety attacks.'"

"And are you?"

"I'm having something, but I don't know what."

Rob was in the car when the appointment finished. He had the engine running, ready for a quick getaway.

"I wanted to keep it warm for you," he said, and Jacey believed him.

There was no room in her head for doubt anymore. Take things at face value, that's what she needed to do. The psychiatrist said as much, and who was she to argue?

"Accept the things you see and hear as real."

She hadn't told him about the little boy, of course. Or the drowning feeling. Just the normal stuff that could happen to anybody.

"Did he give you any medication?" Rob asked.

My husband wants to keep me quiet, Jacey thought. Half awake, or knocked out completely. Once they got home, he led her upstairs, and pulled the covers back for her to get into bed.

"I don't need a nurse," she said.

"I just wanted to—"

"Please. I'm fine on my own."

He left, reluctantly it seemed, and she got undressed and climbed into the bed. She checked her phone for messages. There was one from her mother, asking why she'd forgotten their Skype call the day before, and one from Rael.

Got home from hospital a few days ago, Rael said. *Sorry I didn't text earlier, but a hunky physio called Jackson's been putting me through my paces.* . A few minutes later, when she didn't respond, he sent another text. *You good, hon?*

She gave him an emoji thumbs up.

Her mother couldn't be brushed off that easily, so she sent a longer message.

Sorry, but super busy yesterday, and totally forgot what day it was. I'm a little under the weather – nothing to worry about, just a cold – so can we reschedule for later in the week?

She sent along a gif of a mama sea otter swimming with her baby. That would keep her for a day or two. She'd hold off Skyping until she was sure she could keep her emotions in check. She looked like hell now, too, and who knew what kind of panic that would set off. More letters to Rob, no doubt, her mother's trusted ally.

Jacey had talked to Dr Andrews about her family back in Minnesota; told him about losing her dad, and her English nana living with them, and her mother struggling to cope with the financial side of things, and sometimes with the emotional side, too.

"She would snap for no reason," Jacey said.

"At you?"

"Yes."

Dr Andrews sat still, watching her. Waiting for her to start crying, probably, wondering why she wasn't.

Jacey had glanced at the box of tissues. The white ceramic delftware holder. A blue painted flower design ran along the top. Maybe she could reach for one, pretend to be upset.

"How did that make you feel? Do you remember?"

Yes, she remembered. Her mother's contorted face, mouth open, jaw distended, eyes red and bugging out. "You," she'd scream. "You, you, you." And she remembered the hollowing, the whooshing sound in her ears, and the emptiness that surrounded her, invaded her, penetrating her body until she was nothing.

While she remembered, the hollowing came back, for real. "I still feel it," Jacey said.

"What do you feel?"

His voice was distorted, of course, but she could still hear. She'd clung to the padded arms of the chair, squeezing it with her fingers, and breathing as slowly and quietly as she could. She closed her eyes, even though she didn't want to, even though she was afraid of what was in her mind, her mother in work clothes for doing the chores, and her long greying hair coming undone and falling around her shoulders, and her entire body shaking with rage.

"*You, Jacey. You. You.*"

"Ashamed," Jacey said.

The hollowing gradually thinned. Had the doctor noticed it?

"This seems an important memory," he said. "Judging from your reaction."

"What do you mean?"

"You looked upset, just now."

"Oh."

"Very distressed."

"I guess I was."

He leaned towards her slightly, spoke softly. "Do you know why you were made to feel ashamed by your mother's words?"

"I wasn't made to feel ashamed; I *was* ashamed."

"Why?"

"Because of something that happened."

He inched closer, whispered. "What was that?"

She waited before answering, wondering if his gentle demeanour and soothing speech was a way of hypnotising her, of helping her retrieve important details that she'd blocked from her mind.

She shook her head. "I don't know, but it must have been bad, for my mother to act like that. Shouting and …"

Downstairs, Rob turned on some music. Nothing Jacey could make out, just the thump of bass, turned up loud, and the clattering of percussion. She thought about what her mother had said in the messages to Rob, about some terrible event. What were her exact words?

She leaned over and looked under the bed where she'd left one of the letters; the layer of dust was still there, but there was no sign of anything else. Rob must have moved it, found a better hiding place, unless she'd only imagined finding it, reading those words.

No. What Dr Andrews said was true – if she saw it, it was real; if she felt it, it existed. The boy was real, and the hollowing was real, and the bouncing ball, and the letters from her mother, even if Rob had hidden them from her; even if he'd made everything disappear.

Chapter 32

"Good to see you up again," Rob said.

"Yeah."

Rob's smile was as forced as Jacey's; he looked more nervous than happy, flipping the lid of his laptop closed, putting it in its case, ready for a quick escape, now that his wife had finally emerged from her cocoon.

He looked surprised, too, that she'd showered and untangled her matted hair, that she looked human again, not like some madwoman in the attic of Victorian literature, half creature, half wife. Her jeans were baggy and shapeless, though – she'd lost weight since she got back from her therapy session, having eaten nothing but the ham and cheese sandwiches, that Rob left on the bedside table for her to eat whenever she woke up.

And after five days of Jacey-in-the-bedroom, the kitchen was a mess. The dishwasher was full, and there weren't any detergent tablets left. The sink was overflowing onto the counter, and the floor hadn't been swept. Jacey felt Nana Ivy's disapproving stare burn into her, but she didn't pick up a broom or run water in the sink.

The dishes could go fuck themselves. So could Nana Ivy. Whether she was going mad or not, an unmopped floor was the least of her worries. Besides, it was Rob her dead grandmother should be punishing for being such a slob, not her.

"I'm going to Brighton today," she said. "My friend Rael – you remember – he's home from the hospital."

"Oh," Rob sputtered. "That's good."

She dumped the coffee grounds from the cafetière into the bin and rinsed what was left down the kitchen sink, even though that was a plumbing no-no according to Rob. She couldn't be bothered to go to the bathroom and flush them down, the way he did.

The coffee grounds could go fuck themselves.

So could the toast crumbs.

And the smears of butter on the jam jar lid.

"Right," Rob said. "I thought you had an appointment with the doctor later on. Figured you'd need a lift."

"I can get the bus from Rael's house," she said. "It's pretty close."

"But I took the afternoon off."

"You can do something else then," she said. "Meet up with a friend."

"What's that supposed to mean?"

"Nothing," Jacey answered. "Just what I said."

Rob hesitated, confused by her nonchalance. He made an effort at rinsing his cereal bowl and wiping off the table. He kissed her on the cheek as he passed her, and she did not flinch. *Real*, Jacey thought. Like Dr Andrews said. Rob is kissing me because he cares about me. It is not a lie. It is not a trick. Accept the truth, said the doctor; the reality of the situation. Then you can start to rebuild things: your relationship. Yourself.

When Rob was gone, the house did its usual shudder, as if it was reminding her that she was alone, and there was no one to defend her from whatever it offered up by way of a fright.

She waited for the bells. Nothing. No hollowing either.

She decided that if the boy turned up again, she'd grab him by the scruff of the neck and shake him until he either disappeared or disintegrated into a pile of dust, or started screaming, and demanding that she let him go back home to his mother. It didn't matter if he was an apparition, or a hallucination, or an actual flesh and blood child; he was real, one way or another, and he could fuck right off.

She went up the stairs. No boy. No sounds. She looked up and down the hallway. The side view window showed beyond Helen and Martin's cottage and up the hill. Anyone looking through it the other day would have had a bird's eye view of her tearing down the hill in a state of frenzied fear.

She looked inside the room that was next to it. It was just a linen closet, with what looked to be extra bedding and blankets and pillows stacked up neatly on shelves.

Across the hallway was an open room; small, everything covered with sheets. There was a fireplace with floral tiles surrounding the opening. Dusty rose-coloured curtains that were faded in places and mended with patches. The moths had been at them no doubt. Nothing sinister – no demonic talons, ripping the fabric, scratching at the walls.

And the other bedroom, where Rob allegedly heard the horrible screams. She listened. Silence. She stood in the open doorway and looked at the mirror on the other side of the bed, the one that Rob had got so excited about. Wouldn't it be totally awesome, he'd said, watching ourselves in that mirror? Reaching under her top to unhook her bra, ready to undress her, feeling the heat of her skin. Wouldn't it be fucking *hot*?

She was about to turn around, head for her bedroom, take a shower before going into Brighton, and then she saw it. A flash of colour, like a streak of blurry lights, across the mirror. Real, she thought, and that knowledge kept her fear at bay. The colours reminded her of the little boy – his shirt, the rubber ball – but it wasn't him. It was just a weird trick of the light – a visual form of tinnitus.

She took in a deep breath; strange how calm she was. How totally unafraid.

She blinked a couple of times, waited for the lights to appear again, on the wall, in the mirror, against the window which was reflecting the bed and the lamp table beside it.

Nothing turned up. There was just a sound. Her phone, vibrating in the pocket of her jeans.

Her mother's profile picture was on the screen. Jacey checked the time. Quarter to three. She was supposed to have called her at two, and now her mother was Facetiming her. She'd have to answer; at least she hadn't been crying this morning and wasn't upset.

She smoothed her hair and answered the call, smiling.

"Mom! Hi. I totally forgot."

Her mother had the eyes-furrowed, worried Auntie Em expression again.

"I'm so sorry, Mom. I was just going to get in the shower so I could go out for a while."

"Oh, that's nice to hear. Rob told me you haven't been feeling so hot."

"All better now," Jacey said. She sat on the bed, facing the door, bounced up and down a couple of times to show her mother how energetic she was.

"Good." Her mom said. "I really worry when you don't call."

"I'm just so busy, and time runs away from me. How are things with you?"

"Well, we had a little snowfall last night," her mother said. "Don't know if you can see it."

She held the camera up, so it was pointing out the window. Even on her mother's cheap phone Jacey could see that the ground was light and shimmery and everything outside – all the cars in the parking lot anyway – looked clean and pretty.

"That's nice, Mom."

"What's the weather like over there, honey?"

"Not great," Jacey said. "Gets dark really early and rains an awful lot. Snow would be nice, but it doesn't happen here very often."

"OK," her mother said. "I won't keep you. I'm glad you're getting out and socialising with other people. It's important, Jacey, you know?"

"I know."

"Staying busy and not spending too much time on your own, it's really …"

"I know, Mom." Jacey wondered if her mother was fooled by the plastered-on smile. "And you don't have to worry about me, I'm OK."

"Well, that's not the way Rob made it sound when I talked to him."

Jacey needed to keep up the happy act, although her heart was pounding and her stomach churned. How *dare* her mother call Rob? How dare they talk about her behind her back?

"He made it seem like you were lonely, and struggling and …"

"And what?" Jacey snapped.

"Well, I don't want to say."

"Tell me, Mom, please."

Here it came. Of course. The whoosh of the air, the difficulty breathing.

"He said you were seeing a counsellor."

Jacey felt fluid in her throat, struggled to swallow it back down without her mother seeing.

"Do you think that's a good idea, Jacey?"

She didn't answer. She couldn't speak.

"I mean, to be digging things up? While you're there on your own?"

She cleared her throat. "Digging, Mom?"

"Oh, you know. Like they do. Those … psychiatrists … things from the past, poking around in people's dirty …"

"There's no digging. Nothing to be scared of. Nothing bad, OK? No dirt."

Her mother looked unconvinced. "OK, honey. Whatever you say."

Somehow, Jacey managed to end the call on a friendly note, fake smile plastered on until the final goodbye. But she couldn't stop what had been building up inside her body, burning like a caustic poison, even though she'd managed to hide it.

As soon as she put the phone down, she rushed into the bathroom and threw up in the toilet. She kept her eyes closed until it was over, not daring to look at what she was spewing out, imagining blood and mud, something rotten and foul.

Chapter 33

Lipstick. Mascara. A little bit of an eyebrow tweeze.

She hoped Dr Andrews wouldn't notice that she'd made an effort. Or think that it was for his benefit; that she was a client who'd take the whole transference thing a little too far.

"I'm going to lunch with a friend when I'm finished here," she said, by way of an explanation, not that he needed one.

"Oh, it's good you've made some friends here."

"Well, one, really."

"One's a positive start."

She settled into the chair, greeted the tissue box with a silent "no thanks, not today."

On her way over, she'd spent most of the train journey fretting about how much she should tell him about the conversation with her mother. About her mom talking to Rob. About the hollowing and the bells, about the choking feeling, the taste of mud.

"Where would you like to begin today, Jacey?"

"I don't know."

"Last week we ended with you talking about your mother. A

memory that made you feel as if you'd done something bad when you were young, that you felt ashamed of. Do you remember?"

Jacey nodded.

"And would you like to say anything more about that?"

"OK," Jacey said, and she settled into her chair, slumping down slightly, trying to relax so she could speak freely and not get things mixed up in her head.

"I talked to Mom on the phone today. Well, Facetime. And she told me she was worried about me coming to see a therapist. All that poking around in the past, she said."

Dr John picked up his note pad.

"Any idea of what that meant?"

"No, but I'd never said anything to her about going to a therapist, and she told me it was Rob who told her. She's been talking to him behind my back."

"Oh?"

Dr Andrews wrote something down.

"Did your mother tell you that?"

"She didn't mention the behind my back bit, but that's what it was, obviously."

"And that bothers you?"

"Well, she's my mother, isn't she? She's supposed to talk to me, not Rob. She always did before, so what has changed?"

Jacey stopped talking. She had to be careful. She couldn't let this doctor think she was paranoid, not play into Rob's hands, like her mother was obviously doing.

"Remember you told me that everything is real?" she said. "Even if it's imaginary, or there's no physical reason for something?"

"Yes, I remember."

"Well, I think there's something weird about what they are doing. For real. I found letters, and it was like my mom and Rob were talking to each other before we even moved to England, and why would they do that?"

"I don't know. What do you think? Any ideas?"

"She was worried about me, and she said the same things in her letters, like, not wanting me to be alone, and not wanting me to have time to brood over things and …"

Suddenly Jacey felt the sting of tears in the back of her nose. She glanced at the tissue box. No, she wouldn't be needing them. They could fuck right off.

"She mentioned some trauma when I was young."

"Well, that's certainly interesting."

"But I think, it's like maybe she was making it up."

"Why would she do that?"

"I don't know, but there wasn't any trauma, other than my dad dying when I was pretty little, and lots of money problems and stress for my mother, but that's not a secret. Rob knows all about it."

"You don't seem to trust your mother completely."

Jacey had no answer.

"Is that a fair statement?"

"Well, it's unfair, considering everything my mother has done for me, all her sacrifices, but, I don't know. Those letters. Her acting like I was some kind of burden to Rob, that makes me feel …"

Dr John waited patiently. Jacey sniffed, wiped her nose, glanced at the tissues again.

"Makes me feel like there's something wrong with me. Like I've been sick, or however you want to put it, for a very long time."

* * *

"I went to a shrink before I came out as trans. In the wilds of Lincolnshire."

Rael was struggling to get his cigarette lit against the winds that were blowing up from the grey, heaving sea.

"Or bowels I should say, because the town I grew up in was such a shit-hole."

He turned his back to the sea, pulled up the hood of his sweatshirt to act as a windbreak, and Jacey stood in front of him, like a human shield. He took a big drag, stoking the flame. "Literally. Smelled of manure. Like rotting cow shit, and it covered the landscape, so the fucking potatoes could grow."

They started walking towards the pier, its multi-coloured lights twinkling bright against the grey sky and reflecting on the murky water. At the Old Steine, Rael put his arm around Jacey's shoulder protectively, and the smell of his cigarette smoke blowing straight into her nostrils didn't even bother her.

"So how do you like this guy? The shrink."

"He's OK," she said.

"I sense a 'but' here …"

"I'm not sure if I trust him."

"Have you told him about the house? The weird things you see?"

"That's what I mean. I don't dare, because, what if he thinks I'm really ill, like needing to be institutionalised?"

"You have to be suicidal or on the verge of murdering somebody before they send you to hospital. And even then, you'd have to fight for a bed."

When they passed the Royal Pavilion, Jacey remembered the day she saw Rob at the law practice. Even in her baggy parka, lined with fleece and stuffed with down, she shivered.

Rael must have felt her body shuddering. He pulled her closer and stopped talking. "Hey. You don't feel that way, do you?"

"Suicidal, you mean? No."

And she didn't. Whatever was happening, she was all right. Even her darkest thoughts – what did this all mean? The sounds? The trauma her mother was trying to warn Rob about? None of these things actually made her doubt her sanity, or want to take her life.

Rael sighed and they moved on, cutting through the Pavilion grounds, marvelling at the palace's architecture, the totally incongruous domes and turrets, so unlike anything she'd ever seen, or was likely to see outside India or Southeast Asia.

"Let's try a pub by the station," Rael said. "You OK with that?"

The pub was halfway up another steep hill. Inside it was dark, but not gloomy. The wood was highly polished, reflecting the glow from the fire that was burning in a corner opposite the bar. The seats that ran along the walls were upholstered in soft green velvet, looking comfy and inviting.

The bartender smiled as Jacey stepped inside and Rael fiddled with the door to get it shut properly.

"A pint of Five Points," Jacey said. "And a white wine for me."

The bartender held up a wine glass. "Small? Medium?"

Rael interjected from the doorway. "Make it a large, darling. She's had a rough day."

At first, standing at the bar, Jacey didn't notice the woman sitting at the table next to the fireplace. But when Rael approached her, the woman stood up, and Rael kissed her on both cheeks.

"Ms. Jacey, meet my friend Katherine."

Jacey had no choice but to join them, but the feeling of being deceived wouldn't leave her. Rael could have told her he was setting up a meeting with Katherine; she'd have been more than happy to agree. She was the one who'd wanted to make contact, wasn't she?

Katherine was thin – that's the first thing Jacey noticed. Despite her bright Australian smile and her thick mane of wavy blonde hair, Katherine looked like Jacey would have, if the post therapy depression had lasted months, and not a week. Katherine's hands were delicate and bony, and as she picked up her wine glass – white, definitely a small – they shook slightly.

But for all that, she was very pretty. And Jacey supposed that hollow-eyed look of being ill was appealing in some ways. Added to her vulnerability, would have made men want to take care of her, and women to mother her, and people like Rael to smother her with kindness.

Rael started them off, like the moderator of a debate. "Malin House … shall we begin there?"

Jacey nodded. "You can go first, Katherine. If you don't mind."

Katherine looked at Rael, as if for moral support.

"Well, we moved in at the end of the summer, and things started off pretty much straight away."

She looked at Rael again. He nodded, and turned to Jacey, smiling, as if to say, see? You're not alone, hon.

"I don't know what it was like for you, Jacey, but I heard things before I saw anything."

Jacey didn't respond. She wanted to listen, that was all.

"Rael said that you heard bells tinkling."

She nodded slightly. Katherine was still trembling, and she inched closer to the fire, drawn by its warmth.

"I heard a sort of groaning sound, and for a long time I just thought it was the boiler or something, until I asked Martin about it and he had a look and said everything was fine."

"Martin's very kind," Jacey said.

"Well, I wouldn't be so sure of that," Rael said. "His wife either. Isn't that what you said, Katherine? That they seemed to be involved in what was going on?"

"Yes," Katherine said. "I wish I'd known that at the start."

Jacey wanted to ask about how they were involved; she couldn't think of anything they'd said or done that was other than helpful. There was the time when Helen said she couldn't see the boy, but Jacey had just assumed that Helen was telling the truth, that she couldn't see anything from where she was standing.

"And then the smells," Rael prompted.

"Oh, yes … the smell of smoke … like a fire. And I couldn't find a source for it. And my husband couldn't find anything, either, and he thought I was either imagining it or making it up or …"

"Delusional," Rael said. "That's what he thought, right, Katherine?"

"Yes," Katherine said.

"And he made you go to that shrink."

"Yes."

Jacey's heart pounded. Their stories were so similar, it was uncanny.

"And then I started to see things," Katherine said.

Jacey couldn't help herself. "What kind of things?"

Katherine looked at Rael again. Why was she so afraid of talking? Why did she need so much support? Was she still so vulnerable?

"Tell her about the child, Katherine."

Jacey's heart thumped. Child? Was this the boy, had Katherine seem him, too?

"It was a little girl. First I saw her in town, on the high street. She was dressed in old-fashioned clothes – like Victorian or something – and she was wandering down the street with a doll, one of those creepy ones with painted faces made of porcelain. But I thought, maybe there was a dress-up day at one of the local schools. They love that kind of thing here."

She stopped talking. Pulled her heavy cardigan around her shoulders.

"And then you saw her in the house, didn't you," Rael said, excitedly. "On the stairs."

Katherine nodded. Her face was expressionless. She didn't seem frightened at all, just weary of the whole thing.

"It's not the worst thing, is it, Katherine?"

Katherine shuddered, shaking her head, as if she was reluctant to talk about it, scared to re-live the horrible memory. She hunched over slightly, her blonde curls falling limply across her pale face.

"The fire," Rael whispered.

Katherine nodded. "The little girl was in the kitchen," she said. "I saw her plain as the nose on my face, and then there was a fire."

She took a sip of her drink and stared into the glass as she continued. "And I know the little girl started it, because she was laughing when she did it, giggling the way young children do, only nobody believed me."

"I did," Rael said.

"Nobody else, though. Not the psychiatrist, or my husband, or those women I met, what are their names?"

"Madlyn and Muriel."

"And so I went to a psychiatric hospital, and anything I said, about the girl, about the fires she was starting, just made them think I was crazier than ever."

"You couldn't win, could you, hon?"

Katherine shook her head, almost imperceptibly, as if it caused her physical pain to move her neck. She also glanced again at Rael, who nodded back at her, giving her his approval. It was like he was her coach, and he was happy with her performance.

"You're very brave," Jacey said.

"Thanks." Katherine took a sip of her wine.

"So, do you have any idea who the little girl was?" Jacey asked.

"I'm sorry?"

"Or what she was?"

"Oh, I don't … I'm not sure …"

Rael cleared his throat. "Somebody from the past, isn't that what you said, Katherine?"

"Oh, yes." Katherine nodded.

Rael continued. "Somebody who died in a fire in the outback. One that she started. Or somebody burned at the stake for being a witch, you know, way before your family emigrated to Oz."

Katherine nodded again.

"Yes, that's what I thought. But … I can't be sure, I mean, how could I?"

"The girl was real, that was the main thing." Rael drained his pint. "And dangerous to you, wasn't she, dear?"

Katherine lifted her glass to her mouth with a frail, trembling hand. "That's what it felt like," she said. She whispered the words, as if the hollowing had her by the throat.

"Like she wanted me dead."

Chapter 34

Jacey trudged towards Malin House.

The pavement was slick with wet, fallen leaves, and she watched her feet as she took each step, careful not to slip. Head down, she lumbered forward, humped over, like an old woman with a stooped back. She was tired, and scared of being out after dark, of the forces that could overcome her, now that she was sure they were real.

At least there were plenty of people around, enjoying the last of the afternoon's light, walking through the tunnel on their way home after a day out hiking on the downs. She passed them without saying hello, without even looking up, in case someone recognised her. She didn't want to speak to anyone in Lewes; she didn't want to be known.

As she climbed up the driveway, she saw that the lights were on. Rob was home for a change, waiting for her. Music was playing in the drawing room; one of his Spotify playlists of bands only he and three other people in the world had ever heard of. This one sounded like German trance metal – clanking noises and dissonant thuds. It gave her a headache, even three rooms away.

"I'm home," she shouted as loudly as she could.

It was quieter in the kitchen, her own space. The oven was cold and there were no dirty dishes in the sink so Rob had obviously waited until she got home before deciding what to do for dinner.

She put the kettle on, checked the cookie jar. Or biscuit tin, as Rob insisted it was called. There was a packet of chocolate covered shortbreads inside it. Suddenly she was starving. She put two teabags in the pot and added the water. Rob said it made all the difference, making the tea in the pot, but it tasted the same to her. Still, she humoured him, adding the milk and the sugar, taking out one of the cookies and putting it on a plate for him.

"Honey?"

She brought him the tea, and he glanced up from his books long enough to seem appreciative. Jacey tried not to look at the stack of signed books on the coffee table. She tried not to think about pulling the library apart, finding the letters, all the bad things that happened that terrible night.

"Hope your therapy went OK."

"Helpful, I think."

He looked down again. "And afterwards? The pub?"

Something cut into Jacey when he said those words. His sneering assumption was like a weapon, designed to hurt her, but she wouldn't engage with his passive aggression, or even ask how he knew where she'd gone. "Fine," she said. "Really nice to get out and see people."

"Good," Rob said. He glanced at the stack of books. Did he know that she'd seen them? That she'd read the inscriptions?

"I can put in pizzas for dinner," Jacey said.

"Yeah. Great."

Jacey dug the pizzas out of the freezer, slid them into the hot oven;

no burning of fingers, no dropping of food, no accidentally setting the kitchen on fire.

And there was Rob's laptop on the kitchen table, open. How had she missed it while making the tea?

He hadn't signed out. He hadn't even closed the tab that was open: his email inbox.

All his messages, for anyone to read.

He wants me to see this, she thought. Whatever is on that screen, he wants me to know.

A quick glance told her that most of the names in Rob's inbox were women's, none she recognised, other than from the inscriptions in his book. And Bex was there, too. Dozens of messages. Every day, it seemed there was some kind of communication, but Bex's name wasn't the one that stood out the most, that reached out and grabbed Jacey's attention and caused her heart to beat with fear and dread.

Her mother. Doreen Jeffers. Hotmail.com.

So she'd been sending Rob emails, too, not just letters. Covering all the bases, not wasting any time.

Jacey clicked on the latest message.

I trusted you, Rob, when you married my daughter. I believed your promises to do the right thing and stand by her. That's why I told you about our past – her past – so you'd make sure nothing ever came to light or caused her any pain.

Rob was in the middle of his response.

Jacey's been to the psychiatrist again. She seems worse. Very down and lethargic. Maybe it's just the long dark days, but she's not well, Doreen. Not well at all. I'm not sure how much longer I can …

Jacey adjusted the screen – closed the message and kept the lid open as it had been when she walked into the kitchen. A bottle of cheap Merlot was still on the counter from last week. She poured herself a glass, then closed the door from the den into the hallway. That door was squeaky; she'd hear Rob if he opened it, she'd have time to close whatever message she was reading and back away from the table, so he wouldn't know what she'd done.

Strange how calm she felt. As if the hollowing had come and cleared her of any emotions. She crept back into the kitchen, stood by the table, waited. She took another drink, put down the glass. Finally, she tapped a key on the laptop to bring the screen back to life.

So many messages, flickering in front of her eyes. Where should she start? How much time did she have? She glanced at the door to the den; still closed. She listened for the sound of Rob's feet. She stood still, afraid to breathe. Nothing but silence.

Finally, she scrolled onto the second page, and focused on the screen.

There was a series of messages from the family law practice flashing for her attention, but she opened another one from her mother, sent one week ago.

When you first wanted to take her to England, I didn't say anything, and I wish to God I had. You know the truth now, Rob. Surely that changes everything? Surely that will make you be more careful of her, instead of so reckless and stupid.

Jacey read the words again, unaware of the other sounds around her, not hearing the footsteps on the tile floor, or the sudden opening of the squeaky door. Before she could react, the fire alarm shrieked out a warning, and smoke billowed out from the belly of the stove.

Jacey closed the message, stood away from the laptop. Rob raced into the room, coughing.

"Christ, Jacey. What the hell have you done?"

Rob opened the oven door and more smoke poured into the room. He picked up a wet towel from beside the sink and waved it in the air so he could see enough to open the window over the sink.

When the air cleared he noticed his computer. Half closed. Turned at an angle.

"Jesus."

He closed the lid, picked up the laptop, stormed through the den and into the hallway.

Jacey heard the door to the drawing room slam shut.

He knows that I know, she thought. About him and my mother ganging up on me behind my back. About the two of them, keeping secrets.

She sat down, dizzy, wishing she hadn't drunk the glass of wine on an empty stomach.

What did it matter, Rob knowing that she'd looked at his computer? What did anything matter, other than the fact that something terrible must have happened to her when she was a child, and that Rob knew what it was. What were the words her mother used?

You know the truth.

And what did she mean when she called Rob reckless and stupid? Had he made some kind of confession to her mom about having an affair? He must have; how else would she have known?

Jacey took a deep breath and sat down. The air had cleared, but her head was still fuzzy from the wine, and she felt the air around her move and stir. She heard bells, too, tinkling gently. She wanted to scream at them to shut the fuck up, but they weren't human. They weren't listening to her. They were just things, sensations, lifeless, meaningless.

Gradually, the tinkling grew quieter, and the gentle hollowing stopped. When she dared go into the drawing room, Rob was slumped in a chair, his feet up on the coffee table, like he owned the place. The stack of books had toppled over and were spread out across the table. A few had fallen on the floor: they were lying open, face down, like naked murder victims, randomly sprawled out on the carpet.

"It's not what it looks like," he said, not bothering to look up.

"What?" she said.

"Those messages you were reading."

Two could play this stupid game. "Which ones?"

"The ones you read, Jacey. While you were spying on me. Acting like a goddam Nazi, like the fucking KGB."

"How do you even know which ones I read? There were so many, from so many women. I'd need a week to get through them all."

"I assume you looked at the ones from Bex."

She laughed: a thin, hollow sound. "I don't really care about her."

"Well then, that's just fine."

"I'm talking about my mother. The letters I found, hidden all over the house. The messages on your computer."

"Private messages, Jacey. Nothing there was addressed to you."

"She's *my* mother, Rob, not yours. How can you say that they weren't for me?"

"Because they weren't."

"They were *about* me."

"Not the same thing, is it?"

Rob looked at her triumphantly, like a boy who'd just came first in a classroom debate. He picked the books off the floor, put them back into a neat stack, made sure they were absolutely straight. "I've got some work due tomorrow," he said, yawning. "And I'm hungry, too, so I think I'll just make myself a sandwich and carry on with what I'm doing."

"You can't just fob me off."

When he looked at her, his expression – a cross between a smile and smirk – told her that yes, he could. He could do whatever the fuck he wanted and there was nothing she could say to stop him.

He shoved past her, went through the dining room and serving pantry to the kitchen. Jacey didn't want to follow him. She knew she should stay in the drawing room, keep calm and be still, wait until he came back, but she couldn't stop herself.

She raced into the kitchen. "You brought me here to get a divorce."

Rob didn't even look at her. His head was in the fridge, rooting out mustard and mayonnaise for his sandwich.

"You took me to a place where you knew I'd be vulnerable. Where I'd have no support, and you let me think I was going crazy so you'd have an excuse to get rid of me."

Rob closed the fridge door. "I've tried to help you, Jacey." His voice was calm, smooth, patronising. "I sent you to a psychiatrist."

"You wanted me to be put away. Like Katherine's husband."

"Who's Katherine?"

"Don't tell me you don't know."

"Another one of your imaginary friends?"

She wouldn't rise to it. His facial expression, the way he pushed his hair back out of his eyes, so innocent, the look of a smug teacher who would always know better than her, no matter how much she learned.

"Malin House was your big chance, wasn't it?" she said. "Make me think I was going mad. All you had to do was prime the pump, convince me it was haunted, make out that you heard some terrifying noises."

He found a knife for the bread, cut two thick slices. "That was a joke, Jacey. You knew that was a joke, from the very beginning."

"Making me afraid. Like you did with Trudy."

"What? Why the hell are you bringing her up?"

Now he was acting like the injured party. Scoffing at her big revelation.

"I know about the way you gaslit her. Trying to make her scared and dependent on you."

"This is bullshit, Jacey." He put down the knife, turned to her. "Who told you that?"

"And I know about you going to London. I know about you lying to me and your department. Cancelling classes and all you're doing is going up to meet Bex or somebody else. Some woman, some …"

She couldn't speak anymore. The hollowing had her by the throat, cutting off her air, making her cough and choke so that she had to sit at the table, lay her head down.

"You want to know what *I* know, Jacey? You want to know the actual truth?"

Rob crept across the kitchen. He stood beside her, bending over with his arm around her shoulder, her neck, mouth up to her ear, holding her still so she wouldn't have been able to move, even if the hollowing hadn't already attacked her.

"I know your mom thinks you're crazy."

Jacey tried to get up, fight through the hollowing, but Rob was pinning her down.

"Not me, not your long-suffering husband – but your *mother*."

She felt his hot breath in her ear.

"She thinks you're deluded, Jace."

She heard his whispered words as she struggled to breathe, to speak.

"Your own fucking mother thinks you're insane."

Chapter 35

The hollowing had gone inside her again, twisting her guts, cutting her breath short, spewing liquid into the back of the throat.

Only she knew better this time. A few coughs in the sink and she'd be fine. Empty. A void.

But not dying. Not drowning for real.

She found the carry-on bag from her flight from Chicago. It still had the flight tags on it. She ripped them off, threw them into the wastebasket. She filled the it with as many clothes as she could, pulled on her fake Uggs and grabbed a scarf from a hook in the closet.

Such a long time ago, that flight. So much excitement on the day. Landing at dawn, seeing the green fields of Sussex spread out below them as they passed over Gatwick Airport, and then the excitement of London.

And finally, the thrill of arriving at Malin House, their amazing home.

In the bathroom, she rinsed the sink, and put her toothbrush and few more things into the bag. She looked in the bedside cabinet on Rob's side. There was a spare credit card, somewhere, for emergencies only, that he kept, though it had both their names on it.

Christ, she thought, rummaging through his stuff, the bits of cable and phone chargers, a tube of hydrocortisone for when his eczema flared up – she really was living the life of a captive Victorian wife. The only way to finance her future had been hidden from her, stuck between the pages of her husband's address book.

She grabbed her charger that was still plugged into the wall and headed back downstairs. She crept into the kitchen. His laptop was gone. Hers was still there. She put it in her shoulder bag, ready to leave, but there was Rob, waiting in the hallway, standing between her and the front door, as if he'd known what she was planning to do.

"Look, what your mother told me. I shouldn't have put it like that. She's worried about you, that's all."

"Too bad. I don't care."

"I need to know where you're going, Jace. It's really important."

"Is it?"

"You shouldn't be going anywhere on your own. And besides, it's getting late."

"I'm not scared of the dark."

Rob shook his head. "You don't understand."

She stood still with her hand on the doorknob, looked at the chandelier, up at the dark landing that had brought on so much terror. Rob was wrong. She may not have understood everything, not completely. But she knew the most important thing: whatever was happening, whether it was real or delusional, her husband was not on her side.

"I'll text you," she said.

He made a move for the door. "Jace, you can't."

She flung the door open, stumbled down the veranda steps and soon she was racing across the lawn, slipping on the wet grass, wishing she'd put on her walking boots, something with more grip.

On the dark driveway, something was approaching – someone – but that didn't stop her. Martin and Helen, laden with grocery bags, were trudging up the driveway on their way back from the supermarket.

Jacey managed a smile, a quick wave, but she didn't slow down. Had they been given a signal by Rob, sent by him to block her path? Was this some massive conspiracy, like Rael and Katherine suggested; were Martin and Helen Rob's secret minions? As she rushed past, they turned to look at her, and she heard a voice behind them, shouting.

"Jacey!"

Rob's voice, but she wasn't going to stop for him. And then Helen's too, but she couldn't make out the words, and soon the sounds faded into silence, left behind at the top of the hill.

When she reached the bottom, she slowed down to catch her breath.

Rob would have stopped and chatted to Martin and Helen, made out like he was taking a stroll or something. He wouldn't even mention the fact that his wife had just flown past them. He'd act like everything was normal. Gaslight them, as well as her.

By the time she made it through the tunnel and across the park, there was no sign of Rob. She rushed to the station, and jostled through the crowds of weary commuters who were on their way home from work or school. She fumbled with the ticket machine, panicking in case Rob caught up with her, caused a scene, dragged her back to Malin House with him.

"Can I help you?"

A member of the platform crew – a woman with bright red hair – stood beside her.

"When's the next train to London?" Jacey asked. "I need to get there tonight. As soon as possible."

"If you're in a hurry, go to Brighton and change there. It's a faster service."

"Thank you so much," Jacey gushed.

Jacey looked behind her – there was no one else on the platform, or on the stairs. Rob hadn't followed her. Jacey hopped onto the waiting train and set her bag down on a seat opposite an elderly woman who was wearing a mask and clutching a large plastic shopping bag against her body like a shield. Jacey hoisted the bag onto the overhead rack, and sat down with a deep sigh, ready to settle in and think of what to do next.

And then, outside the window, she saw him.

The boy.

He was standing beside a cast-iron pillar, face turned away, kicking his ball against the brick side of the passenger lounge. His skin looked paler than ever; almost translucent, and his legs seemed too thin to be able to kick with any force.

How had she missed him, when he was right beside the train?

The woman across from her was rummaging in her shopping bag. She'd be able to see the boy, too, if she looked out quickly. He was right next to them; there was no way anyone could miss him.

"I don't believe it," Jacey said,

The woman looked up, a pinched expression on her face, clearly annoyed at the intrusion.

Jacey shook her head. "Do you see that?"

The woman looked out just as the red-headed conductor blew her whistle.

"Wha'?" the woman grunted.

"That boy with the ball. The way he was dressed?"

"Don't know what you mean," the woman said. She looked

suspicious of Jacey. Who was this rude American woman, asking such strange questions?

"I mean a little kid, in this terrible weather, out without a coat, and wearing shorts."

"Oh," the woman said, but the train was moving now, and the platform was left behind.

"Can't say I saw anything unusual."

"But you saw a boy? Three or four years old?"

The woman looked confused. She shook her head, loosened her grip on her bag and rummaged inside it until she found a bottle of water and a tatty-looking paperback.

So had the woman seen him, or not? Jacey wanted to grab the old lady's bottle, beat her over the head with it until she came up with an answer. As if she could read Jacey's mind, the woman flipped through the pages of her book until she found her place, and then put it up to her face, like she was terrified of what Jacey might do next.

By the time the train pulled into Brighton, Jacey knew she couldn't travel any further. London, and any plans for the future, would have to wait until tomorrow.

There was a hotel across the road, part of a budget chain. The room she booked was basic, bland, and she was happy to be alone, to be able to lock and bolt her door and have some peace. The charge had gone on her phone – and she had no desire to plug it in again.

She took a shower and settled into bed. Soon, the white noise hum of the heating system was lulling her to sleep, and her thoughts were floating in the hazy space between wakefulness and sleep.

The little boy. A manifestation of some ancestral crime or guilt, like Katherine's girl, something that living in Malin House seemed to bring to the fore. She thought about meeting Katherine in the pub, how Rael coaxed her along, feeding her prompts and clues as to what she was supposed to say. It seemed strange, looking back.

So did everything else. Two weird sisters pushing a family name on her, claiming it was the source of all her problems. Her husband trying to frighten her about Malin House on the day they first arrived. Bex pretending to be a friend, but committing the ultimate betrayal.

Her own mother colluding with Rob, spreading stories designed to undermine her daughter – *trauma, tragedy*. For what reason, Jacey wondered. To keep her under control, but why?

Seagulls squawked and fought over a yellow and orange pool of what looked suspiciously like vomit that had only been partly washed away by the previous night's heavy rains.

She had time for a cup of coffee before the bus left for London. Bus, not train. She'd never taken a bus anywhere; Rob wouldn't think to look there, if he cared enough to check up on her. She started up her phone, which had charged overnight. There were messages waiting from Rob, from Rael, plus an email from her mother. She deleted them all without bothering to look.

The only number she contacted was David Andrews', cancelling their appointment, and telling the receptionist she was moving away. Minutes later, he called her back, concerned.

"I've left Rob," she said. "My husband."

Dr Andrews said nothing, but she sensed shock and disapproval in his prolonged silence.

"Right." He dragged the word out, as if he was gathering his thoughts, trying to figure out how to respond.

"So, I won't be back in the area for a while."

She tried to sound confident, matter of fact. People move on, don't they? No big deal.

"Sounds like you're at the seafront," he said.

"I'm at the pier. I wanted to wave goodbye to the seagulls. I know you're not supposed to like them if you live in Brighton, but I think they're cute."

She ordered another cup of coffee from the café and went outside. It was cold, but there were plenty of people on the terrace tables, as if they were grateful for the weak sunlight that had pushed through the grey clouds.

She found a spot that faced the entrance to the pier, giving her advance notice in case Rob had put some kind of tail on her. She stashed her bag under her chair and stirred sugar into her coffee. A few minutes later she saw a man striding up to the terrace – not Rob, though. It was Dr Andrews, red faced and puffing from running all the way.

"Hey, Jacey."

He held out his hand, smiling casually, as if he tracked down his clients all the time.

"Are you sure this is all right?" Jacey said.

"What do you mean?"

"Like, is it professional, you turning up outside your office?"

There was an awkward silence, broken by a hassled mother shouting at her two crying twins who were trying to climb out of their stroller.

"You're technically not my client anymore, so I think it's acceptable."

Jacey shrugged; she knew it wasn't, but she had to keep cool.

He pulled up a chair and sat down beside her. "And I found your case so fascinating, I felt we should try to wrap things up before you leave, aim for a bit of closure."

That didn't make sense, Jacey thought. Why would it matter to him? It was her therapy; she had the right to stop whenever she wanted.

"Living in that house, being on your own. The sounds and the things you saw."

He acted like this was another one of his consultations. She expected him to whip out the delft ceramic tissue holder and put it on the table, just in case.

"I need to leave," she said, "or I'm going to miss my train."

"But seeing that child, the way you did. It must mean *something*, Jacey."

There was no hollowing, there were no strange sounds, but a knot was forming in Jacey's stomach, and her throat was starting to tighten.

"No," she said. "It doesn't."

Her breath quickened. She took a sip of her coffee. The taste was like runny mud, but she forced it down, fought the urge to throw up. She couldn't start choking. Not in front of him. Not when she was so close to getting away from everything, not when he might still have some power over her, no matter what he said.

"You all right, Jacey?"

She pushed her chair back slightly, flexed her knees, felt for her bag, ready to jump up and run. "Fine."

"It's just. You seem anxious."

She looked at him, trying to void her face of any expression, conceal her panic and fear.

"Worried about the time. I need to get going."

"And what are you planning to do, Jacey?"

Something in his voice had changed. He didn't sound as friendly. He sounded official, an interrogator. She glanced up, looked at the pier entrance, half expecting Rob and a posse of paramedics to be rushing towards her, with handcuffs or a straitjacket, and a big syringe full of tranquilisers to jab in her arm.

"I haven't made up my mind," she sighed, trying to sound relaxed, a woman with so many options she just didn't know which one to choose.

"I'll wish you well then," Dr Andrews said.

A wind blew up off the sea. Jacey took a deep breath, as if the fresh air could clear her lungs and wash away the taste of dirt and mud that the coffee had left behind, as if it could give her strength to get through the rest of the day. She looked at the pier entrance again, and then the other way, out to the sea end, the Ferris wheel and the tilt-a-whirl, the dodgems and arcades. She listened to the gleeful shrieking of children, the seagulls' angry cries.

Dr Andrews stood up, stretched out his hand. "You're very vulnerable at the moment, you know that, don't you?"

"I'm OK. Like I said."

She should have told this man to fuck himself. She should have left as soon as he turned up.

"But that little boy?" he asked.

Her heart sank. Not *him* again. Why had she ever mentioned that stupid kid?

And then she realised the horrible truth: she hadn't. Not to Dr Andrews at least, she'd never said a word.

She pushed her chair back further. She took a final sip of the horrible coffee, draining the mug. Casually, as if it tasted normal, as if she wasn't in such a hurry after all, as if she wasn't in the least bit scared.

Dr Andrews opened his coat, reached into the top pocket and pulled out a small manila envelope, folded in two. He set the contents on the table in front of her. A piece of paper; a printed photograph.

The Perfect Couple

What kind of trick was this?

"I was just wondering," Dr Andrews said.

He unfolded the paper slowly, carefully holding it open.

"Did your little boy look anything like this?"

Chapter 36

The bus pulled out of the station and, as it passed the pier, Jacey slumped in her seat. They'd be looking for her by now – Rob, Dr Andrews, the two weird sisters. She imagined them all in a pack, racing up and down the seafront, shouting her name, and behind them, the boy, kicking that dirty ball.

But the crowds were sparse – it was early December, after all – and she didn't see anyone she recognised. Even Dr Andrews had disappeared. As soon as he'd unfolded the picture, she picked up her bag and ran. She crossed the road outside the pier entrance, and slipped into one of Brighton's old shopping lanes. She made it to the coach station just as a bus to London was ready to leave. She showed her ticket, jumped on, and soon they were off.

She checked her phone. There were dozens of messages. From Rob, Rael, her mother, even Bex. Had she ever been this popular before? She took out her SIM card; she'd get another phone later on, after the fuss of her leaving had died down.

The bus hit the motorway, and the sound of the engine lulled her to sleep. When the bus stopped at Gatwick Airport to pick up more passengers she woke up with a start. Good, she thought. She needed to stay awake. She needed to make plans. She had nowhere to go, no place to stay, no one to trust.

The picture Dr Andrews showed her. No matter how he'd got it, no matter who had given it to him, a quick glance told her it was the boy, or someone dressed exactly the same.. It was blurry, a cracked old-fashioned photograph, with faded colours. But when was it taken? Recently? Had it been staged and photoshopped and doctored to look old?

Something inside her told her that it wasn't. Something told her that what she had seen – that boy – was what Rael had said.

A ghost. An apparition. Connected in some way to Malin House.

She closed her eyes and tried to remember. Did the boy ever look at her? Did he act like he knew her from somewhere? No. He was either in the distance, or facing away from her like he'd been at the train station in Lewes.

But the clothes he wore were light, for summer. A red and green T-shirt, and it was always the same. His shorts and shoes were always the same, too.

Exactly like the picture.

It had started to rain again, water streaming down the windows of the bus, smearing everything outside into a grey blur. The bus was full after picking up passengers at the airport and she'd had to move her bag so a man could sit next to her. She held it tight against her lap, an extra layer of protection.

When the bus pulled into Victoria Coach station, the feeling of freedom she'd been expecting didn't materialise. She was far away from Malin House now, so why did she feel more trapped than ever. Maybe she needed to travel further than just London; try somewhere more remote, where no one would ever find her, and nobody had ever heard of Malin House or known anyone who'd been haunted there.

She looked into her backpack for the credit card, and behind it in her wallet was the card from the woman at the Cambridgeshire pub where Rael had taken her for a drink of water. It said 'Meals and Rooms'.

If you need help, you can call me, the woman had said. *We're always here.*

There was a number. A name.

Sally.

The pub was empty. The thin grey dog was curled up in front of the fireplace, and Sally was arranging some coloured Christmas lights over the mantel piece, trying to untangle the wires, kicking at the knotted clump of cable at her feet.

The dog looked up as Jacey came into the room and let out a little bark.

"We're not open 'til this afternoon, love," the woman said.

"I was actually looking for a place to stay?" Jacey said.

"We've got a few rooms, but they're not en suite or nothing. You'd have to go down the corridor to use the bathroom. Not that you'd be sharing it with anybody. It not being the height of the tourist season right now."

She laughed and leaned over to pet the dog.

"In't that right, Stanley?"

Stanley licked her hand. "Bit slow at the moment, eh, darling?"

Stanley seemed to sigh resignedly, agreeing with her, and he rested his head back down. The woman carried on petting him, muttering, *good doggy, good Stanley, who's a good boy, eh?*

The woman left the fire and motioned Jacey to the bar. She reached into a cupboard and took out an old black leather notebook.

"It's £40 a night, if you're interested."

"I am," Jacey said.

She put the notebook on the bar and looked up. "Oh, it's you," Sally said, smiling.

"Yeah," Jacey said. She held her hand out in a half wave.

"It's good to see you." Jacey could feel the sincerity in her voice, the warmth. "I was so worried about you that day. I should have insisted on giving you a lift to the station."

"It's OK," Jacey said. "We were fine; it's not that far."

"And where's your lovely friend? The black-haired boy."

"I'm on my own, I'm afraid. And his hair's blue at the moment."

"Well don't you worry, we'll get you set up in a nice cosy room, how's that?"

"That's great."

"How many nights are you staying?"

Jacey didn't know what to say. She hadn't thought any further than making her escape.

Sally put the book down, patted Jacey's hands that were resting on the bar.

"Never mind, love," she said. "You stay as long as you like. We'll take it day by day, how's that?"

Chapter 37

The room overlooked a small car park, the garages of the houses next door and, behind the pub, a fenced off area that led to one of the narrow ditches that criss-crossed the landscape. Bare trees grew on one side of the ditch, and on the other there was a scraggly fringe of trees and shrubs.

She thought about what Muriel had told her about the Kennets. Those children they supposedly killed. "Drowned in the fens," she said.

Is that what these shallow canals were called? Fens?

Despite thinking of Muriel, and drownings, Jacey slept well the first night. No nightmares or strange noises waking her up. There was a different kind of quiet here; no hum of life in the building, no sense of being on the threshold of a busy world. It reminded her of being back in Minnesota – the farm, the village – closed off from everywhere, too far from other towns to register any alternate energy or experience.

As soon as she woke up, she went to the bathroom and saw the dog, Stanley, outside her door, as if he had been waiting all night. He padded after her as she crept down the hallway, sat patiently outside the bathroom door while she peed and washed her hands and face.

He followed her back to her room again, and squeezed in through the door as soon as she opened it.

"Hey, boy," she said, as he went to the window and curled up beneath it. It was nice to have a companion, especially one as calm and silent as Stanley.

The clock on the TV set said it was almost nine, and even without knowing the time, she could make out the breakfast smells of freshly brewed coffee and smoky bacon being fried.

She got dressed, armed with a notebook and a pen, something to occupy her while she waited for breakfast, and Stanley obediently followed her down the stairs. When he saw Sally, he sprang after her joyfully.

"He's been keeping me company this morning," Jacey said.

"I wondered where he'd run off to." Sally smiled. "Shoulda known. Stanley definitely has an eye for a pretty girl, if you don't mind my saying."

"I'm honoured," Jacey laughed. "Stanley's done so much for my self-esteem."

"As if you needed it," Sally said.

There was a place setting at a table near the fireplace, so Jacey sat there. Across the bar, another table was taken by an elderly man who was drinking tea and reading a newspaper.

He put his paper down and watched her for a moment.

"Hi," Jacey said. She wasn't sure what the Rob protocol was on talking to old men in pub dining rooms, but it didn't hurt to be friendly, did it? The old man wasn't likely to judge her, think her un-cool, too much of an American tourist.

"I suppose you're looking for the airbase, or summat," the man said.

"Well, actually—"

"Too late," the man said. "The Yanks closed it down thirty years ago, and the RAF pulled up sticks and moved everything up to Coningsby. There's the museum at Duxford, you might like to take a look at that."

"I was just travelling, actually. Kind of aimlessly, I guess."

"Well, you must have taken a wrong turn somewhere to end up here. You reckon, Sally?"

Sally came to Jacey's table with an individual pot of coffee, and a tiny pitcher of milk. "I reckon it's none of our business, Arthur."

"Sorry about him," Sally whispered. "He's like Stanley. Gets excited when new people arrive."

Jacey ate her breakfast, notebook at her side, writing down everything she saw in the pub. The design on the curtains – old-fashioned rural scene with horses and carts, and farmers on a hay wagon and women bringing them pitchers of milk on a tray – had faded into near-invisibility, and the low beamed ceilings were still nicotine stained from the days when people would have been heavy smokers and could smoke inside.

"God, you're not from some travel website, are you," Sally gasped, when she noticed Jacey looking. "We could use a design update, I know."

"No, this place is wonderful," Jacey said. "Just trying to write it all down so I can imagine it later on, when I go home."

When Sally left, Stanley stayed behind, watching her. Jacey bent over to pet his face, and when she sat back up she saw that Arthur had moved a few tables closer.

"So if it ain't the Air Force you're after, then what is it?"

"Nothing," she laughed. "Just hopped on a bus at Cambridge. Wanted to see where the road would take me."

"Bollocks," Arthur said. "I've known a few Yanks. They don't do nothing by accident. Least of all, start wandering around the fens."

"OK, then," Jacey said. She put down her pen, pushed the notebook aside, and Arthur shuffled his seat closer to her table, leaning over conspiratorially.

"What *is* a fen?"

"What's the fens, you mean?"

Arthur raised his arm and waved it in a circle. "It's all the fens around here. Cambridgeshire, Norfolk, Lincolnshire. All the flatlands and the ditches and dykes that take the water out. Miles and miles, used to be just marshes, and you couldn't farm on it, but now it's all the fens."

Arthur looked pleased with himself. He glanced at the bar, as if he was hoping that Sally had heard his answer.

"Thanks," Jacey said. "I'm glad I asked."

Arthur cleared his throat, sat up straight. "Anything else you want to know?"

Jacey thought for a minute. Arthur would be the right person to ask about the history of this place.

"Yes," she said.

"Fire away, young lady."

"Have you heard of a family called the Kennets?"

Arthur breathed in sharply. Almost a gasp. Underneath the table, Stanley stirred in his sleep.

Sally had come back in from the kitchen. "None of them left around here, I'm afraid." Her voice had lost its friendliness. There was a sharp edge to her words. "Are there, Arthur?"

"And thank God for that," Arthur muttered.

Sally wiped the bar, her eyes glued to Arthur, who looked up at her with an expression of defiance.

"Trouble," Arthur said. "All of them."

"I'm sure she's not interested in the details," Sally said. She managed to get her voice back to that jovial, hospitable place. "You don't want to be boring my guests half to death, now do you?"

Jacey looked at Sally and shrugged, showing her that she wasn't that interested anyway. She picked up her pen and notebook, as if she wanted to get away, as if she had no interest in what Arthur had to tell her, and that she was only hanging back to avoid seeming rude.

But Arthur wanted to speak.

"The girls was trouble, anyway," he said. "They was the ones that brought it in the first place. The boys, well … weren't their fault what happened, was it?"

She looked at Arthur. Her heart was pounding. "What do you mean?"

"They was all killed."

She could feel the air move, and Arthur's voice grow softer, more distant.

"Murdered. The boys."

Jacey gasped. This was exactly what Muriel had said.

"Like, recently?" Jacey said, carefully. It was hard to hear with the disruption of sound; even harder to speak. "Like, a school shooting or something?"

The old man laughed, and his broken teeth look like jagged pieces of milk glass, the kind used in antique lampshades.

"They was picked off. One by one. Over the years. The decades. Centuries, really."

Sally coughed, a sign for the old man to stop talking.

Then she smiled at Jacey. "Don't pay him any mind," she said. "It's so quiet around here that people make up all sorts of things. You know, like all those conspiracy nutters back in your part of the world. If you're bored and ignorant, and you never travel more than twenty miles beyond the town you was born in, you'll believe anything anybody tells you, isn't that right, Stanley?"

Stanley kept his head down low and growled.

"I don't mean Arthur," she said. "He's just telling the stories."

"The wars got most of them," Arthur said, undeterred by Sally's dismissiveness. "Fighting Cromwell's army in Lincoln and Newark, then that Napoleon fellow over in France. The First World War was the worst, all the Kennets in the village lost, more than lads from other families."

He folded his newspaper and put it in the side pocket of his jacket. He stood up, pushed his chair in, tidied the area where he'd been sitting.

"But they're all finished now. The last Kennet girl left during the Second War, and good riddance to them all."

Jacey's stomach churned. At her feet, Stanley growled, and then he stood up, next to her, gently rubbing his head against her legs.

Could Stanley feel it, too? She thought of that little dog in Chicago, who jumped into the water. She'd felt the hollowing then, like a pull of the tide towards the swirling river, as if that had been the cause of the poor creature's death.

"What was that girl's name," Arthur asked the barmaid. "The last Kennet?"

"Nobody can remember," Sally said, and she looked at Jacey, not Arthur. "And it's best that you forget, too."

Sally picked up Arthur's tea things a few minutes after he left.

"You've made two new friends, now," Sally said. "He'll be back tomorrow, you can bet on it, and this young man …" She pointed at Stanley "… won't leave you alone."

"That's OK," Jacey said. "Arthur was so dear. Not as cute as Stanley, of course, but—"

"So…" Sally paused for a moment, a beat. "The Kennets." Her voice was still friendly. Obviously she didn't associate an American woman with a story about witches or whatever the Kennets were. "If you don't mind my asking, how do you know about them?"

"Somebody told me," Jacey said. "Well, the legends surrounding the name, anyway. I mentioned that my grandmother had come from Stanton and—"

"Your grandmother?"

Suddenly, Jacey wasn't sure if she wanted to say anything about Nana Ivy. Arthur's story frightened her. But Sally was waiting to hear it; she couldn't clam up now.

"My grandfather was an American airman, and my grandmother went back to the States with him."

Sally's fixed smile wasn't quite hiding the shock on her face. Arthur said the last Kennet woman had left during the war. The weird coincidence must be freaking Sally out.

"But don't worry," Jacey said. "My Nana wasn't a Kennet."

Sally let out a laugh. "Oh, I didn't think she was."

"Her name was Smith," Jacey said. "Ivy Smith."

"Well that's all right, then."

Underneath the table, Stanley shifted and groaned, trying to get comfortable with his face on Jacey's feet. Sally leaned over and gave his head a gentle rub. "Listen, do you fancy taking Stanley for a walk?"

At the word 'walk', Stanley's ears perked up and he let out a little bark.

"He'll need to be on the lead in town, but if you want to get out on one of the quieter roads, he'll be able to have a good run. Not much traffic here, as I guess you know already."

Jacey went upstairs, dropped her notebook into her bag, added an extra sweater just in case it got colder, and tied her hair back in a ponytail before she headed downstairs. It was strange, being here; the hollowing happened, of course, but it wasn't much, and it didn't frighten her at all. She felt safe, despite what everyone had told her, and what had happened the last time she was here. For the first time since she arrived in England she felt decidedly unhaunted by anything. She'd almost forgotten about Rob, too, in this strange, featureless landscape.

The fens. Drowned in the fens.

She and Stanley left by the back door and crossed the car park. She led the way along the streets of the village, the ones she and Rael had explored during their first fleeting visit. She passed the post office, the general store, the newsagents. What she hadn't noticed before was the church on the other side of the street. It was made of yellow-brown stone bricks and had a square tower and pointed steeple. The gate was open, and Stanley followed her into the churchyard.

She looked carefully at the cemetery headstones that were covered with moss and lichen. She could still make out the names on most of them, but there was nobody named Kennet—there were a few Smiths, Robert and Mavis and their children, plus a baby called Martin, whose parents weren't named, but it would be impossible to know if they were relatives of hers. She checked again; definitely no Kennets. Was the curse so powerful that the churches didn't want anyone by that name buried nearby?

Stanley was still by her side. He lifted his legs on some graves, sniffed around a few others. The sun came out for a moment and he took a rest on the step leading to the church's porch. It was there that Jacey found the war memorial. The longest list of war dead was the one that just said, 'War, 1914–1918'. She scanned the names. There were plenty of the common names she'd read on the graves – Clarke, Jones, Wright – and some more unusual ones: Staves, Allbones, Goy.

She looked at the list for the Second World War. The names weren't as clear, and the lettering looked more chipped and exposed than the World War I names, and some of them had been painted over. The thinning, faded spots revealed the names that were underneath. There were ten in all, with the same number of letters – six.

A few of the letters stood out, but not all. There was an N in the middle, and the second to last letter was an E.

Did it say *Kennet*? Had the name been removed? Replaced by someone else's?

She backed away from the sign. No. What was crossed out was another family's name. After all, she had only the old man Arthur's word that the Kennet family even lived in Stanton. There was no mention of them online; their graves weren't in the churchyard; she'd seen that for herself.

And her being a Kennet was a lie, too. She had no reason to believe anything she was told by Muriel or Madlyn. Her grandmother's name was Ivy Smith. If she dared talk to her mother, she could probably prove it easily, find Nana's birth certificate, and that would settle it. This coming to Cambridgeshire, this following an overgrown path to somebody else's past was stupid, pointless. She had other things to do – a future to plan, with or without her husband – and a relationship with her mother to repair if she wanted to. She needed to get to the bottom of what her mother and Rob had been talking about, too. It was probably nothing more than a minor childhood incident that had been blown up out of proportion, because her mother was lonely and wanted her home.

Pulling Stanley tight by the lead, she headed for the cemetery gates. He stopped a few feet from the end of the path, got down on his haunches, as if he'd seen something that frightened him.

"Come on, Stan," she said. "Let's get you back to the pub so you can have something to eat."

Stanley growled.

"You'd like that, wouldn't you? Maybe Sally's got some sausages left over from breakfast, huh?"

Stanley barked – once, twice – and then he stopped.

He was looking at something behind them. Something nearer the church.

Slowly, Jacey turned around. She felt the hollowing, but only slightly – a faint buzzing, like traffic sounds from far away. Stanley strained at the lead, making her lose her footing.

"Stop it, Stan," she said, tightening her grip, planting her feet more firmly on the ground.

But Stanley wouldn't stop. Something had spooked him, and Jacey was afraid that if she let go, he'd run off in the wrong direction, maybe get hit by a passing car, or get lost and never come back.

She had no choice but to follow in the direction he seemed to want to drag her: towards the church, around the sides of the building, scraping her jacket on the yellow stone wall, and hurtling her beyond the porch where the sign had been re-painted to the back of the building, where there were more graves, and the grass was longer; and there, kicking the ball in the grass, up against an old vault-shaped monument, was the boy.

Finally, Stanley escaped her grip, pulling away, so that the leather burned her hand. He cut through the long grass, leaving a weedy wake behind him, and stood, inches away from the boy, barking and barking.

The boy kept kicking, head down, not bothering to even glance at an angry dog that was growling and snapping, only a few inches from his feet.

Stanley seemed confused. Why wasn't this boy responding?

After a few seconds, the dog backed away, dropping his body defensively. Jacey called his name, and he slunk back to her side. She slipped the lead on again, grasped it tightly. Next to one of the gravestones was a small tree, with a trunk thick enough for Jacey to wrap Stanley's lead around it. She patted him on the head – he was far enough away now to not get frightened again.

She stepped towards the boy.

"Hey," she said.

The boy stopped kicking.

Suddenly, she remembered the picture Dr Andrews had shown her in Brighton. The clothing looked similar, but the boy's face had been unrecognisable, a blur, the cracks in the photograph obscuring what he actually looked like.

"What are you doing so far away from home?"

As the words came out, she realised what a stupid thing it was to say. This boy obviously had no home. Not now, anyway, and the thought of what she was telling herself was terrifying. And he was standing so still. Arms, legs, head, nothing moved, as if he had turned into one of the stone cemetery statues, only hollow, light as a feather.

From the trees behind her, she could hear Stanley growling. Somehow, the sound comforted her. It was real, Stanley's fear, even if the boy wasn't.

She took another step. The smell of damp, dirty mud filled her nostrils and got stronger as she crept closer to the boy. It rose up, as it had done before, from her lungs into the back of her throat. The choke, the cough, the sensation of drowning were all coming back.

She wanted to shout out another question, but the mucky water was strangling her speech. She kept looking at the boy, willing him to turn around.

Why wouldn't he look at her? Why wouldn't he talk?

The water in her throat thickened, and suddenly she was choking on mud, struggling to breathe, staggering away from the boy in a panic, back to the tree where she'd tied Stanley.

The air swirled around her, and the hollowing felt like dry water now, coming in huge waves, washing over her body, while she plunged forward desperately, towards the barking dog, and the tree, and the dry ground, and the freshening air.

She collapsed beside a grave. Stanley whimpered, his voice choking, too, as he strained at his lead. She closed her eyes, focused on breathing, on smelling the clean dirt and the fresh green grass.

A minute later she stood up. Her lungs had cleared, the air smelled sweet, Stanley's tail was wagging happily.

And the boy was gone.

She brushed off her jeans, untied the dog.

But the boy had been here. Real. Alive or dead, it didn't matter.

He'd followed her somehow. He wasn't connected with Sussex, or Lewes, or Malin House.

He was connected to *her*.

Back at the pub a few people were having lunch at the tables, and two men and a woman were perched at the bar. Sally was busy, serving customers. It wasn't the time to ask her about the boy, find out if a lost child had been seen by anyone else in town. It wasn't time to ask about the Kennets, either, why they weren't buried in the churchyard, what happened to their names on the war memorial.

From the way Sally acted in the morning, there might never be a time, unless she could get old Arthur to tell her some more.

"You were gone a long time, thought you and Stanley might have eloped."

"Oh, he's such a nice dog," Jacey laughed, "but I'm probably not ready to settle down right now."

Stanley went to the fire, curled up. He seemed happy again, poor pooch.

"Oh, and there was a phone call for you while you two were gallivanting around the countryside."

"Oh." Jacey's heart lurched, but she couldn't show her fear. "What did you tell them?"

Sally shook her head, pulled the pints that the person at the bar had just ordered.

"Said I'd never heard of you."

Upstairs, after a long soothing bath, she lay on her bed and tried to figure out what to do.

Somebody knew where she was, or guessed anyway.

Coming back to Nana Ivy's hometown had been a stupid mistake. Of course they'd suspect she'd rock up here. She should have gone somewhere else, waited until everyone had forgotten her. Until Rob got his divorce, ran back to America without her, or whatever it was he was planning to do. She didn't have much money, but she could have found a cheap place to rent if she wasn't fussy. Still could, if she had to. Go further away. Scotland or Ireland. Anywhere, really. France. Italy.

The Perfect Couple

But wherever she went, the boy would find her, even if no one else did, and even after everything that had happened, she was no closer to understanding who he was, or why he was there. She should have forced herself to get closer to him in the cemetery, just ignored the drowning sensation. It wasn't real; she knew that. It was just a hysterical reaction to the fear and dread, and the shocking strangeness of seeing the boy again.

A little more courage and she would have been able to look at his face, might have recognised him from somewhere. A school history book, maybe. Some dead prince from the past, but wearing clothes from today.

One thing she was sure of, though. Unless she found out the truth, the boy was never going to leave her; no matter how far she ran, she'd never have peace.

Chapter 38

It was burger night at the pub, and Sally predicted that for the first time ever Arthur would come in. "He says he doesn't like all that American muck, but I think he's smitten with you, if not your country's cuisine."

Sure enough, he came in just after six, while the place was filling up. He sat at the bar, as there were no tables free, until Jacey waved him over to where she was sitting next to the roaring fire, with Stanley snuggled at her feet.

"I see Stanley's taken a shine to you," Arthur said. "That's a good sign in my book. Stanley usually gets things right."

"I don't know about that," Jacey said. "I think I might have startled him today."

"Oh?"

Arthur raised his pint to his lips. His hand shook slightly but he managed a few good sips. Jacey hoped the trembling wasn't anything to do with her, with what they'd talked about before; she hoped that the Kennets weren't terrifying to everyone in Stanton.

"We went to the cemetery."

"Ah, that'll put the frighteners into a body."

"Well, we saw something that scared us both, to be honest."

Arthur took another drink, put his glass down on a beer mat advertising the local ale. He didn't ask her what she meant about being scared, but maybe he hadn't heard her. It was getting crowded now; the tables were full, and people were waiting at the bar.

Someone shouted, "Awright, Arthur. See you finally got yourself a girlfriend."

"Yes," Arthur said. "And she's a Yank. Going to take me back with her to Hollywood."

"Make a star outta you, eh mate? Always had you down as one of them A-listers."

Arthur smiled. His milk-glass teeth glowed in the light of the fire.

"What was you so scared of today?"

"You'll laugh," she said.

"Doubt it."

"A little boy, kicking a football."

"Where?"

"The churchyard. Against one of those tombs behind the church."

Arthur didn't react. He thought for a moment, and then he said, "Did you recognise the boy?"

Jacey shook her head. "I've seen him other places too, far away from here, so I don't think he's a real boy, I mean, like he's alive and needs to be in school or anything."

"So you think he's dead?"

She wasn't sure if having this conversation was a good idea. At least Arthur was taking it seriously. He wasn't laughing at her, or calling a doctor or the police to tell them a delusional woman was running loose in the village.

"A ghost, I mean," Arthur said.

"At first I thought he was just a normal kid," Jacey said. "Like, lost, and he's only wearing summer clothes, so back in Sussex when I first saw him I was worried, in case he was being neglected by his family. Locked out of his house by terrible parents or something, but then …"

Under the table, Stanley sighed and yawned, shifted in his sleep.

"Why did you ask about the Kennets today?" Arthur asked.

"Do you want to know the truth?"

"Of course," Arthur said.

"Because somebody told me I was related to them."

"Who told you a thing like that?"

"A woman in Lewes, Sussex. Two women, actually."

"Hmm. Wonder who they were. No Kennets anywhere near here anymore. There were a few in Lincolnshire, and one tribe over in Norfolk, but …"

Lincolnshire. Where Rael said he was from. Did he know anything about the Kennets?

Arthur took a sip of his pint. "These two women, what did they say?"

"They told me my grandmother was a Kennet, even though that wasn't her name."

"Well, she probably changed it," Arthur said. "Lots of 'em tried that. Never worked, though."

The food arrived, although she wasn't hungry anymore. She took a bite of her burger. It tasted rotten, spoiled. She turned away from the table, spit the food into her napkin

She shouldn't have mentioned the Kennets to anyone. She definitely shouldn't have told Arthur what Muriel and Madlyn said. Soon, the whole village would believe she was a Kennet and try to get rid of her, come around to the pub with pitchforks and torches.

"It doesn't taste good to me," she said.

Arthur looked at her. His eyes seemed younger suddenly. The red lines disappeared, the bags and wrinkles tightened up. "Tastes like mud, I bet."

"Yes," she said. She put down her napkin with the bit of food in it. Set it aside on her plate.

"That's the proof, then," Arthur said. "You got the curse."

What was he talking about? Was he serious? Was this just another example of banter, or what Rob told her was called a wind-up?

"You should get out while you can," Arthur said. He didn't say it cruelly; he didn't mean it as a threat.

It was a warning.

She touched his arm, but he pulled away as if her fingers were poisonous.

"Tell me more," she said. "About the curse. Please."

She couldn't believe she was saying these words. Taking them seriously. "Or the legend, or whatever it is."

"Oh it's a curse all right," he said. He looked around the room to make sure no one was close enough to hear them.

"They was all killed, like I told you," he said. "Except for the girls."

"Who? The Kennets?"

"Oh, no," he said. "Not the Kennets. The Kennets was the ones that done the killing." His face looked old and withered again. His skin hung from the bones in thin, loose flaps. "That's what everybody thought, anyway."

"What did they do … the Kennets?"

"They did away with all the little boys in the village. Hundreds of years ago, before anybody wrote things down."

"That can't be true," she said. "That's just a—"

"Drowned 'em, like puppies, in the ditches and bogs."

"Why?"

"They was witches, you see, and they didn't have any boys of their own. Not in that whole generation. They was jealous. That was the reason, everybody said. Spite. Pure malice."

"I don't believe any of this," Jacey said.

She didn't want to get up and walk out on an old man, especially one who'd been so kind to her, but this was nonsense, even crazier than the stories Katherine told her about the fires in Malin House.

"So the curse was put on them by the villagers, out of revenge, and it followed the Kennets and took things from them that they loved. Sons, like in the wars. All those boys were innocent, so were their mothers by then, but what did that matter? They was Kennets. It was too late."

Jacey felt ill. The horrible tasting food churned in her stomach, and her mouth was dry, as if she'd been eating rotten straw.

"I reckon the boy you saw is a Kennet boy, killed some bad way, by the curse."

"No," Jacey said. She pushed her chair back, her heart pounding, the desire to run away almost overwhelming. "Did someone tell you to say these things to me?"

"I'm wishing I hadn't now," Arthur said. "I imagine you are, too, but I thought you'd want the truth."

"Was it my husband?" Jacey asked. "Rob? Did he put you up to this?"

Arthur looked at her kindly, and his expression took the edge off her panic.

"I don't know anyone by that name," he said. "I'm telling you the truth, because you seem like a nice young lady, and I want you to be safe from this. I don't know your husband, you've got to believe me."

"But why do I need to leave? If I'm not a boy."

"You shouldn't be here, if you're a Kennet. They've all gone, nobody wants them back."

Arthur's face softened again, as if he felt pity for her. "And that little boy you can see, he might be holding a grudge, too."

She felt dizzy, her head swimming with confusion. What on earth was he talking about?

"That boy might be blaming you, for him being dead."

Dinner was over; the pub was empty. Jacey's bill was settled up, with Sally wishing her well, saying she was sorry she couldn't stay longer. Upstairs, Jacey's bag was packed. In the morning, she'd be gone.

Arthur had dawdled at the door, before shuffling outside and making his way home. There was something else he wanted to say, Jacey was sure of it, but what? Before he closed the door and stepped outside, he put his hand up and blew her a kiss.

That was all. Nothing more.

Chapter 39

By the time she got back to Sussex it wasn't even five o'clock, even though it felt like midnight. *How did people live in this country*, Jacey wondered. Darkness and shadows for eighteen hours a day?

She trudged across the parkland, exhausted, like a lost soldier from a defeated army, searching for home in an unfamiliar land. The shadows were long, the streetlights seemed an even paler yellow than before she left; it was colder, more damp. The world seemed to have shrunk somehow, diminished in the darkness.

Malin House was the last place she wanted to be, but she needed to get the rest of her things before her avenues of escape were cut off. Already it seemed as if the harbour of her life had been mined, the railroad tracks blown up, the aeroplanes grounded. The human barriers were the ones that troubled her most; the betrayals of friends, of her husband.

Her own mother.

But she got back to the house without seeing the boy, or hearing any noises, or feeling the hollowing, so maybe things here had changed for the better.

The lights were on next door, and as she looked through the

darkened window of her cosy den, she saw a silhouette in Helen and Martin's kitchen. A still figure, looking out. Watching for something, maybe – keeping an eye out for her.

Safely inside, she shouted for Rob, and when he didn't answer she felt an overwhelming relief, despite the darkness of the house and the unnerving quiet. She crept back through the hallway, into the drawing room, his private sanctum.

"Rob?"

No one there.

She flicked on the light.

The room was back to what it had looked like before. The sofas and chairs were perfectly neat, with the pillows arranged exactly as she remembered when they first threw off the dust coverings. There were no ashtrays or empty beer cans; there was only the slightest trace of cigar smell in the air. Rob's books were gone, too; everything of his.

She turned the lights off, went back out the hallway, flicked on the switches for the huge chandelier, which lit up like a sparkling bonfire, and for the light – less generous – on the top landing. She should have been scared. Anyone could have been waiting for her upstairs, anything.

The boy wouldn't have stayed behind in Cambridgeshire; it didn't work like that. And she could still hear Arthur's warning – *maybe he's blaming you for him being dead.* But what did she have to do with anybody's death? It was pointless to think about. She couldn't defend herself against false accusations, erroneous assumptions. Not to a ghost.

She crept up the stairs. Except for their bedroom, all the doors on the landing were closed.

She poked her head in the partially opened bedroom door.

"Rob?"

He could have been sleeping, or in the shower, but the room was empty. She stepped inside, flicked on a table light.

There were clean sheets on the bed, and the bedside tables and the dressers were dusted and polished. Had Rob hired a cleaner while she was gone? Had he made an effort to welcome her back? Was he hoping for a fresh start?

It was the same in the bathroom. Every surface gleamed.

She looked in the laundry hamper. The linen that had been stripped from the beds was shoved in, and on top of the duvet cover were two damp towels, a wash cloth, and a hand towel that was smeared in make-up. A black strip of mascara, a large smudge of beige foundation. How had it got there? She hadn't done that. She hardly ever wore make-up these days, and if she did, she knew better than to wipe it off her face with a towel. Those stains would never come out, she thought, hearing her mother's voice in her head; hadn't whoever used the towels ever been taught that?

It hit her then. Rob had cleaned up after somebody else. He hadn't been preparing for his wife's return, he'd done it to hide the evidence of what he'd been up to while she was away. And because there was no way of knowing how long she'd be gone, because she hadn't told him, it was obvious he didn't really care if she came home and caught him at it.

Caught *them*.

It could have been a set-up, a trap for her to stumble into, if only they'd got the timing right. Staged for effect, another tool for driving her to madness. She would lash out at him, and his lover, and attack them in a jealous rage. See? He would say. See what she is like, this demented woman I'm married to? Delusional AND violent?

Her throat dry, and her stomach still churning, she went back downstairs to the kitchen. Everything in the house felt strange and disorienting, as if the floor was slanted and the stairs were crooked, and the walls were set at different angles.

She opened the fridge. A bottle of champagne was on the shelf next to the milk. In the dishwasher there were two wine glasses. No lipstick stains, nothing that cliché, but someone had been here, in her place.

She checked her phone.

No new messages, so she texted Rob to tell him she was back.

Straight away the phone rang.

"Jacey, for fuck's sake where have you been?"

There was anger, not worry, in his voice.

"I went away for a few days. Thought you might want a break."

"Why didn't you answer your phone? We were about to call the police. Have you reported as a missing person."

Who was this 'we', she wondered.

"Like I said, I thought you wanted—"

"Don't make this my fault, Jacey. This was about you. It's all been about you. Everything."

She looked around the kitchen. She liked this room; it still felt cosy and safe, in spite of all that had happened. She put the phone on the table for a second, leaving Rob to foam at the mouth, and checked the fridge again. Suddenly, she was hungry.

"Rob? Are you coming back tonight?"

"What?"

"Wherever you are, whoever you're with, are you coming back?"

There was no answer, and at first she thought it was the hollowing, smothering the sound of his voice. But it was just Rob, not knowing what to say. Silenced, for the first time since she'd known him.

"Rob?"

"I don't know."

"Are you in London?"

She couldn't hear any background noise. He wasn't outside, on the street, or in a pub. He was probably at somebody's house. Or in a hotel room, where they didn't mind if your girlfriend wiped her make-up off with a towel.

"OK, Rob," she said. "I understand."

"What do you understand?"

"All your visits to London. Every week, without telling anyone, not even the people you work with."

"Right," he said.

"And your trip to the divorce lawyers."

"Jacey, I …"

He stopped talking. His lies had run out of road.

"It doesn't matter." Jacey turned off her phone before she said the final word. "Goodbye."

Dinner was a frozen meal for one. She'd burned her tongue on the microwave lasagne, but despite that, and the slight chemical tang given off by the tomato sauce, it tasted delicious. She hadn't realised how hungry she was. When was the last time she'd eaten? Dinner last night with Arthur. The mud burger and rotten silage fries.

She ate in the den, enjoying her very last meal in Malin House with a celebratory glass of champagne. The rest of the bottle Rob could drink by himself, warm and flat. He could even share it with his other woman, or women, she didn't mind. The BBC TV queen for the night was Boudicca, the legendary British Celtic warrior, and the presenter was a timid looking white man who seemed generally terrified at the thought of confronting Boudicca's army, and her ways of dealing with her enemies by torture and executions. As he described her methods in graphic detail, his skin seemed to become paler, his hair more grey.

And then, bed. The clean sheets were soft and soothing against her skin, and she was sleeping within minutes of pulling the covers over her body.

And, in the middle of the night …

Woken with a jolt. A rattle of the sticky handle – with more strength than a little boy could ever muster. A kick.

Jacey's heart fluttered. She wanted to jump up to defend herself – there was a rusty key in the lock, never used, that might turn if she used enough strength – but she was frozen with fear. She imagined the boy, grown up and huge, becoming angrier with each knock. She remembered Arthur's words: "Maybe he blames you for him being dead."

Another loud knock and she let out a mewling sigh, like a terrified animal. NO, she thought. No trembling. No crying. She fumbled for her phone at the side of the table. Who was she going to call. 999? What would she say? She clutched her phone, like a miniature Boudicca's shield, squeezing it with her fingers, strengthening her hand.

The handle rattled again. There was another angry kick.

Suddenly, the door flew open and Jacey threw the covers back, ready to run for the bathroom, to lock herself in. Something staggered into the room, dark, solid, not a boy, not a ghost.

Rob.

"Christ," he muttered, as he stumbled over something on the carpet. "Fucking shit."

She could smell him before she could make out his features. She looked at her phone. 2.47. Again, thirteen minutes before three a.m.

He must have got the last train from London, jumped into a taxi. Same timing as before.

She could hear him undressing, belt clinking onto the floor, shoes kicked against the wall, a huge, grunty tussle with his shirt to get it over his head.

He collapsed beside her, and turned his body towards hers.

He put his hand on her hip, moaned gently, pulled his body in closer, tugging at the elastic of her knickers.

Under the covers, she batted his hand away. What was he thinking? Did he even know who she was? Did he think he was in bed with his girlfriend?

He put one arm around her shoulders, the other across her hip, and pulled himself right up against her, skin on skin.

"Mmm …"

His hand ran over the top of her bra, down under her panties.

"No, Rob," she said.

Another drunken groan. She tugged at his hand, slapped his fingers.

"Come on, Rob," she said. "Fuck off."

But he was strong, even if he was drunk. "Jacey," he whispered. "Jacey."

She could feel his hard cock, as he thrust his hips against her body.

"You're fucking gross," she said, twisting her body, trying to inch herself away. "Now stop it."

With one hand between her legs, rubbing her, and the other squeezing her breasts, the grinding motions should have made his attempt to fuck her seem laughable, but it wasn't.

"I mean it, Rob," she said. "You have to stop."

"Fuck me, Jacey." He moved his arm across her chest, pinned her onto the bed. She could smell his breath – the tobacco and booze.

"No, Rob."

"Come on."

His movements grew more pronounced, and he was tugging at her panties now, trying to pull them down.

"I said no, Rob. Didn't you hear me? No."

The more she twisted away from him, sideways on the bed, the tighter he gripped. She thought about screaming, loud enough for Helen and Martin to hear, so that they'd either come to her aid or call the police.

She thought again about calling 999 herself. She still had the phone in her hand.

She thought about Queen Boudicca. That terrible story of rape and humiliation, her hideous revenge. She thought about the queen's shield and sword in battle. Hard. Impenetrable, all those sharp edges.

Rob let out a groan of pleasure, as if this was an act of love, not a brutal assault.

Jacey gripped the phone as tightly as she could and struck its corner against the hand that was tight on her chest.

"Ow," Rob whined.

She hit him again, as he strengthened his grip.

And again, and again, beating it up and down his arm, and then down to his leg, behind her, bashing his cock. And she remembered *The Shining*, the wife who'd stood on the stairs with a baseball bat, while her husband goaded her, taunting her with insults mocking her for her weakness until finally she—

"Christ, Jacey, what are you—"

Wendy. That was her name. *Wendy!* Another smash with the phone against Rob's cock, then on the side of his hip, then on his knuckles, and once more, harder, until he shrieked in pain and his grip loosened enough for her to pull away from him, to get up off the bed and run to the door, panting with outrage and fear.

Rob turned over on the bed and lay silent; within a few seconds he was asleep, snoring. Jacey stood, shaking, phone in hand, still wondering if she should call the police or ask Helen and Martin for help, or contact Rael in Brighton, or Jared in London, or anyone she knew that she could trust, and then she felt the hollowing, and as the air whirled around her she knew she had to leave.

To run, as soon as she could, away from Malin House, away from Rob.

To stay gone, forever this time.

It was almost four a.m. when she put her suitcase and carry-on bag by the front door in the hallway and went into the kitchen. She set her phone alarm for six thirty. That would give her time to sleep, and the chance to get up and out before Rob woke up and somehow got his shit together enough to go into work. Because that's what he would do, without feeling any pangs of remorse or guilt, not caring what crimes he'd committed against his wife.

Work. That's what mattered to Rob. His reputation, his status, the respect of his peers.

He'd left his briefcase on the kitchen table, and his laptop was beside it, lid open, emails on the screen.

A few clicks and she was on his Facebook page, messages blinking, undeleted.

Bex.

There she was, with all her *Love you darling,* and *When can we be together,* like a love-struck teenager. And from Rob, some childish emojis, hearts and kisses and praying hands and sad, crying faces.

Strange, Jacey thought. Seeing the messages didn't bother her. Reading them made her glad that she was leaving Rob so that he could go on to ruin another woman's life. She didn't bother looking for anything else, not in those messages anyway.

She skimmed through his emails, though. More from Bex, one that she replied to, saying, 'Your boyfriend's a rapist, thought you should know'. There were one or two from gushing female students, but she let those slide, along with a message from his solicitor. There was no point telling any them what Rob had done.

Where were the ones from her mother? Those were the one she wanted to read.

She found them in his trash folder. All of them together. One after the other. Chronological.

Rob made it so easy to be a spy.

She opened the most recent message. Her mom had sent it the day before.

So, you think you can get away with this? Just abandoning my daughter, after everything I told you?

Jacey followed the chain, checked the previous email. It was another tongue lashing. *I trusted you. With my daughter's life. You loved her, you said. You couldn't live without her, no matter what.*

You're a lying bastard, Rob.

She went back to an earlier one.

You wanted the story. I told you.

And before.

I've spent my whole life shielding her from what happened, trying to protect her.

There it was again.

Shielding. Protecting.

Maybe it was her mother who'd gone mad?

She doesn't remember, Rob. Not a thing.

Jacey stood back. The hollowing still swirled around her and a terrible taste was building up in the back of her throat. She thought of that day on the pier, the picture the psychiatrist had shown her.

No. That was just another nasty prank, set up by Rob so she'd stay frightened, easier to control. .

Close the lid, she thought. Before it gets worse. Walk away, don't read any more. You don't need any protection, from anyone. Whatever terrible things happened, or had been done to you, it was all in the past.

A final glance at the screen.

And I want to make sure that she never does.

Jacey curled up in the den, wearing sweatpants and a baggy T-shirt, wrapping herself in the extra duvet that was in the linen closet. She slept. No dreams. When the alarm woke her, she was instantly alert. There was no moment of confusion, or forgetfulness. She knew where she was – the den – and why she was there. She quickly got up, padded into the kitchen in bare feet. Outside, the sun was rising, and the sky was turning pink, a pale flicker of hope on the horizon.

It was time to go.

Chapter 40

Rael was waiting for her outside Brighton station, huddled in the doorway of a closed pub, sheltering from the cold and rain, struggling, as usual, to keep his roll-up lit.

She'd called him from the station in Lewes, planning to leave a voicemail, never imagining he'd be awake to answer his phone.

"Are you still in London, Ms. Jace?"

He sounded so happy to hear from her, she felt sorry she had to leave him behind.

"I'm on my way to Brighton. Had to pick up a few things at the house, but I'm heading off. And I wanted to say goodbye, so …"

"Are you at the station?"

"Soon."

"No way am I going to let you go without giving you a proper send-off. I'll jump in a taxi. Won't be long."

He hadn't given her the chance to tell him that she was ready to head through the gates. She looked up at the departure board. There were plenty of trains to London this time of day, and Rob wouldn't be waking up any time soon, not with the amount he'd had to drink last night. So what was the actual hurry?

They went into a café beside the pub. Jacey found a table in the back, away from the steamed-up window, while Rael queued at the counter along with the commuters who were waiting for their takeaway coffees.

"So …" Rael said when he came back with their drinks.

"So, I'm leaving my husband, in case you haven't figured that out."

"And heading back to the States?"

"I want to do some travelling first. I've got a ticket to Paris, and I'll just see where I end up."

"Eurostar? Today?"

She nodded. Rael would never know she was lying. Laying a false trail, whatever you wanted to call it.

"That's amazing. You must be so excited."

"I will be when I get there."

"Oh, you'll love Paris. I know you will."

They sat quietly and sipped their coffees. Jacey felt a stab of guilt for being dishonest, for not opening up to the only friend she'd made here: it hurt, having to lie.

"At least you're out of that bloody house," Rael said. That's the main thing."

Jacey thought about last night. The messages she'd seen; what Rob had done – or tried to do – after he came home. "I can't blame Malin House for all of it," she said.

Rael took a swig of his coffee. He yawned, and turned around, looking across the room, towards the door. His phone was on the table, and he glanced at it.

Instinct, Jacey thought. Habit. She'd have done the same if her phone wasn't tucked away inside her bag, out of sight.

"You sure you don't want another coffee, Jacey?"

He turned around in his chair as if he was going to go order again, and looked over at the door. "When exactly is your train?"

Suddenly, Jacey felt hot in her heavy parka. She was sweating, and her heart was pounding. What she needed was a drink of water, not another coffee. Maybe she was imagining it, but Rael seemed anxious, too. He checked his phone again.

"I really need to go," Jacey said.

"I can walk you to the station."

Jacey pulled the strap of her bag across her shoulder. "Sorry, Rael, but I can't handle long, drawn-out goodbyes. And the station is just across the road, I don't need any help."

When she stood up she felt the hollowing, just slightly; the sounds in the café became distorted and the shifts in the air made her dizzy.

Rael stood, too.

"And I'll definitely stay in touch," she said. "So we can meet up again before I fly back home."

She stepped carefully from behind the table. Rael shifted his body, a slight sideways shuffle, blocking her way. She stepped forward, but Rael didn't move.

"Excuse me, darling," she said. "I need more room for my suitcase."

Rael turned around and looked at the door. Then he took a step towards her, hemming her in. Something didn't feel right – the furtive glances, the blocking moves – but she needed to stay cool, not panic. This was Rael, after all, not Rob.

"It's time for me to go, Rael."

Rael put his hand on the top of her suitcase. "You need to sit down."

She tried to brush him aside. What the hell was he doing? "But I'll miss my train."

"We're worried about you, Jace," he said. "That's why I'm here."

The hollowing thickened. She imagined that the other people in the café were aware of it too, wondering where it was coming from, who was to blame.

"What are you talking about? Who is this 'we'?"

Rael still had his hand on her suitcase, holding it in place. "We know everything, Jacey."

His voice had slowed down with the hollowing, deepened so she had to strain to hear it.

"Muriel and Madlyn," he said. "I was wrong about them. They're on your side. They're trying to help."

Another glance at the door. Who was he looking for?

"Somebody put you up to this," Jacey whispered, afraid to draw attention to herself. She needed to leave, that was all. To get outside as soon as she could. To breathe freely.

"Was it Rob? Trying to scare me again?"

Rael said nothing, didn't react.

"Come on, Rael, you *know* what happened to Katherine," she said, "so how could you—"

"Katherine wasn't real."

She pulled the suitcase, wrestled it from Rael's hands. "I saw her, remember? We had a drink in the fucking pub."

"I mean, her story wasn't real. Her husband being a bully and all that. It was made up. By me."

Jacey remembered how awkward their conversation had been, how Rael seemed to be feeding Katherine lines.

"And that car accident," he said. "The one that nearly killed me. It was my fault, no matter what I told you. Nobody pushed me, I stumbled."

Jacey shook her head in disbelief. "Why would you lie?"?"

He tried to touch her arm, but she pulled away. She didn't want a tussle here, in front of so many people, but she was going to leave, get on the next train, and if she had to push Rael out of the way to do it, if she had to knock him to the floor, she would.

"We know about the boy, Jacey."

"I know you do," Jacey said. "I was the one who told you."

Finally, she shoved past him, pulling the suitcase along the floor.

"I mean, we *know*."

She managed to squeeze through the door, suitcase behind her, and tumble onto the pavement.

"Jacey," Rael shouted.

She didn't stop, even though her bag was weighing her down and the suitcase dragged like an anchor. She wouldn't turn around. All other sounds were lost in the hum of traffic, smothered by the pounding rain that was beating down on the street, but still she heard his voice:

"We know who he is."

Chapter 41

She hurried across the concourse, fumbled with Rob's credit card at the ticket machine. London. All stations. Single.

She clutched her bag, tightened the grip on her suitcase.

She looked up at the departure boards. *London Bridge, London Victoria*, none of them leaving immediately.

Cambridge. A direct train, in five minutes' time.

Get on it. Don't think about the ticket. Tell the conductor you made a mistake. Lie. Cry. Deny.

She shoved through the waiting passengers, using her suitcase as a shield, Boudicca style, and pushed her ticket through the machine at the barrier. She struggled along the platform to the train, and managed to heave her heavy suitcase through the sliding doors just before the conductor blew the whistle for departure.

She found a seat in a quiet, empty carriage.

She had no idea what she was going to do, but she had time to think, and for now at least, she was safe.

None of what Rael had said to her made sense. Rael knew Rob was full of shit, so why would he be helping him. Or Muriel? Or

Madlyn? Rael knew it was all lies. Tricks. Sharp sticks to poke Jacey over the cliff edge of sanity so that Rob could … what?

After last night, it didn't matter. She would never go back to Rob. The affairs, the scheming to get rid of her, those things were nothing compared to what he'd tried to do to her in their bed.

The shame of Rael's betrayal stung, too, as if he'd reached over the café table and slapped her in the face. Rob, her mother, and now Rael – this was a conspiracy. It wasn't paranoia; she wasn't delusional.

Real, Dr Andrews would have said, except that he was in on it, too, obviously. Showing her that crumpled old picture, trying to scare her.

But why were they doing it? Unless it was to help Rob have her put away?

The countryside rolled by past the small towns on the way to Gatwick Airport. Then the suburban stations, all looking the same, with their supermarket chains and auto parts depots and big box furniture stores. The villages in the distance were lovely though, nestled between green rolling hills. The farms reaching almost to the edge of the tracks, the grey-brown earth, with yellow stubs of crops that had been harvested months before. The sheep in fields, their white coats dirty and grubby looking, shaggy cows and blanketed horses.

It was prettier here, in the Sussex downlands, than it was in Cambridgeshire. But she thought about the cosy fire in the pub, the friendly faces, and the whippet Stanley nuzzling her underneath the table.

She'd go back to Stanton. Just for one night. She'd told Rael she was going to London for the Eurostar. That's what her ticket said, in case someone checked the machine. In case they could do that.

She closed her eyes, sleepily remembering the way Stanley looked up at her, his brown eyes full of loyalty and love. The gentle roll and rumble of the train lulled her into a dream-like state. Another memory tugged at her brain, nothing to do with pubs, or dogs, or the English countryside.

Her mother crying, for no reason that Jacey understood. And her mother slapping her, hard, so that the skin on her face turned red, and that was for no reason either. Jacey had asked a question, that was it, while she and her mother were crossing the barnyard in the rain. She couldn't remember the question, only the slap, and the force of it that made Jacey slip on a pile of damp straw that had fallen off the hay wagon. Then her mother helped her up and held her and rocked her back and forth, even though it was raining and Jacey was cold and wet and totally confused.

And the hollowing came. She remembered that, too, the terrifying strangeness of it.

Was that the first time? Her mother was telling her things she could not hear, could not understand, because the sounds were distorted and caused her to wince in pain, as if she'd be deaf forever because her eardrums had burst.

The train rattled her awake. The conductor came through, cleared his throat.

He glanced at the ticket.

"You'll need to change at East Croydon."

"Fine," Jacey said.

He walked away, on his way to the next carriage, and then he turned around.

"And you, Miss?" he said. "Are you fine?"

Jacey shook her head. "I don't really know."

"You should have rung me," Sally said. "I'd have had your room ready."

"My room," Jacey thought. As if she was one of the family.

"Look at you, poor thing. You're soaked through." Sally nodded towards the fire that Stanley was curled up in front of. "Wait there, and I'll bring you a cup of tea." As Jacey made her way towards the table next to the fire, Sally shouted, "Stanley. Look who's here to see you."

Stanley's ears perked up, and he raised his head. When he saw Jacey he sprang towards her, tail wagging, jumping up at her, with his paws on her knees.

Jacey leaned down and let Stanley nuzzle his face against hers.

"Good boy, Stanley. Good boy."

The fire gradually warmed her. The tea Sally brought was comforting and delicious.

"We had a phone call a little earlier," she said. "Somebody asking for you."

Jacey's heart sank. "What did you tell them?"

"That nobody by that name was staying here."

"And that was it?"

"Oh, they asked me a few other things. Had I seen you, was I expecting you at any time?"

"What did you tell them?"

"I said sorry, but I'd never heard of you. Said we hadn't had an American here since they closed the US airbase."

Finally, Jacey felt herself relax. She reached over and stroked Stanley's soft, fire-warmed fur. "I'm not an escaped criminal or anything," she said, "but thanks anyway."

"More like a runaway bride, I expect," Sally chuckled.

"Yes. Something like that."

Sally had put a hot water bottle in the bed, and left more sugary tea in a metal flask on the dresser.

Jacey undressed. Slipped into tracksuit bottoms and T-shirt. She double locked the door, checked the view over the car park, before climbing into bed. She told Sally she'd be down for dinner, after she had a nap, and Sally said she'd reserved a table by the fire so she could sit beside Stanley again.

If only she could stay here longer than one night. Being looked after, cared for by Sally, felt so unusual. But surely her mother had always cared for her?

Jacey closed her eyes. Even now, what she remembered was not care, but a constant series of warnings – *don't go there, be careful doing that*. There'd been a harshness in her mother's love, the way she was always admonishing her daughter, as if Jacey couldn't be trusted not to mess things up.

And what she'd said to Rob. "I have spent my life protecting my daughter."

Had she? Really? From what?

When Jacey got up she looked outside again. The ditch beyond the car park appeared to be freezing over, a thin crust of ice forming on the top. It was getting bitterly cold, and Jacey thought about the fire that would be blazing downstairs in the pub, and of Stanley, and something called 'hot pot' which was that night's special for dinner.

"Arthur's favourite," Sally said. "He'll be delighted to see you again."

The hot pot didn't taste of mud.

It was delicious, with soft chunks of meat and thick bits of potato and carrot. She was finished with her bowl when Arthur came in. He noticed her – he must have – but he stayed at the bar. Jacey remembered their last conversation. The thought that she might be related to the Kennets had made Arthur uneasy, to say the least. He'd obviously said nothing to Sally though, judging by her friendly welcome; or else she'd thought nothing of it, laughed off his superstitions.

Finally, when she was about to go back upstairs, he came to her table, carrying a half-finished glass of beer.

"Good to see you again, Arthur," she said, standing up, making room.

"Aye," he said. "It's good to see you, too."

"I'm just here for one night," she said. "So don't worry about the curse. I'll make sure I don't spread it to anyone."

He looked sheepishly into his beer.

"Aye ..." He shook his head. "I don't know why I spoke to you like that. Weren't at all fair on you."

"I haven't seen the boy since I left here," she said. "So I figure that's a good sign."

"Aye, I'm sure it is."

She felt stupid even mentioning the boy now. It seemed ludicrous in this warm, inviting pub, to be talking about centuries-long family curses, and strange phantom children. "Maybe talking to you about him settled things."

It was obvious from his expression that he wasn't convinced, but still he nodded and said, "Aye. Maybe."

As the pub filled with people, they moved their conversation on to other things. Where she would go next on her travels. She told him exactly what she'd told Rael – Paris, then the south of France to escape the worst of the winter. She didn't think anyone would ask Arthur about her, but it was good to tell the same story. Back to London. Eurostar to Paris. TGV to Marseille, and who knew, maybe a ferry to Corsica, if they ran in the winter months.

"Sounds exciting," Arthur said.

"Can't wait," she said.

"And what about your husband?"

Jacey's heart raced for a second. She'd never told Arthur, or Sally, that she was married. Arthur glanced at her ring finger and grinned. "I'm an old fool, but I'm not a blind old fool."

"I'm sure he'll find out soon enough," she said. "One way or another."

"Reckon he will."

She left him then, hoping that he'd come in for breakfast so she could say a proper goodbye. Her heart swelled as she went back up the stairs. If only she could take these feelings with her – Arthur's kindness, Stanley's calm affection, Sally's warm laugh.

When she got upstairs she emptied the suitcase and packed just the carry-on. She'd be travelling light from now on; she'd explain to Sally that she was leaving the big bag behind. She wouldn't need all those heavy sweaters when she got to the south of France, would she?

She put on her sleeping things and crept to the bathroom in the corridor to brush her teeth. There was light spilling out from under another room's door, so she wasn't the only guest this time around. Was Stanley as affectionate with the others as he was to her, she wondered? Did Arthur talk to them, too? Or join them for dinner or a pint?

She hoped not; she liked feeling special.

Back in bed she checked her phone. All charged. No messages waiting. Not even from Rael. The radio silence from Rob was to be expected. He didn't really care what happened to her, so why would he try to get in touch?

She thought about messaging her mother, telling her that she'd left Rob and wouldn't be going back to America any time soon, but that would have meant explaining things for which there was no real explanation, or demanding answers to questions she didn't want to ask.

* * *

With all those things running through her head she found sleep impossible. The lies she'd told Rael and Arthur about travelling to France and possibly Corsica, were now exciting her for real. Why shouldn't she go to Paris? Why shouldn't she take the TGV to Marseille and travel on from there? Italy, Croatia, Naples, Monaco. She imagined the bright blue water of the Mediterranean, being in these places that she'd only seen in pictures or movies.

Eventually, she must have fallen asleep, because something woke her when it was still dark.

She stayed in bed, totally still, and listened again. Was the sound inside her room? No. Was it in the hallway outside? It seemed to be, unless the hollowing was back and disturbing her hearing. No. There were definite footsteps, followed by a strange shuffling sound.

She thought about the lights she'd seen under the other door. Maybe the new guest had gone to the bathroom and was stumbling along the dark hallway.

The sound continued. And whoever it was seemed to have stopped outside her door.

She turned on the light, making sure that she remembered to turn both locks. Despite her precautions, her heart was pounding. She held her breath, waiting for the sound that she knew would come.

The bang against the bottom of the door.

The *thwack* of a ball being kicked.

The boy, she thought.

She remembered what Arthur said. He'd known the boy would be waiting for her. Maybe he'd seen him. Maybe he knew who he was!

She stayed completely still. Another knock, another soft kick, then the sound of footsteps retreating, down the hall, then on the stairs, down, down, down.

The side door to the outside opened and closed.

Could the boy do that?

Go in and out like a guest?

She was hot in her sweatshirt and jogging pants. The hot water bottle had gone cold, but it was clammy and warm at her feet, so she kicked it away. Outside, the wind blew, rattling the window, lifting the curtains in a strong draught that she felt even on the bed.

The shaking continued, too strong for the wind.

Then it went quiet again. The wind calmed, and there was no one outside her room.

She got up. Crept to the window. Without touching the curtain she managed to look outside onto the yard. She couldn't see anyone, but she heard the sound of the ball being kicked. Louder, a stronger strike, on a harder surface, the parking lot tarmac or against a car.

She looked again. Then she gently pulled the curtain aside, only an inch, not daring to throw it wide.

By the yard light. Kicking the ball on the fence.

The boy.

He was trembling – she'd never noticed that before – and his clothes seemed damp. She could see the outline of his face, so pale and featureless, but also malnourished, the bones beneath the translucent skin.

Could she bring him inside? Like a stray animal? Could she give him a mug of hot tea and feed him leftover hot pot, fatten him up before letting him out into the wild again?

No. She would have to go to him.

Could he eat and drink? Would he get warm if he had better clothes?

There was a small blanket on the top of the wardrobe. In her bag she had a KitKat that she'd forgotten to eat on the train. There was an electric kettle in her room, and hot chocolate mix, and the empty tea flask that she could take outside.

She could help him, even if he wasn't able to come inside and sit by the fire. She could try, anyway.

When she was ready, she opened the door, looked cautiously out into the hallway. Nothing. Nobody. She crept down the stairs, looked into the empty pub. There was Stanley, asleep by the fire, the embers still glowing slightly. When she opened the door to the car park she saw his head raise up and in an instant he was at her side, nudging her leg.

"Go, Stanley," she whispered, "back to bed."

She opened the door, and Stanley went with her outside, following at her feet, almost clinging to her legs.

Poor Stanley whimpered when he saw the boy, as if he knew that something was not right.

"Hey," Jacey whispered. The boy was ten metres away from her, the ball at his feet. He stood still, facing her this time – for the first time? Had she actually seen his face before?

Blonde. The eyes, she could see, were a pale blue.

A pretty boy, or at least he had been once.

She took a step closer to him, and felt the familiar disorientation of the hollowing. The air seemed to be gone, and it was hard to breathe without panting. There was no noise to distort, but her ears hurt and she was reminded of her mother's brutal slap, the one that had brought her to her knees so many years before.

She took another step.

The boy did not move. His eyes were still, staring.

And Jacey heard a scream, echoing in the darkness. And her name was somewhere in the scream. *Jacey!* Loud and hollow and riding on a wave of sound that was in her ears, inside and outside, hearing and remembering.

Another step, and the boy moved away from her, slipping through the fence.

She looked back at the pub. Still no lights, other than the one in her room. No one was awake; it was not time yet to be making fires or brewing coffee, or frying bacon. She held on to Stanley's collar, and he guided her around the cars, out of the car park onto the road beside the ditch, and there was the boy, kicking the ball, walking beside it.

Kicking and strolling, and Jacey and Stanley followed, moving faster, as the boy seemed to hover over the road, and the ball got bigger, blowing up like a balloon, and Jacey remembered.

A shop.

A toy store.

She was there in the toy store and she'd chosen the ball from all the other toys that were on display – the trains and cars and wooden blocks and yoyos and she was holding the ball tightly as if she couldn't let it go because it was hers; hers to share.

Hers to *give*.

The boy stopped moving. He turned, looked back at her.

The boy crossed the road. Moved towards the ditch full of cold, icy water.

Beside her, Stanley growled, pulled away, so she had to tighten her grip on the lead.

And the boy moved closer to the water.

"Stop," Jacey said. The boy turned around and she held up the blanket, an offering, something to distract him at least, but the boy was running towards the ditch, kicking the ball, going too fast for Jacey to be able to catch him.

He'll fall in, she thought. *The water is deeper than he thinks. He'll freeze to death or drown. I've got to stop him.*

She heard a sound behind her.

The hollowing of course, getting louder and louder, and a play of light getting brighter, and she let go of Stanley's lead, heard the distorted sound of his barking, and as she ran across the road, chasing the boy who was almost at the edge of the ditch, she heard the sounds get louder and the lights became blinding and she realised for just a second that it was not the hollowing that was hurtling towards her, but something solid, something terrifyingly *real*.

The impact sent her flying. She was awake, her eyes closed, as the car that hit her sped away; she was suspended in the darkness, waiting for the thud, the pain, bracing herself for the brutal crunch of bones on tarmac.

Chapter 42

A mouth full of something. Unable to move.
No breath.
The ball. Where was the ball? Where did it go?
He needed to find it.
Sister gave him.
The ball was floating away.
Where sister?
Sinking in the black water. Quick. Grab it.
Sister?
Sister?

She could not move. She could only see.
The ball was gone.
The boy was in the water.
Not kicking. Not moving.
Head stuck under a crust of ice.
She wanted to run, but the air wouldn't let her; it was holding her in place, like invisible chains.
She wanted to scream but it was like she was choking on the

icy mud, along with her brother. Like she was sucking in the water that was drowning him, while she stood by and watched, unable to move.

Chapter 43

Jacey woke up to the beeping of a monitor somewhere near her, and as her vision cleared she saw a needle in her arm that was attached to a drip. She shifted her head on the pillow. There was pain, but there was also movement. Same with her shoulders, her fingers, her toes. She was alive, and her body was obeying commands from her brain.

A nurse came into the room. Bright blue uniform, tall handsome man with dark black hair like some kind of Byronic angel.

"Stanley?" she said.

"Nope," the nurse said. "My name's Daniel."

"The dog," she whispered.

"Sorry?"

"I was with a dog when I got hit, and …"

She remembered.

The road.

The boy.

The vision.

Who the boy was, and what happened to him.

The truth.

And she heard the sound of her mother crying, somewhere, in

the past, in the present, in the barn of her childhood, in the hospital room, beside her bed.

Then.

Now.

"You have people waiting for you," the dark angel said, adjusting the drip, checking her stats.

"People?"

"From far and wide, Jacey," he said. "You are one popular woman."

"But Stanley," she said. "The dog."

"I'll ask."

Chapter 44

Weeks later, and Malin House was empty, except for the furniture that had been there when they arrived. Rob had moved into a flat in Brighton on his own, but Jacey was allowed to stay on until her injuries – a cracked pelvis, two broken ribs, a fractured wrist – healed.

For some of the time her mother was with her, arriving in London a few days after the accident, as soon as she was able to get a flight, and spending Christmas and New Year in the orthopaedic ward. As soon as Jacey was out of danger, fully conscious and able to understand, her mother told her about her twin brother's death, how he had drowned in a half-frozen irrigation ditch when he was three-and-a-half years old, exactly as Jacey remembered the night she'd been hit by the car.

"Michael," her mother said, clutching a tissue, looking out the hospital window at the featureless Cambridgeshire landscape, grey and gloomy under heavy clouds. "His name was Michael James, and he was younger than you by five minutes."

Jacey didn't say anything about the boy in her visions, or how she had been haunted by him, but she told her mother what she'd seen when she was unconscious – a drowning boy – and she'd explained how at times in her life she'd been taken over by something she called the hollowing that seemed to have begun when she was a child.

Maybe the hollowing was why she hadn't gone for help when Michael went through the ice, she said to her mother. Why she hadn't run home screaming. Why she couldn't remember anything about what happened, not even being found hours later, huddled on the ground, half-frozen herself, next to the ditch.

They were snug in Jacey's cosy den, and her mother was curled up on the sofa beside her daughter, holding her hand, but failing to warm it. They were both shivering, as if still haunted by the events of the past few months, and the deeper trauma that had blighted their lives.

"We thought it was good, your not being able to remember," her mother said, her eyes red and wet with tears. "We thought we were doing the right thing, all those years, keeping you from knowing the truth."

Jacey's back stiffened. Her mother's weepy voice was making her bristle with resentment. "By lying to me," she said. "That's what you mean, so why not just say it?"

"I wanted to protect you, especially when you were so isolated. Over here, on your own."

"By making me think I was going mad?"

"No, darling. That wasn't the plan."

"Making me think I was living under some sort of curse?"

Her mother's mouth opened, but she was unable to find any words, or make any excuses. She inched away from Jacey, as if the thought of what she'd done embarrassed her. Good, Jacey thought. You *should* be ashamed.

Her mother cleared her throat. "You remember Nana Ivy?"

"Of course."

"Well, she was always going on about ghosts, you remember that?"

Jacey nodded.

"And that stupid curse was another thing, that so-called Kennet curse that made her so desperate to marry my father and get out of England."

"That curse wasn't real," Jacey said.

"No, of course not, but to your Nana it was, silly as that sounds, and to the people who lived in that horrible village. Anything bad that happened in Stanton, especially if it happened to a boy, it was all down to Nana's family, from hundreds of years before. And so, when poor little Michael died, that's what she blamed – the curse that she'd been trying to escape from her entire life."

Her mother stopped talking, took a sip of the tea they'd made earlier; it had long gone cold, but was better than nothing. Jacey thought about how Arthur had acted in the pub, despite his kindness, when she mentioned the Kennets. How he'd seemed frightened for her, but frightened *of* her, too. On some level, even to him, the curse was real.

"Your poor father absolutely forbade Nana to mention it, threatened to kick her off the farm, turn his back on her forever if she said another word about those stupid Kennets, but the damage had been done. I half-believed in the curse, too, and so I blamed myself when Michael died. As if, somehow, I had brought on the death of my own son, just by who I was."

Her mother was sobbing now, and she leaned over and crumpled into Jacey's body.

"And that's why I never told you," she cried. "I didn't want my only daughter's life ruined by this, I didn't want her driving herself crazy with guilt, the way I almost did."

Jacey knew she was meant to put her arms around her mother, to tut and mutter something like *there, there,* but she couldn't do anything other than sit rigid, while her mother cried herself out.

Eventually her mother sat up, wiped her eyes with a tissue, blew her nose and moved away again, towards the window, as if needing to create some distance between them.

"I know that you saw him," she said.

"What?"

"Rob told me you'd been seeing a lost little boy, and I knew it had to be Michael. Like a memory, a fragment. And when you started hearing things, those strange sounds Rob told me about, I thought you'd remember."

She stayed at the window, touched the curtains, pulled them back so she could see outside. She took a deep breath and turned around again. "And once I realised what Rob was up to – that business with the other woman – I was terrified he'd tell you about Michael, just to be cruel."

"So why didn't *you* tell me? Why did you get these other people involved, those horrible women?"

"I knew Madlyn from a family history group."

Jacey's stomach twisted. "What family?"

Her mother looked sheepish, ashamed again. "Madlyn and Muriel were actually distant relatives of Nana's. They were researching the history of the so-called Kennet curse, and tracked our family down, so we became pen-pals, I guess you could say."

"So you knew who Madlyn was before I even got here?"

"Yes, long before, and I told her my dilemma, my fears for you, when I couldn't keep an eye on things – on you, on Rob – like I could at home."

Her mother's defensive tone made Jacey feel sick, and every word she spoke made things worse.

"Madlyn could tell you weren't happy; she knew about the sounds you heard, she'd seen how anxious you were around Rob, how cold he was to you. And then, completely by accident, she saw him on the train to London, alone, and she overheard his conversation and …"

Jacey felt her heartbeat slow, and her skin grew cold. "And what?"

Her mother shrugged. "She knew he was up to something. She wasn't sure what, but it was bad enough for her to contact me, and we decided it would be a good idea to make you feel like Malin House was haunted, because of all the local rumours. She thought that might send you back home, away from Rob, and …"

Her mother sat back down on the sofa, and her body fell limp, as if she'd collapsed with exhaustion.

"And you could keep lying to me about what happened to Michael," Jacey said.

"No, darling," her mother cried, as if she couldn't understand the anger in Jacey's voice. As if she was shocked by it, insulted even. How dare her daughter question her fine intentions?

"I just wanted you away from that horrible man. What the others did, talking about the curse, frightening you like that, it was nothing to do with me."

Her mother reached for her hand; Jacey fought the urge to slap it away.

"I would have told you as soon as you got better, but you were so vulnerable."

Jacey knew the words were meant to sound sympathetic – *oh, poor, frail, little you* – but she felt them as accusations, as being tinged with contempt.

"You always were fragile, ever since …"

Jacey held her breath, waiting, as her mother's voice trailed off, overcome with emotion, her body wracked with sobs. Jacey imagined the words, heard them spoken, although her mother couldn't talk. *Ever since you watched your brother die* is what she wanted to say. *Ever since you silently stood by, frozen with fear, doing nothing to help.*

A few minutes later, something moved. The anger and resentment – hers, her mother's – seemed to lift, like a bird, and rise up from their weeping, shuddering bodies, and fly away, out the window, across the wide lawn of Malin House, up the hill to the windy downs, and far across to the glittering sea.

Chapter 45

It was spring when Jacey was finally able to leave Malin House and travel to France and Italy, or anywhere she liked. She had her tickets to Paris. Her route from there all planned. The thought of so much freedom made her dizzy, but with excitement, not fear.

Before she left, she felt the urge to hike up to the downs, one last time, catch the sight of sunshine on the distant sea.

She put on her boots, packed a few things in her backpack – just in case she had a use for them – and headed out. The day was clear and warm, and the ground was firm under her feet. She saw Helen in the garden, planting flowers, wearing her straw sunhat and chambray skirt.

"I'm sorry things didn't work out for you here," Helen said. "I mean, with your husband."

"Well, they did, in a weird way, I guess."

She looked up at Malin House.

"I got to live in a haunted mansion in England," she said. "Not many people can say that."

"Did you ever actually see any ghosts?"

Jacey smiled and shook her head. "Not really. No."

At the top of the hill she stopped and looked back down over the town. The river was in the foreground, the ruins of a castle were up on the hill, and above the tall looming hill on the other side of the valley, was a bright blue sky. She knew she wouldn't miss this place, but still, it was lovely.

She smiled; she was thinking like the English now. *Lovely* instead of nice. Not that she'd ever tell Rob that. Not that she'd say anything, ever again, to that arrogant, abusive prick.

She strolled towards the hilltop café, thinking about Muriel and John and Madlyn; those eccentrics she'd blamed for hurting her when all the time they'd been helping. Or thinking they were helping; trying at least.

And Rael, who she'd thought was her friend.

Who *was* her friend, really, despite everything, who wanted to tell her the truth, before she pushed him away. He'd sent her messages that she didn't respond to, explaining that he was a distant relative, too. Nana Ivy's great-great-grand-nephew, twice removed, if you could believe that, he said. Of course his mum believed all that curse bollocks, so when he transitioned, became a boy...

But he hadn't meant to lie to her, that was the main thing. He honestly felt it was dangerous for her, living in Malin House with Rob, so he went along with the others, until he realised that not knowing the truth about Michael was bad for her, too.

She'd send Rael a postcard from the south of France. He deserved that at least, and maybe a text or two from time to time. Later, when she was back in England, they could arrange a meet-up, make their peace, say a proper goodbye, and stay friends somehow

As she turned off the path, towards the sea, she remembered the flatness of the Cambridgeshire fens. She thought about that final night, how Sally had found her at the side of the road, and called for an ambulance, how loyal Stanley had been the one who'd sounded the alarm, waking up half the village with his barking. She thought of the letter Arthur had written to her at Malin House, apologising for frightening her with his foolish talk about the Kennets, that silly old story, and wishing her well.

She thought of her mother, back in Minnesota; the grief she bore, the years of silence that stemmed from kindness, not cruelty, and were well-intentioned, deserving of Jacey's forgiveness.

She thought about the hollowing, the bells that almost drove her mad, the choking and drowning. All of them had stopped since that night on a dark road in Cambridgeshire, since learning the truth about her little ghost, about the trauma of her past.

After a short hike she turned back in the direction of Malin House.

In front of her, something was waiting on the soft, muddy path. At first she wasn't sure if it was real, or if she was hallucinating. Her heart lurched, then swelled with emotion.

It was a boy. *The* boy. Almost four years old. Wearing a T-shirt and shorts, kicking a stone.

Her boy.

She took a few steps towards him. He stayed still, looking at her.

"Michael," she said, taking another step.

She waited. Would he recognise his name? Would he speak to her? Would he know who she was?

Of course not. That was not how this worked.

But he was watching her. She was sure he could see her in some way, and that in some way he understood.

She took another step, almost close enough that she could touch him if she wanted.

"Michael," she said.

She set her bag down, opened the zip, took out something she'd bought specially for today. Just in case.

It was a child's hoody. Fleece-lined. Comfy and warm. Light blue, to match his eyes.

"For when it's cold," she said, setting it on the path.

The boy didn't move.

She reached into her bag again, and took out a ball. It was the same size as the one he'd been kicking when he'd drowned, in the same bright colours, with numbers instead of letters.

It was brand new, and shining.

She kicked it gently along the path towards him.

He was looking, watching her, totally still.

"Goodbye, Michael," she whispered. "I'm going now."

She turned around slowly, then walked away, ten metres or so. She stopped. Waited.

After a minute, bells sounded, faint and sweet, and when she looked back again, the hoodie was gone.

The ball was gone.

Michael was gone, too.

THE END

Acknowledgements

First thanks go to my children, and my family crew: Sean, Hannah, Alexa, Racheal. I'm so lucky to have such wonderful people in my life. Special thanks to my daughter Hannah for being an enthusiastic, insightful and encouraging early reader.

Thanks to John and Cath McLoughlin, for allowing me to include Bella and Stanley; Rosie and Jim Pannett for the use of Bramble; and Julie Scudiero, for letting me bring Thora back to life. Any resemblance in this book to real-life pooches is entirely coincidental!

I am extremely grateful for my many friends, writing colleagues, and wider family, both in the UK and the US. Thanks for your interest and support. Thanks to Harry Scantlebury for casting an eye on certain parts of the book, and offering advice.

Special thanks go to my agent Sallyanne Sweeney, and everyone at Lume/Joffe Books, especially Aubrie Artiano, who commissioned the book for Lume, and Becky Slorach at Joffe for her superb editorial guidance and support. I'm so happy to have found such a fabulous home for *The Perfect Couple*.

PRAISE FOR *ALIYA TO THE INFINITE CITY*

'This book – this book!!! An epic adventure packed with richness and history and a brilliant new magical school. I can't wait for children to find this story.'
ZOHRA NABI, AUTHOR OF *THE KINGDOM OVER THE SEA*

'Perfect for fans of *Nura and the Immortal Palace* and set in a magical alternate Egypt, the first instalment of Rifaat's enchanting fantasy series finds Aliya discover her time-travelling abilities and enrol at a remarkable academy.'
WATERSTONES.COM

'Including interesting moral dilemmas and embracing diversity, this is a powerful reading experience introducing a vivid and intriguing fantasy world – one where magic is corrupted and the impossible is powered by science.'
BOOKTRUST

'Poisonings, disappearances, and the importance of family and friendship keep the plot flying along.'
THE GUARDIAN

'An inventive new fantasy adventure, with its roots in the stories of the Middle East, *Aliya to the Infinite City* is a treat for fans of the magical school genre.'
BOOKS FOR KEEPS

'With a brave and relatable heroine, a stunning Egyptian setting, magic, history, mystery and adventure, this book has it all!'
PARROT STREET BOOK CLUB

'This lively adventure story set in a richly imagined world is a great read for anyone who loves magic and myth.'
THE WEEK JUNIOR

'Completely engrossing and fantastic!'
@ERINLYNHAMILTON ON X

'This is a middle grade fantasy that feels like a future classic of the genre.'
@GOLDENBOOKSGIRL ON INSTAGRAM

A MESSAGE FROM CHICKEN HOUSE

Laila Rifaat has conjured up another adventure rich with magic, mystery and heaps of courage in this brilliant finale! I've been lost in this awesome parallel world since the beginning, at once familiar from all the magical childhood stories, with genies, enchantment and sinister secrets – but now refreshingly new with fantastic friendships and cool beasts! So jump aboard the magic carpet . . . the race is about to begin!

BARRY CUNNINGHAM
Publisher
Chicken House